T.L. BODINE

House of Lazarus

For my dad, who's always been my #1 fan

DEATH DOESN'T HAVE TO INTERRUPT YOUR LIFE!

If you or a loved one is living among the Undead, you have options. You deserve the 24-7 care and skill of the specialized staff at one of our Lazarus House facilities across the country!

With the help of Lazarus, you can retain your humanity and your dignity. Our trained staff are known for their care and compassion. And now, in a limited time offer, the US government is offering vouchers for 100% FREE subsidized inpatient care at one of our dozen facilities across the country. Don't delay. Reach out to your healthcare provider or speak with your local Coalition office to secure a spot for your loved one today.

They cared for you in life. Isn't it only fair that you care for them in death?

Undead "Miracle" Drug Under Scrutiny, Prescriptions Suspended as Scientists Evaluate Claims of Violence

CDC Suggests All Undead Receive In-Patient Treatment Only, Effective Immediately

ATLANTA — The Centers for Disease Control has issued a blanket warning for the drug locomotis lazalus, sold under the brand name Lazarus. Effective immediately, the drug is no longer available on an outpatient basis and now must be administered under the oversight of a trained healthcare provider at a designated care facility.

Over the past several years, the steady increase in post-mortem resurrection has necessitated a comprehensive treatment solution combining pharmaceutical interventions with practical therapies and containment protocols. Pyadox, a pharmaceutical company previously specializing in novel cancer research, released locomotis lazalus (Lazarus) to help with mitigating reported symptoms of pain, tissue degradation, memory loss and mood swings. Lazarus was previously available by prescription from any healthcare practitioner, with family members or loved ones frequently in charge of providing patient care within the home. However, a recent uptick in reports of Undead violence and erratic behavior has caused authorities to rethink the strategy.

"There has been a lot of misinformation surrounding the use and efficacy of Lazarus," said Brandon Smithers, Coalition spokesperson. "What we know is that the product works, but only when it's used correctly. And from what we've seen, that just isn't happening when people are asked to dose themselves."

Effective immediately, in compliance with the Undead Registration Act, all Undead must be moved to in-patient care facilities where their treatment and response to Lazarus can be most effectively monitored.

Chapter 1

I've stopped dreaming since I died.

Or, I guess to be more specific, my dreams have all been replaced with nothing. When I sleep, I descend into a vast and empty blackness that stretches out in all directions. There is a spotlight over me, the only light in the world, and I spend the night huddled in its thin puddle of light, staring out at an ocean as black as void, and I wait.

I don't know what I'm waiting for. I only know that, after so many hours, I open my eyes and take in the first deep rattling breaths of the day and listen to the sluggish, intermittent timing of my heart's lazy beat and I come back to life. Each morning is its own resurrection.

A tiny miracle, except I've stopped believing in miracles.

"Randy?" I reach across the bed, my fingers searching for him, but he's gone. The sheets are cold and rumpled, the pillow a vague lump under the blanket. Randy's been sleeping over more nights than not these past few weeks, but he's rarely here come morning. I haven't gotten used to it yet. Not his being here, and not his absence.

I never meant to hook up with him, much less date him — if that's even what we're doing. He won't put a label on it. It's not a thing we talk about. We're just a couple dead guys trying to figure out what all of this means, I guess.

I groan and roll out of bed, feeling my joints ache and creak and give off the dull, wood-splintered sound of dry bones being forced to move. Every time I swing my long legs over the side of the bed and stand up, I worry that the bones will snap with the effort, that I'll pitch forward onto my knees and feel my limbs dissolving beneath me, the stress just too much for dead bones to handle.

This has never happened, but I worry about it anyway.

There's noise coming from down the hall, movement and voices. I frown. There's an odor, too, and I'm so far removed from hunger that I don't recognize it at first. But then I hear the sizzle, and I can place the scent: bacon.

There was a time when my stomach would have rolled in anticipation, when my mouth might have watered at the salt-fat odor of the sizzling meat, but none of those systems work anymore. I died with a steering column jammed into my torso, and my guts rearranged themselves and came back up through my throat once I was up — not great circumstances for eating.

On the bright side, the Undead don't need to eat, anyway.

I don't know what it is that keeps us moving. Electricity, I guess. I'm not a biologist. I just know that my heart beats when it wants to, that my blood sludges and sluices through my veins, that I breathe when I remember or when I need to talk. I'm like an old-school animatronic, all hydraulics and creaking joints. But my brain's still up there, still intact, doing what brains do. Keeping me awake and aware and with a head crammed full of memories.

Past that? All those other organs and systems, all those pieces that handle digestion and nutrient absorption and waste removal and filtration? As far as I know they're all just jostling around in there, useless and redundant as an appendix. Whichever ones are left, anyway, the ones I haven't coughed out in pieces.

Undeath is nothing if not efficient, I guess.

I find pants and shuffle out into the hall, my socks stirring up static on the carpet. I don't bother with a shirt. My bare torso is all weird bumps and angles, the faded but ever-present bruises, the places where ribs have broken or organs have gone missing. There are places Randy helped me stitch up when I was freshly dead, the jagged edges of skin still puckered with black thread and weeping some kind of clear fluid. I guess they'll always ooze a little. Small price to pay for keeping your guts inside.

"Zoe?" I call, squinting down the hall to the kitchen.

Zoe is my sister. She's just shy of 17 and has accomplished more with her life than most anyone I know, even considering that Los Ojos, New Mexico grades on a curve when it comes to lifetime achievements. She's finishing up her high school through online classes, which gives her plenty of free time to pursue her real passion as a YouTuber — excuse me, citizen journalist. She's turned her bedroom into a one-person TV station, green screen and all, and she covers news about the Undead.

"In here," she calls back from down the hall.

There's a rattle of pots and pans, the clang of metal on a burner, and I reflexively pick up speed. Zoe's not especially well-known for her culinary skills. She's more like the type to get distracted chasing theories or yelling at the news while things boil over and catch fire on the stove. I shuffle into the kitchen half-envisioning another grease fire incident like the one that left the little splatter of pock-marks burned down into the linoleum.

But it's not Zoe standing at the stove — it's Randy, his pale skin practically glowing under the overhead light. He's wearing a pair of my boxers and not much else. They're too long in the leg, hanging down almost like shorts, and they cling precariously on the points of his hips.

His hair, a shade of pink best described as "bubblegum," is extra tousled, jutting up in all directions.

"Morning, Davin," he says, with an air of theatric formality.

"What are you doing?"

"Making breakfast."

"In your underwear?"

"No, in *your* underwear." He has a skillet in one hand and is staring down at it with great concentration. A mess of eggs and cheese is spread over the pan, an attempt at an omelet, and from the way it's crumpled it looks like he tried to flip it and managed instead just to make it mad.

Zoe sits at the kitchen bar, elbows propped up, watching with interest as he wrestles with the eggs. She's looking much more put-together than either of us; I guess she's been awake for a while. Her wild black curls are held back in barrettes, and her glasses are clean and smudge-free for a change. She's wearing a low-cut top that, had our father been here, she most certainly would not be allowed to leave the house in.

"Well, can you maybe not play naked chef in front of my sister?"

"If you don't want me here, say the word and I'm gone."

"That's not what I meant. You know it's not…" I glance over at Zoe, irritated that she's here watching, irritated that he's playing this game. I let the rancid air out of my dead lungs, an exaggerated sigh, and move past the kitchen to the back door. "I need a smoke."

There's a battered picnic table on the back porch, and I sit on it, knees folded up, and light up a cigarette. It's cool out, the morning brisk with the promise of fall. The trees haven't decided whether to turn their leaves yet, but the seasons are shy in New Mexico. Up in the mountains, you get the dramatic shift, the bright gold of the shivering aspens and the deep red of the oakbrush. But down in the valley, the cottonwoods are capricious. Sometimes fall skips over Los Ojos entirely, trees shifting from green to dead without lingering on the beautiful in-between.

The back door opens and I spare a glance over my shoulder, lifting a brow at Randy as he approaches. He's still in nothing but my boxers, his nipples stiff in the cold, his skin almost bluish. The livid purple-black bruise around his throat, the reminder of his suicide, is impossible to ignore.

You don't ask people how they died, but the story usually comes out one way or another. What I know is that Randy committed suicide by hanging. His neck didn't break; he strangled to death, slowly, all alone, and went for a long time undiscovered. When he came back as Undead, he was still hanging, still alone. I can only imagine how it must have been. I can imagine him desperately kicking, his feet thrashing for some kind of foothold, unable to call out or get loose, unable even to just let himself die.

Eventually, the maid found him and cut him down.

And his father, a rich and influential man who could hardly bear the shame of a gay son, much less a dead one, made arrangements to ship him out to New Mexico with a sports car and a savings account.

I know all of this because Randy told me, but I don't know if he remembers doing it. We were in a dark place at the time, suffering the bitter withdrawals of the drug we'd been relying on to feel alive. Going off Lazarus is like dying all over again, but with more nightmares. We found each other in the darkness, reaching and grasping, and huddled together like the last survivors of a disaster, and we shared things that night, things neither of us have mentioned or addressed since.

It's better that way, I think. Probably.

But worse, too, because now I don't know how to talk to him. That's the thing with relationships born out of a tragedy, I guess: once the disaster is over, once that immediate rush of emotion is gone, what can you possibly have left to talk about?

So now we look at each other in the backyard, and neither of us say anything. I have things I want to say, but I don't, maybe because a part of me is afraid he'll leave if I let him get too close; like a delicate hot-house flower, too much handling would cause him to wilt.

"I'll head out," he says, coming close but not quite touching.

"You don't have to."

He gives a wry smile. "Nah. Wouldn't want to overstay my welcome. And," he adds, lifting a finger before I can interrupt, "I've got things to do today, anyway. It's cool."

What things? I narrow my eyes. The cigarette cherry has gone gray, smoldering out from neglect. I can't tell whether Randy's being vague to irritate me or if he's doing something he doesn't want me knowing about.

In a former life — hah — Randy was at the epicenter of an Undead drug ring. Most Undead exist under the watchful eye of The Coalition, a government-sponsored healthcare and public safety organization created to keep tabs on the freshly deceased. There are laws in place to keep everyone accounted for: mandatory registration, monthly required doctor visits, government-mandated treatment programs. These days, the Undead are mostly housed in treatment facilities, Lazarus Houses where they're kept medicated on the drug that's supposed to keep them on an even keel and protect them from losing their humanity and going on a rampage.

The rest of us — The Underground, the Undead who live under the government's radar and try to pass for Breathers — were skating by on stolen drugs, and Randy was the hookup for the greater Los Ojos area. He'd offered me a job as a way to pay back the favor of finding me on the side of the highway, freshly Undead, and introducing me to The Underground.

But the off-the-books Lazarus supply dried up, forcing us into withdrawal. And, unlike what the official government statements would have you believe, the withdrawal didn't leave us as mindless killing machines. In fact, once we got through a torturous three days of symp, we came out on the other side feeling…well, dead. But mostly fine. More tired than we'd been on the drug, more filled with the bitter ache of occupying a body you can feel actively decaying around you…but mostly fine.

"What kind of stuff?" I ask, not expecting a straight answer.

He shrugs. His dark eyes glitter. "Wouldn't you like to know. A man must keep his secrets."

As if as an afterthought, he leans in for a kiss, and his lips have brushed past mine and pulled away before I even have a moment to react. He's retreated into the house before I catch up with the lingering sensation of his touch.

***

When I go back inside, Zoe is ignoring a plate of mostly untouched eggs. Instead, she's on her phone, leaning her chair back on two legs and rocking it gently back and forth, a thoughtless rhythm while she stays engrossed with her screen.

"Stop that," I say, reflexively. "You'll break the chair."

She doesn't look up, but after a moment she does ease it down to all four legs. She slouches forward instead, sprawling out and keeping her eyes locked on the screen.

Most teenagers, you have to worry about them texting boys and arranging illicit hookups or sending nudes. With Zoe, I'm more afraid that she's plotting a political revolution from her iPhone.

"Randy left," she says, and her tone is accusatory.

I try for a joke. "I hope he put clothes on first."

She ignores me. Instead, she types something out with her thumbs, then sets the phone down and looks at the eggs with a vaguely surprised expression, as if she's not quite sure how they got there. They're burnt, a caramel-brown skin clinging to their rubbery sides.

"The party is the 28th at 8," she says.

"What party?"

"My birthday?" She lets out an exaggerated noise. If an eye-roll made a sound, that was it. "Unless you forgot."

"I was there when you were born, maggot," I say mildly. "I just didn't know we were doing a party."

Her nose wrinkles. "Well, whatever. CJ's at 8. Don't forget."

"CJ's?" I can't hide the surprise in my voice. CJ's is a local coffee shop, known in Los Ojos for its ethically sourced dark roast and fresh-baked danishes. It also happens to be the meeting place of the local Undead and headquarters of The Underground. When Randy and I were running Lazarus all over town, CJ's was the front we laundered all the money through. It's a weird choice of meetup destination for a birthday party. But then, Zoe's got some unusual friends. "Is that a good idea?"

"It'll be fine," she says, and sounds annoyed that I'm questioning her about it. "We're just hanging out."

"Who's coming?"

"The regular crowd. You know. Jo and Andrea and Ash and Lilith and everybody."

So, The Underground. Does Zoe have any regular friends? I try to think of one, a name I can suggest, but my memory's drawing a blank.

"Well, if that's what you want."

"I figure I can get some really good footage, too. For the documentary."

"Zoe —"

"I know, I know. I'm not releasing anything yet, I'm not an idiot. But, you know. One of these days, the time will be right, and it'll be safe to go public. And when that happens, we'll all want to remember where we've been. Where we came from. We'll want to remember…everything." She gestures vaguely around our kitchen.

Zoe's been obsessed with this idea of making a documentary for weeks now. It started the night Randy and I locked ourselves up, waiting for withdrawals.

At the time, neither of us knew for sure what might happen. We knew that The Undead who go off Lazarus are supposed to lose their minds and become mindless, vicious zombies.

So we locked ourselves away, just in case. Zoe had set up a webcam, snaking its cord through the door, pointing it at the room so she would have some warning if things went wrong.

Unfortunately, Zoe's footage turned out too dark and grainy to be of much use, and she was devastated about it. Here she was, sitting on definitive evidence that The Undead were not the monsters the media made us out to be — that we didn't need their drugs or their treatment centers — and she couldn't use it.

So she's taken to recording everything else that she can, all the brief moments of humanity and existence, just in case. Building up a case for Undead rights.

There's just one small flaw to her plan, something I haven't told her about yet because I'm still trying to wrap my head around it myself: I've seen an Undead turn inhuman. I watched it with my own eyes.

"Davin?"

"Huh?"

"You okay? You kind of…zoned out there for a second."

"Oh. yeah. Sorry." I don't know why I haven't told her everything about what happened the night Randy and I first went off Lazarus. At the time, there had just been so much going on — Randy and I barely making it home, feverish and sweating blood and hitting that crisis stage of withdrawal, and the emergency of our uncertain futures was more important than what had happened to bring us to that point. And after, for the first couple of weeks, I hadn't brought it up because the trauma was too fresh, the memories too upsetting. It was hard to dredge it back up.

But how long could that excuse hold?

Shielding Zoe from the truth is a laughable concept. Zoe lives and breathes the truth. She knows more about what's going on in the world than probably anyone. At this point she could brief the president about the Undead crisis.

"Just thinking about some stuff. No big."

"Randy?" A sly look.

"No."

An exaggerated pout. "You need to be nicer to him."

"I am nice!"

Eye-roll. "Whatever. I'm just saying. He's sensitive."

"He's...complicated." And then, humiliated that I'm even thinking of beginning to have this conversation with my baby sister, I forcibly turn the subject. "Anyway. I'm going into town. I'm going to see about putting in some more job applications. You want to tag along?"

"Nah. I'm working on some stuff."

"Documentary stuff?"

She shakes her head. "College applications."

What little blood I have left in my veins turns icy. My voice goes high, a strangled squeak as I wrestle with my gut reaction, which sounds a lot like: *No, absolutely not.* "Oh yeah? Where you thinking?"

She shrugs. "I've got a few. UNM and NMSU and the Colorado Art Institute..."

"Colorado," I echo, and feel myself forcing a smile so cheerful it hurts. "That's, um, how far away is that?"

"Denver." She gives me a withering look, clearly not believing my poor attempt at cheer. "It's like an eight hour drive, so it's not that far. And it's not exactly like Los Ojos has a film program. Or a college. Or literally anything to do."

She has a point. Los Ojos is a shithole. It's a wide spot in the road between other small towns. Nobody chooses to live in a town like this. You just sort of end up here because it's where you were born and you never got a chance to leave, or else something clawed at you to drag you back.

"I'm really proud of you," I say, but there's been so much delay it sounds fake as hell. "I am! And you can go anywhere! I just..."

"Don't want me to leave," she finishes for me.

"I just figured you'd go to NMSU," I say. New Mexico State University down in Las Cruces — still a drive, but not as bad as eight hours across state lines. It's where I'd gone to school for a year before I dropped out and came home to help out when Mom died. In my head, I'd almost forgotten that there were any other schools, or that Zoe might be planning a future that would take her to the kind of place she wouldn't want to come back from.

I don't want her to stay in Los Ojos, don't get me wrong. I just, until this exact moment, haven't thought much about what happens after she graduates. So much has happened in the last few months that thinking ahead feels completely impossible.

But I can see from the look on her face that she's gone on the defensive. "Dad said I should go for it."

Of course he did.

Per Undead Registration Act regulations, Dad isn't allowed within 500 yards of a minor, even his own kid. But there's nothing stopping him from calling, and Zoe's ear is always more sympathetic than mine.

I'd like to say he was okay before he died, or at least before Mom died, but that would be bullshit. I mean, he was better, obviously, before he hit rock bottom and set up camp there. He held down a job, for the most part. He paid some bills and was alive, which as it turns out makes a pretty big difference. But he was still a drunk, even before Mom was in the ground, and not even his death managed to change that.

A lot of my memories from my teens involve sitting in the car in a bar parking lot at odd hours, waiting for Dad to finish up so I could drive his stinking body back home because he couldn't afford another DUI. I was an expert designated driver by age 15.

His death hasn't improved our relationship, to put it mildly.

He doesn't get to be a father anymore, not on my watch, not when he's so flagrantly abandoned his post, and the idea that Zoe would talk to him about college before talking to me sends a flare of white-hot anger through my ruined body.

But I don't like trash-talking him to Zoe. Not when she still has good memories, somehow, not when she's managed to hold onto something like respect or love for the guy. So I swallow down the anger as best I can, my gaze floating off to the empty space next to her head because I can't bear to look her in the eye.

"Well, good luck," I say, and that fake cheerfulness is gone now, replaced with something awful and hollow. "I mean it. You'll do great wherever you end up."

She shrugs, noncommittal, and moves to collect her phone and dump the rubbery failed eggs in the trash. Without another word, she pads off down the hall, leaving me alone in the kitchen.

Chapter 2

"Wow. You were gone for a while." Zoe meets me at the door. I guess she heard me pulling into the drive. "You get an interview or something? You land a job?"

I sigh, nudging past her and into the living room. Being unemployed is like its own full-time job sometimes. I don't even know how I've managed to lose most of a day to driving around one tiny, dusty town looking for "Help Wanted" signs and asking for managers and filling out applications that will be immediately put in a drawer and forgotten, but I have. It's late afternoon already, angling toward suppertime, and I've accomplished a lot of nothing.

The TV is on, turned to the national news, the precursor to the local broadcast that Zoe always watches with dinner. You'd assume that a teenager with a smartphone and a bedroom full of computer equipment would get her news off social media — and she does — but watching it on television is something she does for fun. She and Dad used to watch the news all the time together when she was really little, when Mom was alive and Dad was still working for the newspaper. They used to snuggle up on the couch, her leaning against him with a stuffed animal in her arms, watching with rapt attention as broadcasters went into all the grisly details of the world's problems, and Dad would answer her questions and point out little tidbits and trivia, especially about local stories whenever one happened to overlap with something he'd worked on. It didn't happen all the time — the news station would broadcast from a bigger town an hour or so away, covering all the little villages and holes-in-the-highway in the surrounding area — but once in a while he could point to something on the screen and say, "Hey, I broke that story!"

Los Ojos has always run about a decade behind the rest of the civilized world, so writing for the town newspaper actually remained a pretty viable gig here even while people in big cities were losing journalism jobs left and right.

I don't know for sure if it was his paranoia about world events that lost him the job, or if losing it was the thing that made him start to snap. Either way: It had been good while it lasted, and maybe that's a reason why Zoe clings so hard to her own journalistic ambitions, why she watches the news the way that some people watch sports.

The TV's on mute, so I can't hear the audio, but the picture on the screen is a middle-aged Black woman. She's giving what appears to be a passionate statement, with lots of looking off-camera and talking with her hands. The caption beneath her reads LOCAL WOMAN REFUSES TO BURY SON, INSISTS HE WILL COME BACK TO LIFE.

"No, no job." I go into the kitchen and open the fridge, not really knowing why. Habit, I guess. Reflex. I stare into the comforting glow and try to exhale my disappointment.

Before I died, I was working at a gas station. Not exactly glamorous work, but it added up with the Social Security checks that Dad was getting, and between the two we could keep the lights on and food in the fridge. But once Dad went into the Lazarus House, his money got eaten up with treatment costs. As it turns out, those government subsidies for "free" treatment are actually mostly just reallocated SSI. I lost my job — disappearing for days when you can't explain where you've been will do that — and finding a replacement has been hard. Looking for work while hiding your identity as a shambling corpse is bad enough. Doing it as a college drop-out in a small town full of other drop-outs makes it worse.

Randy's money has mostly been paying the bills. At first, because he was paying me for my role in our Lazarus-selling scheme. When that went to shit, he kept trying to chip in for bills or food costs, leaving money on the counter or stuck to the fridge with a magnet when I'd refuse to take it from him. I hate it, but I hate not paying the utilities even more.

"Davin? You okay? You look…"

I blink, realizing I've been standing and staring into the fridge for a long time, long enough that my skin's picked up a chill. I close the fridge door and step away, exhausted. "Yeah. Sorry. It's nothing."

"Well, cool. The facility called. Dad's place, I mean. They wouldn't tell me anything because I'm under age," here she adopts a nasally falsetto, "but it sounded like maybe it was important."

Why didn't they just call me? I pull my phone from my pocket and frown at the missed call. Oh. I guess I wasn't paying attention while I was out trolling for applications.

"Thanks for the heads up."

"Yep. Keep me posted on what's going on." She tilts her head, looking up at me like she's about to say something else, then changes her mind. "I'm going back to working on some footage. I found this new video editing software that's supposedly really good for correcting artifacting — going to see if I can salvage any of the webcam footage from that night. Fingers crossed!"

"Yeah," I echo, hollow-voiced. "Fingers crossed."

***

I take the phone out back and claim my usual perch on the picnic table. The wood is gently grooved, worn smooth from sitting on it for years. I light up a cigarette and punch in the numbers for the Lazarus House.

Before I can get them to understand that I don't want to talk to him — that I'm just calling to see what they wanted — the front desk forwards me over to Dad. There's a pause as they keep me on hold, explaining who I am, and the hesitant waiting noise of dead air as the phone connects. Did they put a phone in his room, I wonder? I can see it clearly in my mind's eye, a private room that looks as much like a jail cell as anything: the metal cot and chair, bolted to the floor so he can't throw them around anymore when he gets angry. Or is there a communal phone bank, pay phones lined up along the wall? Does Dad have to earn the privilege to use them, or can he run to them any time he feels the urge to call?

Before I can say anything, Dad's voice on the line:

"Davin. Finally, you answered. You have to listen to me. You have to come, right now."

"Dad —"

"You have to come. You have to get me. They're doing terrible things to us."

I've heard this before, enough times it's lost all its teeth.

There's a bunch of different kinds of drunks. There's angry drunks, happy drunks, sad drunks — and paranoid drunks. It's a chicken-and-egg thing: coming up with excuses for all the reasons his life has gone to shit; drinking to escape how miserable he's made himself; falling deeper into stupid delusions from a liquor-addled brain. Lather, rinse, repeat. Dad's been like this for years, and his death didn't help. It's only gotten worse the more time he has on his hands, time to sit and think and stew and worry. He can't drink anymore, obviously, not while he's locked up in a facility, but an Undead's wounds never really heal, and that seems as true for drinking yourself to death as for anything else. So, as the saying goes I guess, once a drunk, always a drunk.

So, once upon a time, Dad would nurse a beer and rant about the cell towers that were giving us cancer, about the shadow government that was surveiling us through our television, about the person who had stolen his identity and ruined his credit and his good name until no one in town wanted to hire him.

There had not, for the record, been anyone stealing Dad's identity. He fucked up his life all by himself.

"Calm down, Dad. Explain it to me."

"I can't," he says. He drops his voice, conspiratorially. "Not over the phone. I have to talk to you. Face to face. Come over, please. Please come."

"I'll visit you this weekend. Like always."

"It can't wait. Please. Come now."

"Okay, okay," I say, dropping my voice although I don't know why. "First thing in the morning, then. I'll come tomorrow."

"Today," he insists, plaintive like a little boy.

"Dad, I can't come right now. I've got — "

"What if there's an emergency?" he says, and I don't like the sudden shift in his voice, a tone that suggests he's about to _make_ an emergency.

"Fine." I hear the resignation in my voice and hate myself for it. I tell him I'll be there in an hour and not to do anything stupid in the meantime, and end the call before he can start to argue.

Zoe is lingering in the kitchen when I come back inside. She's heating up a tortilla over the stove burner, smoke curling up from the edges as the surface starts to bubble up and char.

"You going somewhere?"

"Yeah." I hesitate. "I need to swing by Dad's."

She flips her tortilla with her fingertips, then jerks her hand away quickly and shakes it. She turns off the burner. "The Hospice of the Damned?"

"That's the place. You need anything while I'm out?"

"Nope." She reaches for the tortilla again, sliding it off onto a plate, dropping it quickly and shaking her hand again. "Ow! Shit!"

"All right, asbestos hands," I tease, but my heart's not in it. "It'll be a while. You can order a pizza or something if you get hungry. Just try not to burn the house down."

Zoe's buttering up the tortilla and folding it over in fourths, trying to eat it quickly before the butter melts out but mostly succeeding in just getting it all over her hands. Butter drips down her wrist. She ungracefully tries to lick it off before dropping the whole burnt-and-oily tortilla onto her plate and rubbing her hand on the dish towel hanging off the oven door.

"What the fuck? We have pizza money? Since when?"

"Check the cookie bear."

There's a cookie jar on the kitchen counter, an old-fashioned ceramic bear with a chipped ear. I keep him because he reminds me of Mom, who couldn't bake for shit, who would fill him up with dollar store duplex cremes instead. When I got older, it was mostly a place to hide Dad's keys and store loose change. Randy's been in the habit of dropping bills in there sometimes, hiding money like some kind of sugar daddy Easter Bunny.

She gives me a thumbs-up, temporarily silenced by a renewed attempt to cram the rest of the dripping tortilla in her mouth.

"Keep the door locked. I'll probably be a while." I leave and then linger on the doorstep, listening for the click of the deadbolt that would prove she listens. It takes a minute, but I hear it slide home and I go out to the truck, trying to summon the energy to make the drive to the Lazarus House. An hour of driving, and I know before I even pull out of the driveway that this will be a waste of gas.

I think, briefly, of calling Randy, seeing if he could tag along for the company. But what's the point? The Lazarus House won't let Zoe in except for special visitation days. I can't imagine they'd be too excited to have some stranger there. And it's a big enough risk already having me show up, trying to pretend I'm not just as dead as the patients inside; having a pair of rogue Undead roll up is just asking for trouble.

And despite the way things have gone since I died, trouble is usually something I try to avoid.

***

The sun goes down early now, stretching out the night, and today sundown is ushered in by a thick blanket of clouds. The dying sunlight reflects off them, orange fire licking the undersides of purple clouds, and it would be beautiful if it weren't so ominous. I'm waiting to see the lightning flicker through those heavy clouds, waiting for the sky to open up with late-monsoon rain, waiting on the highway to flood and my truck to hydroplane and send me skidding.

Wouldn't that be funny, I think, easing off the gas a bit as the tires touch the bridge that crosses the Rio de Animas. *What are the odds that someone can die twice in two separate car accidents on the same lonely stretch of road?*

The guard rail is still busted out from when my last car went sailing through it. They've put up caution tape, blocking out a space around it with orange traffic barrels, but who knows when someone will bother to get it properly fixed. Somewhere down there, swept downstream, is the mangled steel corpse of my car. Somewhere down there is the place I woke up, muddy and aching, to puke up my guts and feel the death that had settled down in my heart and lungs.

But the truck bumps over the bridge easily, without incident, and then it's behind me. I remember to breathe again and suck in a hungry gulp of air. I don't know whether it actually means anything, now, or if oxygen is some new kind of placebo for the Undead. But the threatened gorge of panic abates all the same, and I finish the drive to the Lazarus House without exhaling. The sky darkens but does not storm.

One day, maybe, I'll cross the bridge without feeling that tightening in my body, the ache in my chest. Maybe after enough weekly trips across this stretch of desolate highway, the memory of my death will fade and loosen its hooks in me.

I'd like to think so, anyway.

What I know is I've driven so much today, I've brokered in so much disappointment and tension, that the morning with its empty bed and burnt eggs feels like an eternity ago.

But at least I'm here.

I can see the facility looming large ahead of me, set back from the highway by a long path and a pair of fences, one chain link, the other hastily threaded barbed wire.

Fun fact: Back in the day, a leper colony used to be called a "Lazar House" or "Lazaretto." Not named for the dead guy who came back to life, but for the other Lazarus in the Bible — the poor leper who died a beggar outside a rich man's shop.

I wonder if the people running this place have a taste for irony.

This modern House of Lazarus is a collection of worn-down adobe buildings clustered around a dusty central courtyard. The structure itself is very old, Spanish Colonial in style and origin, and it's been a lot of things over the centuries. That's another fun fact about the old Lazarettos. At first they were for the lepers, and then the tuberculosis patients, and once the diseases were cured, people needed someone new to put in those buildings, so they started locking up their lunatics, their hysterical women, their sufferers of chronic melancholia. As long as there are asylums that need to be filled, society will always have some group of undesirables to put in them.

I stop at the gate, and the guard approaches from his little security box.

I roll down my window. "I'm Davin Montoya," I say, digging out an ID. "My dad…lives here." I stumble over the word 'lives,' choking on the inaccuracy, and try again. "He's a resident — Ignacio."

The guard glances at my ID, then hands it back with an approving grunt and moves to open the gate, waving me through. I pull up the gravel drive and stop at the "visitor's parking" area in front of the office, which is actually a single-wide trailer sitting awkwardly in front of the crumbling old historic building.

The door creaks when I open it, and the receptionist looks up at me with suspicion, like she's expecting me to rob the place. She's a middle-aged woman with her hair tied back, gray at the temples. If you don't look closely enough to see how thick her makeup is caked on, you might think she's about 20 years younger than she is. I don't recognize her, but then, I'm not usually here in the middle of the week. The whole staff is probably different than the weekends.

"I'm here to see my dad," I say, because she's just staring at me. I pull out my ID again. "Ignacio Montoya?"

"We don't hold open visitation on weekdays. Did you make an appointment?"

"Well, no, but —"

"We'll have to ask you to come back another time."

"I'm sorry," I say, shifting uneasily. "I'm just — I got off the phone with him a little while ago. He sounded very upset. I'm worried he might…" I trail off, start again. "Just let me see him for five minutes?"

Her eyes narrow. "Ignacio Montoya?" she repeats.

I nod.

She looks down. She keys something into a computer. She's got one of those screen protectors on it, the kind that makes it impossible to see anything from an angle, so from here it just looks like she's peering into the an empty screen. In the silence of the office, I can hear that low, quiet plastic creak of the computer doing its thinking, the small sounds of electronics groaning with effort. The receptionist taps long acrylic nails against the desk, impatiently waiting for something to load, and then looks back at me with an expression of recognition. It's not a happy look. "Oh, yes. Your father, you said."

I nod.

"He's caused us a lot of trouble."

"I know. I'm sorry." I hate that I'm apologizing. I hate that she's making me apologize. I would have figured that apologizing for my dad's bullshit would end when one or both of us died, but it turns out that some things are actually more certain than death and taxes. "Look. He called me about an hour ago. He sounded worked up over something. I was thinking if I came down I could talk to him before he tried something stupid."

Something stupid — like the time he escaped from 'outside time' and scaled the fence, planning to hitch a ride to the casino bar for a drink. Or like the time he bit an orderly, not because he'd gone mad from Lazarus withdrawal but just because he didn't want to get his injection that day. Some patients have roommates or make friends in here; sometimes you see them playing chess out in the courtyard. Dad isn't one of those patients.

Judging from the look on the receptionist's face, she knows these same stories, or at least just pulled them up on her computer. He's probably got an incident report a mile long.

"Let me phone down to the floor and see if anyone is available to check in on him," she says, coolly, and then turns away from me to make a call, as if facing away is going to erect a soundproof wall between us.

I wait, awkward and exposed and increasingly angry about this whole situation. The reason I even turned my dad over to this place — the whole point in locking him up — was so I could get my life back, so I didn't have to spend my days babysitting him, keeping him penned up in the master bedroom and dealing with his insane angry rambling. Now, well, it's a little late, isn't it? You can come back from the dead, but you'll never get your life back the way it was; every moment gets chewed up and discarded as soon as you pass through it.

The receptionist sets down the phone, and I realize I've zoned out most of the conversation, her half of the exchange mostly just a dull buzzing drone in my head — my name, my dad's name, something about a status, something about a visitation. But she's looking at me now, wary and tight-lipped, the way a dog looks at you when you've got it cornered and it's thinking about biting. I think she's going to tell me something she knows I won't want to hear.

"Mr. Montoya, your father is sleeping now."

"So go wake him up."

"I'm afraid we don't advise that." Her jaw clenches, teeth gritting behind that tight lipsticked smile, and I can see the ball-joint of her cheek pulsing under the skin. Her eyes are cold. "We ask that you come back during your appointed visiting hours."

"I drove all the way out here," I say, trying hard to keep my voice level, trying hard to keep my nails from digging crescents that won't heal into my palms as my fists tighten. "I just want to see him for a minute. Just to be sure he's okay."

"Your father is fine, Mr. Montoya, and if you had called ahead we would have saved you the trip. Now I must kindly ask you to leave, and refrain from any unexpected, unscheduled visits in the future. It will save all of us some time and trouble."

Would I have fought this, in a previous life? Was there a time when the stakes were lower — when I did not have a terrible secret of my own to keep hidden — when I would have raged at her, when I would have waited for guards to appear and usher me from the premises? I might tell myself that, but in my heart I know I wouldn't. I'm not a guy who sends food back at a restaurant; I'm not a guy who starts fights over what I want. If I were that guy, a lot of things in my life would have gone differently.

And right now, with a foot in the grave and staring down the specter of my future in mandatory lock-up if they catch on about my Undeath, well, now isn't the time to indulge in ill-timed courage.

I mutter something scathingly polite and back away from the front desk, trudging back out to the pickup, seething with an anger that crawls up through my body like some living thing. I'm done with his shit. I can't get my old life back, but I can keep him from screwing up this one any worse than it already is.

I fish my phone out of my pocket as I start up the truck, pulling up Dad's recent calls, and block the number.

Chapter 3

You'd think that even just waking up each morning after your death would feel like a miracle, but the reality is that just about anything becomes routine once you've gotten used to it.

There's this theory I heard about once in a psychology class, before I pulled out mid-semester to come tend to my dying mom, called the hedonic treadmill. The basic idea is that happiness and misery are fixed states of being, more internal than external. Some scientist studied it by looking at people who had undergone a life-altering tragedy, like a death in the family or becoming disabled, and then people who had won the lottery.

What he figured out is, in both cases, the subjects returned to their baseline levels of happiness within just a few months. It doesn't really matter, it turns out, what happens in your life: however happy you are is just how you're going to be. Misery is a thing that soaks deep into the fabric of our lives. It's unavoidable and inescapable. When you grow up with unhappiness, when that unhappiness is all that you've ever known, you'll find the misery wherever you look because you don't know how to be happy. That's the hedonic treadmill.

Then again, maybe the scientist was full of shit. I feel like if I won the lottery right now, it'd solve a whole lot of problems. I'd still be dead, but at least I wouldn't be dead and broke. Whoever said money can't buy happiness probably never had his electricity cut off.

September is swiftly giving way to October, days getting eaten up in job searches and hassling Zoe about her homework, and the bills slowly accumulating on the kitchen table are the most reliable way of marking the passage of time. I've opened all the envelopes and laid them all out on the table like pieces of a very boring jigsaw puzzle, staring at them as if maybe if I can see them all at once I'll have some kind of epiphany about how they can get paid.

I catch Zoe out of the corner of my eye, approaching with a kind of cat-like slyness that makes me immediately suspicious. She's carrying a sheet of printer paper, held carefully so I can only see the blank side.

"What's that?"

Zoe's pushes a paper at me, looking somehow both sheepish and utterly pleased with herself.

I take it, having to read it a couple times to make sense of it.

There's her name up at the top — Zoe Montoya — and right below that, UNDEAD LIVES. Then, in table form, a list of names, aliases, and usernames with numbers out beside them. Most of them small dollar amounts, some of them bigger, the final balance tipping out at just under a thousand bucks. I stare.

"Is this…?"

"My donor's page!"

"Your…what?"

"My donation page. I've got subscribers who get to see my videos before I post them, and they get some extras like footage I didn't use or stray research or whatever — don't worry, it's not like *real* behind the scenes stuff, it's all still really anonymous and under this persona I've got."

Partly for theatrics and partly to satisfy my paranoia, Zoe has always taken pains to dissociate her journalistic activities from her identity — voice-changers and VPNs and a green screen and dramatic lighting and all sorts of other tricks. But I can't see how any of that is going to do her any good if her name is printed right here at the top of the page, and that's not even touching on the insanity of the amount tallied at the bottom.

"All of these people are giving you money for your 'Undead Lives' channel? The one where you post videos about Undead rights and conspiracies and stuff?"

"Well they're not getting nudes, if that's what you're asking," she huffs.

I can tell I'm not reacting to this the way she expected; this conversation isn't going the way either of us probably want. Also the idea of her selling nudes hadn't even entered my mind, but now that she's suggested it that's adding a whole extra layer of things to worry about.

"I'm not trying to imply anything! I'm just. Surprised. I didn't realize you were doing this."

"Are you mad?" Sulky, defensive. She snatches the paper back and holds it close to her chest, like she thinks I'm going to do something to it.

"I'm not mad. I would have liked you to tell me before you did it, though. I'm a little concerned —"

"Davin, the literal title of your autobiography would be 'I'm a little concerned.'"

She's not wrong, but it kind of pisses me off to hear it. "And for good reason! That's your real name, tied right there to this content —"

"It's only stored on the donor site! And it's not even like, a big-name site, it's set up *specifically* for people who are doing stuff discreetly..." She blushes, suddenly averting her eyes.

"Zoe..."

"I *told* you, I'm not selling nudes or anything! There are people there who do sex work, okay, that's kind of what the platform caters to. But there's people doing all kinds of stuff! Real grass-roots stuff and advocacy work and all kinds. I'm not an *idiot*, I vetted it and made sure it would be totally safe! But people love my videos. And I can make money at it, _real_ money! Which we need, last I checked."

My temple starts to throb, a phantom pain of a body helpfully remembering only the worst details of how it feels to be alive. I lay a hand over my eyes and massage my temples. Nobody ever gave me any kind of rule book for raising little sisters. And if they had, I strongly doubt that this specific scenario would have been included in it. *How to talk to your sister about her anti-government advocacy work on a sexworker website when it threatens your identity as an extra-legal zombie.*

But I can also practically hear her heart breaking with disappointment, so I have to say something.

"I'm really proud of the work you do," I say carefully. "And it's really impressive that you've got so many passionate fans. I'm just worried —"

"The *reason* I came out here to show you this is because I want to help. And also, I can't set up a bank account or cash out any of this money without a guardian's legal approval." She mumbles this last part pretty fast, like she's hoping I won't notice. "I know we're hurting for money."

"We're not…" okay, that's a lie, and I can't even finish saying it without feeling like an asshole. I squeeze my temples harder. I wonder if being dead has softened my bones. What if I squeeze too hard? What if my fingers break right through my skull and plunge into my brains like jello? It would, at least, save me from needing to finish this conversation. "I don't want to take your money, Zoe. You worked for that. It should at least go into a college fund or…something."

That gets her attention. "So you'll sign off on it? You'll let me open an account and everything? I can show you the tax forms…"

I don't think that's what I actually said, but now I'm going to be double the asshole if I turn her down. "Is there, like. A time limit to this? Is this something I can think about and get back to you?"

Instantly deflated. "No…I guess. The money just sits there until I cash it out. In escrow or whatever."

As surreal as everything in my life is, the fact that I'm dangerously close to needing my 17-year-old sister to explain what the fuck an 'escrow' is just about pushes me over the edge. "Let me think on it, okay? Just a couple days. Can you give me that?"

Big sigh. "Fiiiiine."

"I am really proud of you though."

"Whatever."

God damn it. There's no coming back from 'whatever' town. I'm claiming this as a victory while I can.

***

I give up on the bills, carefully piling them up into two little stacks: empty envelopes on one side, bills on the other. This doesn't really accomplish anything, but it almost feels like it does. Anyway, it looks better. Zoe's relocated to the couch and is clicking through the recordings on the DVR, looking for something. Apparently she finds it, because she makes a little triumphant noise and clicks it on.

"On tonight's special report — the Reanimation Virus. It's been two years since the dead began to return. What do we know, and what's still a mystery?"

The news program plays its little opening jingle, and the camera pans over a carefully staged studio before settling on a table set in the middle of a dark room, the background blotted out to really amplify the 'talking heads' motif. The newscaster is a woman with gray hair carefully cut into a mid-length bob, her pantsuit aggressively neutral. Across from her is a dark-haired woman with olive skin and high cheekbones. She's wearing a pair of dark-rimmed cats-eye glasses, her hair twisted up into a bun like she's getting her fashion advice from Ruth Bader Ginsburg.

A name plate hovers on the screen, introducing her as Olivia Nez, Disease Researcher.

"Dr. Nez —"

"Olivia is fine," she cuts in, as smoothly as if they'd rehearsed this a dozen times, which I'm sure they have.

"Olivia. Right. Tell our viewers how you came to be involved in this research."

"Well, Suzie, it's really an honor to even get the chance. Those of us who study infectious diseases can spend a lifetime without ever seeing some of the things we learn about in theory really come through in practice — but here, we have something truly special. I don't think anyone has ever seen anything quite like what we've seen with the Undead, as they're being called."

"Do you feel that 'Undead' is a misnomer?"

Olivia shifts in her seat, adjusting her weight carefully so as not to cut off any of the cameras poised on her. "I mean, what you're seeing with these individuals is an immune response unlike anything we even have a name for. We have patients who are clinically dead by every metric — heart rate, brain wave activity — for hours, sometimes even days, before resuming some limited bodily function. Now, would I call that a resurrection, or a return to life? I guess that depends on how you define 'life' and 'death,' and that gets into a philosophical or religious place. I can't speak to that. But from a clinical perspective, what we're really talking about is a prolonged period of apparent death followed by a chronic state of immune suppression and some unique symptoms."

"By symptoms, you mean things like their apparent lack of pain and super strength?"

"I think calling it 'super strength' is a bit of a stretch, but yes." Olivia reaches for the glass of water on the table and takes a drink in three small, measured sips, like she's buying herself time to think of the next thing to say. "What I think is important to understand, to really contextualize this, is that none of the things we're seeing with this so-called Reanimation Syndrome are really all that unusual in the natural world. There is a species of frog that can have its body literally frozen for several weeks, then resume normal functioning. There are reports of people who have endured suppression of various body systems due to cold temperatures or poisons who are apparently dead but do manage to resume a normal life afterward."

"Haitian zombie powder, for example,"

"Sure." Olivia looks annoyed. I see her take another sip of water and wonder if this interview is veering away from what they'd rehearsed.

Suzie tilts her head, expression one of polite skepticism. "But — from a clinical perspective — the people we know of as Undead have, in fact, died. The Supreme Court ruled that the Undead, as non-living persons, have the rights of corpses rather than citizens. You're not suggesting otherwise?"

Olivia's lip twitches. "I would say that science and politics are not always in agreement. Science, for one, draws its conclusions from a body of evidence, and scientists continually revise our understanding based upon new analysis of that evidence."

I like this Olivia Nez, I decide. I glance over at Zoe, who's watching with rapt attention, her phone lying forgotten in her lap. I cross over from the kitchen and settle down on the other end of the couch. I'm not usually one to get sucked into the news shows like she is, but I've also never heard anyone on television ever talk about the Undead like this.

"Hey Zoe, what do you know —"

"Shhh!" She flaps a hand in my direction, silencing me, and then pointedly turns up the volume.

Suzie's talking again. "Speaking of research," she says, a clumsy attempt to steer the discussion back on track. "We're here today to answer the question that I know has been on everyone's minds since the event first began: What actually causes this Reanimation Syndrome?"

"Well, Suzie, we've known from the beginning that there was a viral component. I think the media latched on very early with calling it the Reanimation Virus. In samples taken from patients, we did find the presence of a certain previously unidentified retrovirus."

"For the viewers at home —"

"A retrovirus," Olivia continues, cutting off the question, "is one that rewrites the DNA of the host. The best-known of these of course is the human-immunodeficiency virus, or HIV. When one of these viruses invades the host, its genetic material interacts with the host's cells in such a way that the host might experience a permanent state of infection or lifelong symptoms of some kind. What we're discovering is that many of these retroviruses affect the immune system. HIV of course can lead to acquired immune deficiency syndrome, or AIDs. But it's theorized that retroviruses could also be to blame for other degenerative diseases like ALS. And that's what we're seeing with the Reanimation Syndrome."

"So — just to be sure we're understanding this correctly — you're saying that a virus is responsible for the resurrection?"

"That seems to be the case. Our current working hypothesis is that, at one point, this novel retrovirus began to spread through the population, and a certain percentage of people who were infected developed a specific immune response that would explain the posthumous symptoms."

"But the virus itself is not the cause of death? It seems like we're seeing Undead dying predominantly of trauma."

"That's right. And I think that probably we'll be seeing more cases in the future. What I think is most likely is that the actual viral agent responsible for the disease causes a very minor illness during a patient's lifetime. The initial infection occurs with little or no symptoms, or perhaps the symptoms are easily written off as being a mild cold or flu. Regardless, patients get sick, and then they seem to get better, and they have no idea that their DNA has been altered. When a patient dies after experiencing this infection, the immune response is triggered, or the viral DNA is activated in some way — we're still not entirely sure of the mechanisms here — and the Reanimation Syndrome symptoms become apparent."

Suzie looks directly at the television screen, smiling in that wide, dead-eyed way that the talking heads always seem to, like a mannequin that someone put in front of a teleprompter.

"We'll be right back with more questions for Dr. Nez after this commercial break!"

Zoe reaches for the remote, fiddling around to find the fast-forward button.

"Hey Zoe," I try again. "What do you know about this Olivia Nez person?"

She shrugs. "I've seen her name come up a few times on some scholarly stuff. I honestly haven't been following the science side of things as much as the politics. I think I like her, though."

"Me, too. She seems pretty sharp."

I hadn't really given a lot of thought to the type of research that must still be going on with the Undead. In my mind, I always sort of assumed that as soon as they came up with Lazarus that all the scientists just packed up and went home. But then again, with Lazarus not really working the way everyone said it would, maybe they're still researching like crazy.

If I were the one on that sound stage, I'd be asking Olivia a different set of questions. *Why did I see somebody rip someone's guts open with their teeth after taking Lazarus,* would probably be the first one.

But I guess they probably didn't have any Undead in the writer's room coming up with the programming for the night.

Zoe hits play again, now that she's passed the commercials.

Suzie jumps right back in with the questions: "The internet is alive and well with conspiracy theories regarding this issue. Would you be able to speak to the veracity of some of these claims?"

"Conspiracy theories are more a matter of social science than immunology," Olivia says. "I am not qualified to speak to how these ideas spread. My understanding is that these theories are a response to the unknown, as a way to tie up the loose ends of what we cannot reliably explain. I think it's best to avoid giving them too much consideration and focus instead on the hard science. Once we have answers, the conspiracies will die off or be relegated to the trash heap of history with Flat Earthers and Holocaust deniers."

I think it's pretty bold of her to assume that those ideas have been so fully discredited, but I guess even scientists are prone to some wish fulfillment fantasies. I know from experience that getting someone to stop believing in some crazy bullshit is harder than just showing them why they're wrong. But maybe it works better if the person is sober.

"What about the idea that the Reanimation Event is tied to some sort of bio-weapon?" Suzie presses.

"There is no credible evidence to suggest that the virus is man-made." Olivia hesitates, frowning, and it's the first time she seems to lose her total confidence. "What I would ask anyone entertaining that thought is, to what end? The purpose of biological warfare is to control a population through genocide. I would say that ensuring that people do not die is the opposite of genocide. What possible political reason could exist to create a population who were harder to kill? These patients do not require food. They have a limited capacity for pain. They have shown an amazing resilience and physical strength. I don't think those are qualities anyone would want to foster in their political opponents."

Suze's eyebrows have gone so high they threaten to disappear into her hairline. "What about the super soldier theory?"

Olivia makes an irritated noise, setting her water down heavily. "Look. This is not some kind of comic book story or blockbuster movie. These are real people who are suffering the long-term debilitating effects of an illness that science is only barely beginning to understand. Any conversation speculating about anything other than giving them the treatment they need and preventing undue suffering is a distraction. You brought me here to discuss science, Suzie. If you want to talk about these other issues, I suggest you interview a science fiction writer."

"All right. So perhaps the biggest question for many of our viewers: Is there any evidence that these patients are contagious?"

"That's another thing that we don't know for certain. Based on the sudden emergence of cases, it seems very likely to me that we're looking at a novel mutation that occurred in nature and spread. There are certain trends that we are still trying to understand. For one, the virus seems to have overwhelmingly affected a younger population, teens and young adults, which might suggest a sexual mode of transmission. But we are also seeing it in children and the elderly, so…" Olivia shrugs, and reaches for her water again, looking momentarily dismayed at how little is left in the small cup. "But as the virus itself appears to transmit asymptomatically, there's really no way of knowing for sure how widespread it is, or if everyone infected will reanimate. The only way to know for sure would be to conduct massively widespread testing, and there simply hasn't been funding for that."

"Why is that, do you think?"

Suzie has to know that this question is a trap, but she keeps her expression neutrally curious, perfectly calm.

"It seems that the government has been minimally interested in a preventative response," Olivia says, carefully, measuring her words. "The model has seemed to be entirely reactive, and generally hands-off, leaving the practical details up to healthcare providers and pharmaceutical companies. Due, I imagine, to the government's assertion that these patients are not people."

"And that's all the time we have today!" Suzie says quickly, clapping her hands together. "Thank you so much for your time. Olivia Nez, ladies and gentlemen! Stay tuned for this sponsor break. When we get back, Republican presidential candidate Ezra Lynch—"

Zoe shuts off the sound and picks up her phone, rapidly tapping something into the screen.

I crane my neck, trying to get a look, but she shifts her weight to angle away from me, frowning. I can't tell if she's trying to hide something or just deeply engrossed in whatever it is she's looking up. I'm thinking back now to her apparently huge fanbase, how eager they are to send her money. I don't think she'd be stupid enough to hand her phone number over to anybody like that, but then, a few hours ago I wouldn't have thought she was making money on a donation site either.

"Did you eat today?" I ask, instead.

"I think so."

How can you *think* you ate? It seems like something you'd remember. I miss food, and I miss taking food for granted almost as much. "Want me to make a sandwich or something?"

"No, that's okay." A moment's pause. She glances up. Her phone screen reflects in her glasses, a tiny little postage-stamp-sized inverted reflection of a tan-skinned woman's face. Because she's looking up Olivia Nez — of course she is. "Grilled cheese?"

"I make the sandwich, you take out the trash. Deal?"

"Deal."

You'd think that waking up each day after your death would be a miracle. But honestly, the times when everything feels normal are the best.

Chapter 4

Sometimes social workers drop in unannounced.

That's how you know that you're not doing so well in the eyes of the state. They stop by to catch you off-guard. They've got a quota of visits they have to make, and they've got to make it sound convincing that what they're reporting back is the truth, unvarnished, without rehearsal or preparation. So they swing by, pretending they were in the neighborhood, pretending that the visit is a matter of convenience and not a trap to catch you at your worst.

But our case worker's not usually one to pull that shit.

His name is Adrian, and he's usually a pretty stand-up guy. We met him the first time not long after Dad died, and he's always been pretty good to us, dropping as much of the bullshit as possible. One of the first times we met, after Dad resurrected, he pulled me aside and gave me the spiel — how I'd been under so much pressure taking care of my dad and my sister. How it wouldn't be so bad if I couldn't handle the strain, if I got a little help, if I let the state intervene. He laid it all out right there, without saying as much, that gentle warning if I fucked it up that Zoe would vanish into the foster care system.

But that was the last time he made the offer. Ever since, he's kept to his boundaries.

So I'm surprised to see his car in the driveway when I get home from another day of dropping off job applications. I was in a pretty good mood until about two seconds ago. I'd gotten a call-back to go interview at a tire store, despite knowing essentially nothing about tires, and that seemed like a promising sign, but there's just something about pulling up to your house and seeing a social worker parked there that makes a day go sour.

I pull the truck into the drive, parking half in gravel so his car won't be hemmed in. I don't want anything standing between him and getting out of here; I'd rather not give him any excuses to stay longer than necessary.

How long has he been here, I wonder? What is he talking with Zoe about?

I ease open the door, quiet, as if that'd make any difference — as if it's possible to sneak into a house this small, when the door opens right into that shared space between kitchen and living room. Zoe and Adrian are at the kitchen table, cups of coffee in front of them. The house smells like a diner at 3AM, all acrid coffee and old grease. Adrian's mug sits, mostly neglected, the coffee developing a shimmering oilslick film on top; Zoe's cradling hers, looking down into it like she's trying to read a fortune in tea leaves. It's hard to gauge how long the two of them have been sitting here. There's a little manilla folder on the table, and a small leather notebook, both closed and stacked neatly atop one another. I notice that nobody's moved my bills-and-envelopes stack from the corner of the table, but at least that probably means nobody went pawing through them, either.

"Oh. Hey," I say, false-casual. "I wasn't expecting you."

"It's all right, I just was in the neighborhood and figured I'd drop in for an informal little visit." Adrian leans back in his kitchen chair, tenting his fingers. He's a clean-cut white guy, rust-colored hair and fair skin, bony hands and long fingers, prominent knots of sinew and blue-green veins working up the underside of both wrists. His chinos, I notice, have an ironed-in crease, a pleat down the center line. I imagine having the free time to be fussy about wrinkles. His gaze flickers to me only for a second before settling back on Zoe. "We won't be seeing much of each other soon enough. You're just about to turn 17, right?"

Zoe meets his eyes, her glasses catching the light and flashing, drawing a momentary blankness over her expression. "Yeah."

"You've come a long way." He looks down at his coffee cup, his expression unreadable. It's hard to tell whether this statement is meant as praise or a leading question, something meant to invite commentary.

If it's the latter, Zoe isn't taking the bait. She lifts her brows, an answering challenge, and waits for him to continue.

I'm still lingering awkwardly in the threshold, not sure what to do with myself. I'm suddenly self-conscious of my appearance, the jagged scar of sewn-up tissue up one side of my face, a mark that won't ever really heal. I'm hyper-aware of the way my permanently broken ribs create a concave divot in my chest, wonder if it's visible under my t-shirt. I tug nervously at the hem, suddenly thinking of that scene in every action movie where they catch the bad guys and start torturing them for information. I'd be a hopeless villain, I think. I'd crack under pressure before the torture even started. I imagine myself in some small, dimly lit cell. Would I start screaming confessions the moment the door opened? Guilty conscience, the kind of urge toward honesty that would make me confess to wrong-doing to my dad even knowing the ass-beating that might follow. Confessing even to things that weren't my fault, taking the blame onto myself, equal parts noble gesture and compulsive self-flagellation.

I cross the threshold and pass the table, moving into the kitchen, and open the fridge. Act normal, I think. Food is normal. Food is a thing that normal people do, when their guts aren't a tangle of shredded meat.

"Well." Adrian continues, losing the silence game. "You seem to be adjusting well. You said you've already gotten some college applications out?"

"Yeah. A couple."

"Your brother must be very proud," he says, gently, and I try hard not to listen for an edge in his words. "And your dad? What's he think?"

"We haven't talked much lately," Zoe admits.

I stare harder into the fridge, feeling my grip tighten on the door handle.

"Oh, that's right," Adrian says, as if there were any way he could have forgotten this little detail, as if Dad's death and resurrection and Lazarus House incarceration were not the defining foundations of our family, were not the whole reason he was being paid to sit at our table and talk to us. "He's at the Lazarus House now, isn't he. How is that going?"

The atmosphere in the room shifts. It seems to grow a few degrees colder, like a draft has blown through an open window somewhere. I drag a pot of beans out of the refrigerator and pull off the lid, examining them. They seem fresh enough. No mold growing on them, anyway. I take them to the stove to heat them, distract my hands, but I catch Zoe's glance on the way. A wary look, like she's waiting on me to take point. Like she wants me to weigh in now or forever hold my peace, and I'm real anxious about whatever she might say, so I say instead, "It seems all right. We don't get to visit often."

"No…I guess you wouldn't." That feels cryptic, but I can't guess at what he means. He sighs, though, and there's a weariness in it that seems genuine. Something in his voice shifts, or his bearing, like somebody's who's been sucking in their stomach and finally relaxes, letting out all the tension in one slumping breath. "It's all a bit of a mess right now, isn't it?"

That's the first thing he's said that doesn't feel like a leading question, and I glance over my shoulder to exchange a look with Zoe. She meets my gaze, briefly, and gives the smallest of shrugs, nearly imperceptible. Her poker face is better than mine. There's no question which one of us is more competent at being interrogated. Which one of us, for that matter, got less of a paddling.

"The Lazarus recall, the policy changes…it's been hell on the child welfare system, I'll tell you that much," Adrian says, and drags a hand down his face, seeming to age ten years in the space of a few words. "We've got more kids than space already, and all the damned paperwork. There's some light at the end of it, though, I think. It seems to be slowing down."

Zoe perks up like a dog to a whistle. "What do you mean?"

A guilty sort of look passes over Adrian's features, a look like he's just realized he's said too much, and I think it's genuine. I notice the dark circles under his gray eyes. "The epidemic seems to be slowing down. I couldn't tell you for certain, it's not like I've got any numbers to back me up, just an impression. Folks seem to be staying dead more often now, anyway, than a couple years ago. Which makes sense I guess. Any virus is bound to run its course, one way or another."

I think about the story on the news — Olivia Nez and her retrovirus explanation, Undeath as a type of autoimmune disease. Just as simple and mundane as celiac, death instead of gluten.

I think: It's too good to be true. It's too much to hope for this to be some blip on the radar of history, an inexplicable moment rather than a permanent change in the fabric of life and death.

I also think: So what does it fucking matter? If the thing's run its course, or it hasn't, it doesn't make me any less dead, and it doesn't make Dad any less gone.

Feeling suddenly gloomy, I pull the now-bubbling beans off the stove and start heating up a tortilla on the burner, the blue gas flames tickling its underside.

"Well, anyway. Zoe." Adrian reaches for his papers, shuffling them like a nervous gesture. "You're almost seventeen. You are still technically under my case load, and you're certainly entitled to assistance if you want it, and I trust you're smart enough to get that help if you need it." From the corner of my eye I can see him looking over at me, perhaps inviting me to weigh in. "But I think we can dispense with these formal visits, if you're okay with that?"

Zoe nods, maybe too enthusiastically, and rises up from her chair. "I think that's a great idea," she says, with something resembling graciousness.

"I'll see you out," I offer, starting away from the stove, but Adrian waves me off.

"It's all right. I know my way from here, I promise. Take care, both of you."

And then he's up and out and gone, and Zoe's sliding the bolt into the latch behind him, and I'm exhaling a long and anxious breath and feeling my not-beating heart plummet down to my toes before lurching back up to my throat.

"That was fucking weird," Zoe comments, coming up beside me. She takes the two burritos I've rolled up and set on a plate and heads back to the table with them.

"I was going to eat that," I protest.

She rolls her eyes. "Jesus Christ, Davin, you were not."

She's right, of course. The last time I ate a bean burrito I was puking up my internal organs for half the night, and that was with Lazarus keeping me on a mostly even keel. Still, it stings more than it should that she didn't stop to offer me any. Just another inarguable proof of how thoroughly dead I am, how utterly irreversible this state of affairs truly is.

"So, Adrian, huh."

She shrugs. "I don't know what all that was about, but I don't think I'll like the answer when we finally figure it out."

"You think he's hiding something?"

"No, I think he was trying to deliver a message. But what, and why, I have no idea." She frowns. "Maybe he knows about you."

"I was afraid of that." How would he know, I wonder? Some tell, some sign? Or could somebody have told him?

She shrugs again, and takes a big, un-dainty bite of her burrito, spending a long time chewing and swallowing before continuing. "If he does, he's on our side, though. That's the message, I think. That he's got our back. I just can't imagine why he'd feel like he had to tell us that."

But my mind has wandered back to that other thing, the too-good-to-be-real thing.

Is it possible?

Are we really coming to the end of all this?

***

"All right, birthday girl. Where are we headed?"

Zoe's cradling the new video camera in her arms like it's a literal atomic football — like she's afraid one wrong move and the thing will explode. That cheesy grin hasn't come off her face since she pulled it from the wrapping. With the party still a few days away, I don't think she was expecting any birthday treats, and it feels good to surprise her with something good for a change instead of some cataclysmic bad news.

I don't like taking hand-outs, especially not from my let's-not-put-a-label-on-it zombie boyfriend, but the camera was worth the money. I can't remember the last time I saw Zoe this happy. Besides: It feels better, somehow, to get Randy's help with paying for a gift than for paying the utilities. He's Zoe's friend too, sort of.

"Can we go up onto the mesa?" she asks with uncharacteristic shyness, like she's afraid she's already asked for too much and doesn't want to press her luck. "I'd love to get some establishment shots of the town for the documentary. And...you know..."

I do know. When we were kids, Mom and Dad used to take us up there, picnicking in the little state park at the scenic overlook. There's an old Indian pueblo nestled among the rocks, long empty now, the remains of a city built into the stone. Someone, nameless now and forgotten by time, painted a wordless history on those stones: people and animals and thunderbolts, glyphs of a time long past. It's probably the coolest thing anywhere near Los Ojos, full of good memories for our family — even if memories of colonization and genocide and rewritten history cling to the place like ghosts.

The truck isn't really made to seat three. I wasn't thinking about that when I bought it. At the time, I couldn't conceive of a future where there was anyone in our little family but me and Zoe. It never occurred to me we'd need seating space for more.

Randy had offered to drive, but the Mercedes is a sports car, hardly more spacious than this and certainly not well-suited to mountain roads. So instead we're all three squeezed into the cab, a pretty ridiculous trio playing at being a family.

Zoe insists on riding shotgun so she can film out the window as we pass through the town, even though the only things to look at are laundromats and auto repair shops built in the husk of buildings that were once drive-thru liquor stores. But she's enjoying it, and Randy's not complaining about being squished into the middle seat, even if he won't stop fiddling with the radio.

He rests a hand, lightly, casually, on my knee, his fingertips tapping an idle beat. I don't know whether he notices.

"Actually," Zoe says, shifting and squirming in her seat to angle her head toward me. "Can we stop and get something to eat on the way?"

There's a Blake's near the highway exit, a semi-local burger joint known mostly for its breakfast burritos. The sign looms, the restaurant's mascot: a figure in a top-hat and pinstripe coat, smiling broadly. His legs are two long, slender blue poles, and he rises like a giant up against the horizon, towering over the building and throwing a shadow over our car as I pull into the drive-through. There's something vaguely sinister about him, his faded red-white-and-blue uniform, his dead white eyes. But he's comforting, too, in a way, like a promise that there's at least a few things in the world that will never change. Most things in my life have gone sideways since I was a kid, but the Blakes sign is as creepy as ever.

Zoe orders a green chile cheeseburger and a Pepsi. Randy, leaning over me, calls out to the window for a large strawberry milkshake before I can stop him.

"Seriously?" I hiss, more amused than agitated.

"Let a guy have his vices," he replies, sullen.

I roll my eyes, but sigh, and there's a brief scuffle as I try to go for my wallet and Randy grabs my hand and pins it to the seat, capturing it midway into my pocket. He's climbing over me again, an excitable spider monkey, handing a crisp $20 to the cashier. She looks at us with an impossible to discern expression, her real brows replaced by thin, drawn-on arches that give her a perpetually bemused look.

"I could've paid," I mutter.

Before Randy can offer a retort — and I can see it there, glimmering in his eyes, some bawdy commentary waiting to roll off — the food is getting shoved through the window at us, and I take it and the change and disseminate all of it, pulling away from the drive-through before I can field any more weird looks from the person at the register.

Randy happily stabs the straw into his milkshake and parks it in the corner of his mouth, slurping it in long, continuous gulps, not surfacing for air. He sucks on the straw like a calf nursing at a teat, stopping only long enough to dislodge chunks of strawberry that get wedged up inside.

About ten minutes later, on the road that winds up the side of the mesa, we pull over so he can throw up.

Ten minutes after that, we're pulled over again, and he's doubled over this time, coughing and hacking, his whole body spasming with the effort of expelling the offending invader. It comes up in a thick puddle, red-pink ice cream swirled through with black goo, some rancid fluid from deep down inside.

I watch, arms folded, trying not to let the sight of it send me into a retching fit of my own. Zoe, while he's distracted, dumps the remainder of the milkshake out from the passenger side door.

"Now what have we learned?" I ask, gently chiding.

Randy flips me off, still spitting up chunks of strawberry.

When he's finished, he stands up shakily, wiping his mouth on the back of his hand. He frowns. "Never used to be this bad," he mutters. "Used to be I could eat a little, sometimes."

"Lazarus probably helped," I say.

He nods, stone-faced. I make him ride the rest of the way up the mesa in the bed of the truck.

Chapter 5

From the top of the mesa, you can see pretty much all of Los Ojos, a scrappy patchwork of houses and trailer parks, highways and desert. We don't have a skyline, not really, but you can make out the crest of ambitious buildings, a bank office with pretensions of something grand.

Randy is sulking in the back of the truck, legs dangling over the edge of the open tailgate. Zoe's in her element, though, climbing around in dirt and scraggly desert grass, pointing the camera in every direction as she messes with settings for focus, color balance, sound quality. There's a little picnic area up here, plants growing feral up between the cracks of cement, the wood of the picnic table and benches gone driftwood gray with time and weather. I sit on one of these splintery benches and light up a cigarette.

"The quiet town of Los Ojos," Zoe narrates, panning the camera. She's standing near the cliff edge, peering out past the safety divider, camcorder poised to record the townscape below. "An unexpected epicenter for the Undead, home of one of the nation's first Lazarus houses, but also home to secrets?"

She looks up, pointing the camera at me. I hold a hand up in front of my face in protest, and she pouts.

"Come on, Davin. For posterity."

"Why do I have to be in this documentary, anyway?"

She rolls her eyes, making an impatient sound. "Because you're what the whole subject is about?"

"Oh, you're doing a documentary on excellent older brothers? That's so sweet."

She shoots me a cutting look, not even gratifying me with a comment. To think, she used to think I was funny.

"So, Davin Montoya. Twenty-four years old and recently deceased." She keeps the camera trained on me, peering at me through the viewfinder. "You also once played a pivotal role in delivering Lazarus to the city's most vulnerable Undead population."

Well, that's one way to put it. I raise a brow. What kind of documentary is she envisioning this as, anyway?

"But a Lazarus shortage forced you to change all of that and, in the process, discover the truth about this so-called miracle drug. Correct?"

She's staring at me expectantly, all big dark puppy dog eyes behind her glasses.

"I don't really know..."

"Come on, Davin! You never told me the whole story! So tell me now. For the camera. It'll be great!"

I sigh. "All right, all right. Just because it's your birthday. And if you use any of this footage before I give you permission, I will kill you."

She finger-traces a hasty cross over her heart.

I take a long drag on my cigarette, stubbing out the cherry on the worn wood of the picnic table. "Okay. Fine. So. We're Undead off the books. Unregistered. Nobody knows we're dead, so we can't get Lazarus the normal way, right? So instead what we would do is buy some from people who were registered — they'd get the drugs from their doctors, skim some doses off the top to give to us, and it all worked out okay because doctors were always prescribing them way too much."

I glance over at Randy, who's now perked up with interest, watching me as I describe the job that he had trained me to do.

"But then people weren't getting treated as outpatients anymore. So it was harder to get the drugs, and we were starting to feel withdrawal."

"And what does the withdrawal feel like?" Zoe fiddles with something on the side of the camera, I guess zooming in on my face. "According to the media, Undead who don't take their Lazarus start to lose their minds and go violent. Is that what you were experiencing?"

I shake my head. I light another cigarette to give my hands something to do. "No. Lazarus withdrawal isn't…it feels like dying. Although…" I frown, trying to remember through the blur. "No. There's parts where you miss time, where things go dim and you don't know what happens. There's nightmares. It's like being the sickest you've ever felt in your life. But, I mean, I didn't try to eat any brains or anything, as far as I know. And neither did the other person with me at the time."

I hedge, not sure if I should talk about Randy. If Zoe ever actually does use this footage, it's not my choice whether or not he gets outed in it. I figure he'll wander over here to get in front of the camera if he wants to be part of this. Honestly, I'm a little surprised he hasn't already — I'd have assumed he was the kind of guy who can't resist being the center of attention, no matter what.

"So the stories of Undead going vicious and turning into brainless zombies are fake," Zoe is saying, with satisfaction.

I glance over her shoulder, beyond her, making brief eye contact with Randy, who's leaning forward with interest from his perch on the tailgate. I take a long drag off the cigarette and shake my head. "No, that's not entirely true, either."

Zoe, who's halfway to shutting off the camera, snaps her focus back on me, rapt. "What do you mean?"

This is the part I haven't told her, the part she doesn't know. But it's the part I haven't been able to stop working over and over in my mind. "I have seen it. We have. An Undead losing his mind, going vicious like an animal."

Zoe's eyes go wide behind the camera, but she keeps it trained on me.

"We were arranging to buy some doses from a friend who works at the Lazarus House. These two other Undead followed us there and tried to get in on the deal. It got kind of tense. But one of the guys, he wanted to check that it was the real deal, I guess, and he tried some, and…" I feel my heart jolt, like a dead engine trying hard to turn over. I look up at Randy, seeing a look of sudden understanding on his face, a mirror image for what I feel on mine.

"Oh shit," he says, and hops down from the truck to come close, starting to pace just behind Zoe. "It's the Lazarus House?"

"What?" Zoe lowers the camera, looking between us without understanding.

"The Lazarus House. Fuck." I touch my hand to my head, feeling sick and stupid but a little giddy, too, as if I were standing too close to the edge of the mesa and staring down at the jagged cliff below. "We'd been skimming from doctors and outpatients for months, years. Nobody goes nuts. But the stuff that Chuy gets us from the Lazarus house — one dose of that and Javier went crazy, remember?"

"Wait," Zoe says, and she's fumbling with the buttons on the side of the camera. "So you're saying that they're giving…that there's something wrong with what they're giving at the Lazarus House?"

"They could be?" I look between them, a sick sort of horror at realizing I'd never put it together until this moment. That I'd slept on this for weeks without thinking through the implications. "Look. I just know that we were all fine. And then Javier took something from Chuy, and the next thing I know he's ripping the guy's guts out."

For years, the narrative has been the same: The Undead are violent by nature, and only Lazarus keeps them from losing their minds and becoming killing machines. A rash of violence, the attacks on the news, they've been proof in living color that Undead and their caretakers could never be trusted to do what needed to be done in order to stay safe. That was the whole thing, the core argument, the reason why Lazarus had to be controlled, the reason why the Undead had to be put into institutions.

"So it seems to me," Randy's saying, his thoughts clearly following the same train that mine are, "that the narrative's been a little backwards all this time. Keep the Undead in the Lazarus House! They'll be safe there! But surprise, it's their drugs that make them go crazy."

"We don't know that," I say, thinking about Dad, thinking about what kind of monster I'd have to be to send him there, to keep him there, if what we're saying is right. "It could…there could be something else going on." *They're doing terrible things to us*, Dad had said, and I thought he was just being dramatic, paranoid. "I mean, there's dozens of Undead in that facility. Maybe hundreds. Coming in from all over the country. There's no reason they'd be giving them monster juice on purpose."

"So the government is experimenting," Randy says, with the nonchalance of someone talking about a horror movie, not real life. He holds up a hand, ticking off possibilities on his fingers. He turns one down, then a second. "Or your pal tried to screw us over somehow, giving us a bad batch or something."

"Yeah, that's probably it," I say, latching onto the second explanation like a lifeline. "Or it was something wrong with Javier. Dude was a gangster, maybe he was high on something."

Randy holds up a third finger, looking at it thoughtfully. "Drug interaction? Interesting theory, but sure, let's throw it in the pile."

"Anyway, forget I said anything. I was just talking for the video. I don't actually know anything."

Randy drops it, surprisingly, but maybe just because he can see the gears spinning in Zoe's head already, knows if anybody's going to dig in deep on this that it'll be her and that'll save him the trouble of fighting with me for answers. We wrap it up pretty quick after, Zoe suddenly itching to get off the mesa and back to her computer — gee, I can't imagine why — and me eager to be anywhere else, doing anything else, distracting my thoughts from this new and terrible idea.

***

"Davin. We have to go public with everything. We *have* to."

We've been home for hours at this point, but I know exactly what she's talking about. She'd gone quiet on the drive home, staring thoughtfully out the window as the trailer parks and laundromats passed us by in reverse-order from what she'd filmed, I guess mulling over the story. Maybe wondering why I hadn't told her everything earlier. Maybe wondering what else I'm not telling her. Or maybe not wondering about that at all — maybe just thinking about the whole Lazarus puzzle, like all the problems in the world are something that she, specifically, can tackle and solve.

"And then what? The Coalition comes swooping in to raid the place? I know you're passionate about this, but as soon as my face goes online, we're painting a target on our house."

Randy had been about halfway in my lap, kissing, the kind of kissing that was leading up to something more, but now he's retreated to the opposite side of the couch and I'm glad because I'm not feeling like PDA in front of my sister, but my skin is also feeling the absence of his touch.

At least Zoe seems too fired up to pay a lot of attention.

"Because they made everybody in the world believe the Undead were dangerous! That's *exactly* why we need to go public with this! If people could just see the truth —"

"Zoe, I hate to tell you this," Randy says, shifting his weight on the couch. He fidgets with a loose thread on a throw pillow. "But the truth won't set you free. Do you really think the government made up its own secret police force because they *really thought* the Undead were all a bunch of murderous zombies? We're talking about people's grandmas, here, their husbands and friends and cousins. People know the whole violence narrative is bullshit. It's just a really convenient excuse for folks who are sick of takin' care of their relatives to shuttle them off and skip out on any responsibility."

His eyes roll in my direction, brows lifting. He smirks, an affable smile, but there's teeth behind it.

"No offense."

"Fuck you." I mean it to come out lighthearted, some gentle banter, but there's a hard edge in my voice. "Look. We've been over this. We know the Undead *can* be dangerous. We've seen it."

"One time."

"One time was enough for me. And besides — it's *not* just one time. It's all over the country. It's all over the news. Sometimes people go nuts and start attacking people. That's a fact."

"And they said that was happening because they weren't taking Lazarus," Zoe presses, raising her voice. "They *said* that. And they're using that as an excuse to round people up and put them in prison!"

"Hospitals aren't prisons!" I shout back, and then flinch, recoiling from my own anger. I close my eyes and force a breath out through my nose. Behind my eyelids, I can see the Lazarus House, its crumbling old Spanish Mission architecture, its weedy courtyard, its spaces for socialization and privacy. Just because Dad hates it there doesn't mean it's a bad place. Dad hated it here, too — so what's that say about us?

Zoe blinks at me, surprised. I don't remember the last time I raised my voice at her. From the look on her face, I don't think she can remember it either.

"Does it matter how nice the prison is if you're not even guilty?" Randy asks. "They say, 'Take this drug, it keeps you from being a monster.' Well, maybe that's bullshit. Maybe the drug doesn't stop you from being a monster, and maybe it even turns you into one. But what's *not* bullshit is that it makes you feel good. It makes you feel like a whole person, more or less. An' the government just can't keep its claws out of anythin' that makes you feel good, can it?"

"But that's the whole point. It's called a Lazarus House for a reason. You go there, you get your drugs, you feel better, they stop you from hurting anybody."

"Except the one time we ever saw somebody go nuts on Lazarus, it came right from their stock room," Randy says, dropping the pillow now and examining his black-painted nails. The edges are starting to chip from picking at them.

"Christ, Randy, are you just going to play Devil's Advocate all night?"

"You're the one flip-flopping around like a spineless ragdoll," he snaps back.

Zoe looks between us, going suddenly stiff and silent, like a rabbit caught under the shadow of a hawk. She looks like she did when she was little and I'd be fighting with Dad, that way she'd draw up and get real small and linger in the hall to run away at the first sign of an impending ass-whooping.

"Which is it, Davin?" Randy presses. "If you're going to be a bootlicker, you have to admit that the drugs really work, or else the Lazarus House is just a prison. Otherwise, if you're going to sit here and say, 'Oh, I'm fine, I don't need any drugs,' then you have to admit that the whole Lazarus House is bullshit."

He says this so confidently, so simply, that it almost sounds like it has to be right. But he's full of shit. Not every choice is a binary, easily divided out into two neat piles. Everything is complicated and messy, with frayed ends and soft edges, and I can feel it with absolute certainty, a pressure in my chest: The Lazarus House has to be okay, because I sent my dad there, I made that choice, and it has to be the right choice. But it's also not what I want for myself, because I can't leave Zoe to fend for herself in this world, because I can't live with myself knowing that my comfort is more important than her safety, and if I can get by without Lazarus then that's what I need to do — and I need that to be the right choice, too.

I don't say any of these things. I can't make myself spit out the words.

"Whatever. It doesn't matter. Zoe, what did you want for dinner? C'mon, anything you want, it's still your birthday."

She's still hunkered down in rabbit mode, but she slowly starts to loosen her shoulders from around her ears. "I'm not hungry."

"I'm sorry I yelled." I pause. Randy gets up without saying anything and heads for the back door. He's lighting his cigarette before he's even all the way outside, but I wait for the door to latch before I turn back to Zoe. "Can you promise me you're not going to use that footage?"

She grumbles something.

"Zoe, I need you to *promise* me. No identifying details. No names, no videos, no media, nada."

"*Fine.*"

'Fine' is better than 'Whatever,' so I'll take that as a win.

"Besides," I say. "It'd be irresponsible to break the news without having all the facts, right? You at least have to wait until you know for sure what the whole deal is or you blow your chance, right?"

That gets through to her. I could sit here and tell her all night how important it is to be safe, how dangerous it is to risk having me outed — how if I go to the Lazarus House, she lands in foster care or shuffled off to some relative neither of us even know. How she could lose everything, from that bedroom film studio to the YouTube channel to her chances at college. But that's all an acceptable risk.

Sacrificing journalistic integrity, though? Apparently that's still something.

"You're right. I'll work on the story. Until I've got something they absolutely can't ignore."

"That's the ticket." I glance at the back door. "You got your school work done for the day?"

"It's my birthdaaaaay," she whines, but I think it's mostly artifice.

"All right, all right, you win. No homework and no starting revolutions. Compromise?"

She sticks her tongue out at me, but smiles, and the tension's gone, that scared-rabbit response gone, and things are mostly okay again.

Chapter 6

It's the screaming that gets my attention.

In this neighborhood, it's not uncommon to hear people yelling in the middle of the night — domestic disturbances, dust-ups that start and resolve as quickly as a dog fight over a meal. Sometimes you call the cops, but mostly you just check the lock on the door and pull the curtains tighter. In the morning, when the husband's sobered up or the wife is finding the money to post baby-daddy's bail, neither of them are looking at the long arm of the law as the hero.

Usually when the cops get called, nobody's happy to see them. There was a lady who lived across the street from us for a while whose ex-boyfriend had a real bad habit of coming around and begging forgiveness in the middle of the night. I know, because everyone in the neighborhood knows; we could all hear their discussion points debated loudly through closed doors for the neighbors to overhear.

It got nasty one night, the ex yelling some ugly threats, and he took a tire iron to her car. When the window got smashed, that's when I called the cops. You have to have a firm set of rules in place, guidelines for your boundaries on what risks are acceptable. That tire iron could just as easy have gone through a house window, or through a skull. You don't want to be the guy who witnesses your neighbor getting murdered, and you really don't want to be the guy who gets brained trying to help.

Anyway, the cops showed up, guns drawn, yelling at him to drop the tire iron and get on the ground and then, next thing you know, the lady was out through the front door and running down the driveway, screaming at the cops. She came out swinging, caught one in the side of the head, and it took both of them to wrestle her down to the pavement so she'd stop hitting them. They didn't shoot either of them — small mercies — but the end of it was both of them getting man-handled into a patrol car.

So, no, you don't call the cops.

Zoe's at the living room window peeking out through the curtains, trying to get a clear look at what's going on outside. I come up behind her, looking over the top of her head. It's hard to make out much in the dark, but I don't want to turn on the porch light, don't want to make it any more obvious that we're rubber-necking.

At first I think somebody's already called the police, but the car pulled up to the curb isn't a squad car. It's the same make and model, the sleek angles of a Dodge Charger, souped-up muscle car with its killer whale paint job: white and black, the warning colors of nature. But there's no light bar on top, and the logo painted on the side bears a different government seal.

Coalition.

"Davin…" Zoe says, her voice a low warning, and she reaches a hand back, catches at the hem of my shirt. For comfort, or to keep me from bolting like a frightened rabbit? Hard to say. I'm frozen stiff where I stand, squinting out into the dark.

The car is parked in front of our house, the tail lights two red eyes in the dark, and I'm bracing myself for the sound of knocking, the barking of Undead-sniffing dogs, the bouncing beam of a flashlight, but none of it comes.

They're not here for me.

Then a scream, and my attention snaps to the house across the street, a house where there hasn't been any trouble in years, its old tenant long gone and replaced with an elderly couple.

That's who's outside now. An old woman on her knees on the porch, her hands clasped close to her chest. The porch light casts a sickly glow over her form, and the long shadows of two Coalition officers cut through the pool of light.

An officer reaches for her, grasping her at the elbow and wrenching her to her feet, and when he does a brittle bone snaps in his grasp. I can see it, the unnatural angle of her limb, and even across the street and through the closed window I can hear it in the wail of protest she calls out into the night. I can imagine her bones, addled with osteoporosis, melting into grit inside the pockets of her flesh.

Zoe turns away from the window and for a moment I think she's going to bury her face in my chest, I think she's going to cry it out, but I keep forgetting she's not a little kid anymore. Zoe's traded her sadness for anger, her fear for action, and she's ducked under my arm and made a dive for the door before I can think of stopping her.

She shoves through the door and is running to the end of the driveway before I can get my corpse coordinated enough to follow.

"What the FUCK are you doing?!" she yells, and her words ring in the night. Somewhere down the block, a light goes out. A dog barks.

"Go back inside, ma'am," one of the officers says, holding up a gloved hand in a dismissive gesture. "Everything's under control here."

"Like hell it is!"

I reach the door and the cold air outside is like a shock to the system. I hit an invisible wall, some kind of division between worlds, and I freeze in place in the doorway, caught between inertia and indecision.

"Zoe —"

"What are you DOING?" Zoe repeats. She's standing at the foot of the driveway, maybe held there by her own invisible wall. "You're hurting her!"

"She's fine, ma'am."

The old woman lets out a yell, a wild animal snarl, and wrenches around, twisting her boneless broken arm like stretched taffy in her attempts to break free. Her teeth snap together, a dog biting at the air, the unnatural whiteness of dentures capturing the light.

"This woman is sick, and she needs treatment."

"That woman is Undead," Zoe snaps back, crossing her arms over her chest, either in defense or to ward off the cold. "And you're a goddamn liar."

I finally manage to get myself moving again, like breaking loose from some quicksand, and I close the gap in the driveway.

"Sorry!" I call, and hate the appeasement in my voice, hate the cringing puppy that's using my mouth and throat. Zoe's going to be furious, but what the fuck else am I supposed to do? I grab her by the shoulders and try to steer her away.

The Coalition officer manages to get both of the old lady's arms behind her back, and the other maneuvers to stand between us, stepping out into the curb and waiting for us to retreat.

I think, wildly: *Wouldn't it be funny if a car came right now. If it hit him and knocked him into the pavement and then he was the corpse, and he had to sit up and get into handcuffs for the crime of being alive past his expiration date. Wouldn't that just be fucking hilarious.*

But the thought is a fleeting daydream, and I'm backpedaling, hauling Zoe back into the house like an over-eager guard dog, and I want so badly to apologize because she's not the one who's wrong here; everything is fucked but she's in the right and it hurts so bad knowing that and also knowing that it doesn't make any difference.

"Damn it, Davin," she snaps, breaking out of my grip, but she storms inside the house anyway, and I lock up the door behind her. "God DAMN it!"

"We can't do anything," I say. "We can't, and it's…"

She closes her eyes, letting out a long breath through her nose. She clutches fistfuls of curly hair at her temples and tugs, eyes squeezed against the bubbling rage, but she gets it under control. She inherited our dad's temper, but she was always a thousand times better at keeping it contained.

"Dangerous," she finishes for me, on the exhaled breath. "I know. I know. I wasn't thinking. I'm sorry."

And then it ripples through her, the spasm of anger, and her balled fist strikes backward, thumping heavily into the wall. "I didn't even think to grab my fucking camera."

The Coalition car pulls away from the curb, sliding out into the night, and I try not to think of the old woman inside and her brittle, dead bones.

You did the right thing, I tell myself, but I can't really believe it.

***

Morning comes too quick, miserable in its silence. I lie in bed for a long time, staring at the ceiling, listening to the sounds of the house settling around me, the distant noises of cars and the rattle of a garbage truck. It's early. I can tell because there's nothing but silence coming from Zoe's room, and because the light creeping in around the edges of my blackout curtains is more gray than gold.

The side of the bed that I've started thinking of as "Randy's side" is empty, cold from a night of vacancy. I reach out to touch it, surprised at how smooth the blankets are, how un-rumpled the sheets.

I used to thrash around a lot in my sleep, cocooning like a burrito, blankets and sheets ending in a pile, sweat staining the edges of a mattress I couldn't keep covered for a full night.

Now I sleep like the dead.

Sliding out of the bed, I listen to my bones creak and groan, night-stiffened tendons quivering and threatening to snap. I stretch slowly, gently, trying not to think about things pulling out of socket, of bones cracking like dry twigs.

Last night rushes back into my memory: The old lady across the street, her arm twisted impossibly, her dentures flashing in the dark.

I wish Randy had stayed the night. He'd been distracted since we talked about the Lazarus, leaving almost as soon as he came back in from smoking. Probably for the best, though; I wouldn't have wanted him here when the Coalition showed up last night, not so he and Zoe could both turn on me for my cowardice.

Of all the good memories from yesterday — the trip up to the mesa, Zoe's excitement about the camera — it's that awful image of the Coalition raid that's burned into my memory. Figures.

I try hard to shove it from my mind, forcing myself to stay here in the moment as I start to paw through the pile of clean clothes on my dresser, looking for something that looks like job interview apparel. You don't want to over-dress for the kind of jobs I'm looking for. You show up looking for work at a tire store in a suit and tie and they'll pretty much turn you away at the door for being a try-hard. You have to put just enough effort in that they think you're taking it seriously, but not so much that they figure you're making fun of them.

I try to distract myself from last night's memories by practicing interview questions in my head.

Name a time you handled a difficult customer.

What is your biggest flaw.

What was a time you went above and beyond at your job.

It's a little hard to concentrate when all my brain wants to do is show me pictures of awful things: that old lady; Javier digging his teeth and nails into Chuy's guts; my dad, the way I found him when he died; the guardrail on the bridge rushing impossibly fast toward my car as I skidded off the highway.

My phone buzzes, muffled but insistent.

I frown, looking for it first on my night stand, then in the pile of clothes next to the bed until I find it.

Not a text message — a public safety warning.

ALERT!

The Undead Registration Office has issued the following warning to residents of Los Ojos, NM: An Undead has broken containment. He was last seen in the area of Alameda and South Valley. Coalition officials are coordinating with local police to contain the situation. The suspect is described as a middle-aged Hispanic male. He may be acting erratically.

If you see the suspect, do not approach or engage. He may be dangerous.

I watch as the message makes a final journey down the screen, feeling an uneasy certainty that I'm about to get a call. The description could easily fit my dad. Could he have slipped out of his room, I wonder? Attacked a guard? Hitch-hiked all the way here?

I blocked the number, I remember. If he was the escapee, would I even know?

They have Zoe's number. They'd call her.

Wouldn't they?

Guiltily, a wave of cold nausea lurching up from my chewed-up guts, I pull up the Lazarus House in my contacts and unblock it. A moment later, my screen populates with notifications, missed calls and voicemails previously hidden and now uncovered.

I grimace and set the phone on speaker while I finish getting dressed, letting the messages auto play.

"Shit, Davin, I need a drink. Please. Bring me something, anything, I can't think, I can't do anything. If I just had a little something to take the edge off, just a little bit, I could actually figure this out, please, they won't let me have anything."

Beep. Next message.

"I can hear them sobbing in the walls. The rats are crawling from their mouths and they're choking on their tails and oh god oh Jesus please come get me let me out of here please I want to go home."

Beep. Next message.

"Davin you son of a whore answer your goddamn phone I did everything for you I worked my fingers to the bone and you're letting me sit in here and rot you worthless shit I wish you'd never been born I wish your mother had aborted you I wouldn't be here right now if I had how could you do this to me."

Paranoia, pleading, anger — the messages cycle a roulette wheel of emotions, and by the time they're finished I'm feeling shaky and queasy in a way that has nothing to do with being dead. Perfect. Just what I needed before trying to put on a happy face and trying to convince Ted's Quality Used Tires why I would be an asset to their team.

But, I remind myself, the silver lining: The most recent message is less than an hour old. No way Dad could've called from the Lazarus House and gotten all the way here. Whoever the escapee is, he's not my problem.

***

Ted's Quality Used Tires has a hand-written sign in the window, scribbled on the back of an old invoice: Now hiring friendly, dependable staff!

Trying to call on my deep reserves of friendliness and dependability, I take a steadying breath and walk inside. I look as good as I ever will. Pale, but my natural complexion helps counteract it a bit; under the right light, I just look like some young guy who's stayed up too late playing video games and hasn't seen the sun in a while. I've got my hair slicked back and I'm wearing a polo shirt and khaki pants, evergreen uniform of the underemployed. There's a twisted, puckered scar of hastily stitched-together flesh on my cheek, but there's nothing to do for that. The only blessing is that it mostly healed, the edges sealing like raw dough pressed together and left to rise. It doesn't ooze or weep fluid like the scars in my gut.

Deep breath. Inhale, exhale. I should have brought some tic-tacs. I wonder if my breath smells fetid and corpselike. I don't think it does. Randy's doesn't when I kiss him. Not really. He would have told me if I tasted like grave dirt. He tastes like cigarettes and cinnamon gum. But maybe it's like house-funk; maybe you get used to it, olfactory exhaustion from smelling the same environment day after day.

I should have asked Zoe if I smelled before I left, but I hadn't wanted to wake her, not after the whole mess that woke us up last night, not after all the arguing before that, a shitty end to what was almost a great birthday. She'd tell me, though, if I smelled. I'm sure of it.

Randy doesn't smell. Well, he does, but it's not an unpleasant odor. He smells like expensive cologne and that ever-present chemical tang of hair dye.

I'm stalling.

I make my way up to the counter and arrange my features in what I hope is a friendly, dependable smile.

The kid behind the counter looks young enough to make me feel ancient. Zoe's age, maybe. The kind of guy she might have crushed on, if she were still in public school and was the type of girl to crush on guys like this.

The manager isn't here.

There's nothing in the schedule saying there are any interviews schedule for today, and nothing with my name on it.

He has no idea where the manager is. He doesn't know whether they're hiring. When I point out the sign out front, he looks thoughtful and admits it's been there as long as he's worked here — which is, he rapidly explains, three and a half weeks. He's not sure where they keep the applications. He suggests that maybe I should come back later. No, he won't look for my application. No, he doesn't know when the manager might be back, or who I'm supposed to talk to.

He keeps looking at me nervously, clicking the pen he's pulled from under the counter, forgetting to use it to write down a message. I can't tell if he's just oblivious, or if he's trying to play coy with me; if he thinks I'm some kind of drunk or insane squatter, someone looking to start trouble.

And this is with me freshly showered. I wonder what he'd think of me bloody and mud-spattered, crawling up the banks of a river. I wonder what he'd think of me coughing up my insides, sweating blood from Lazarus withdrawal.

The thought brings a twisted, wry smile to my lips.

"You know what?" I say, finally, feeling like I'm getting nowhere. "Never mind. You have a great day."

He eyes me suspiciously and I head back outside, around the corner of the building in the space between the tire store and the gas station next door, far enough from the door that he won't see me lighting up a cigarette and decide to panic about zoning restrictions. I try to think through my options.

I can try calling the number that called to set up the interview and hope it goes to someone other than the guy currently inside. I can stand out here and wait until someone who looks authoritative goes inside. I can try canvassing the streets looking for other "help wanted" signs. I can go home and try applying online again. I can go home and admit defeat. I can call Randy and beg for a favor, tell him Zoe ate up our data limits on the internet again so we're paying the fees.

He'll pay it, is the worst thing.

He'll pay it, the same as he gave me the money to buy the pickup, the same as he's been slipping money into the cookie jar, the same as he paid for the camera. He grew up with money so it doesn't mean anything for him to hand it out, and it all comes from his dad anyway — hush money, an allowance he gets in exchange for staying quiet and out of trouble so nobody back home finds out that he's dead. Randy's happy to spend his dad's money on anything I ask, and I'm the asshole who's too proud to accept it.

Overhead, the sky threatens rain. The sun slides behind clouds, mid-morning light growing prematurely shaded. The temperature drops, the wind changing from crisp to bone-chilling, a cutting knife-point. My skin takes on that itching, crawling feeling of anxiety, the sensation that leaves you rolling your shoulders and fidgeting in an effort to escape.

It feels like the early stages of Lazarus withdrawal, but that's not possible. I haven't had the drug in my system for weeks.

I don't immediately notice the dark shape a few feet to my left – until it moves.

"Hey," a voice that sounds like wind over dry leaves. "Sorry if I startled you."

The speaker is huddled against the side of the building, thin knees drawn to his chest, his body mostly enfolded in layers of clothes. What I can make out beneath the bulk of the clothing looks more akin to a living skeleton than a person. It's impossible to tell how old he is; his skin has that thin, mottled look of the elderly, but it's also pulled tight against his skull, not wrinkled or sagging. His hair is long and limp, hanging around his collar in scraggly black strands, and his eyes seem much too large against the protuberant cheekbones of his gaunt face.

He's missing a hand. The dirty cuff of a sleeve stops just short of his wrist; the exposed bone is yellowed with age.

"You shouldn't be here," I say. "Out of containment."

Is this the guy the alert was about?

Either way, he's not one of the Underground. There's no way this guy could pass as a Breather, and besides, Randy and I had Lazarus deals with just about every Unregistered Undead in the city. Los Ojos isn't a big town — if this guy was one of us, I'd know him.

He inclines his head, fixing me with one over-large eye, and smiles a rictus grin. "I could say the same to you."

My heart falters. It stutters to a stop and is still in my chest for a few seconds before lurching back to life.

"I know, son," he rasps. "Don't kid yourself. You think you're the only one who can spot our kind in a crowd? You spend enough time around the dead, you start to know them by smell. You can call me Julian, by the way."

I don't offer him my name in reply. I stay quiet, not having much of anything to say, hoping maybe he'll leave me alone if I seem disinterested.

"You look good, though. And fresh. Lucky. Must have died quiet."

The scream of torn metal, the thrust of the steering column against my abdomen. Climbing on my hands and knees through the muddy arroyo, pausing to vomit chunks of flesh and red-black blood. Yeah. Quiet.

"A nice, steady supply of Lazarus, too, I expect. Light me one of those cigarettes."

I shake one out, light it for him, not knowing anything else to do. If he decides to make a scene here, out in the open, we could both be found out. The Coalition dragging me into the back of a patrol car. Or the cops, like one of Zoe's videos, fanning out to circle us. Imagining my blood and brains on the pavement.

"No Lazarus," I say, because I'm worried that's what he's going to ask next, because I'm afraid bumming the cigarette was just the first of many favors he's going to try to ask. "Not for a while."

He takes the cigarette from me, holding it between two skeletal fingers of his remaining hand. The skin is scraped off in places, showing sinew and bone beneath, but the fingers still flex – more or less. He takes a long, deep drag and begins coughing, that dry rattling cough that accompanies late-stage pneumonia; the cough of someone who will never be able to dislodge the things in his chest. A moment later, he recovers, spitting a gob of something black and sticky onto the pavement.

"So if you're off the Laz," he says, eyeing me sidelong, "then you know how it is. You know what they say is all so much bullshit."

"You need to leave," I tell him. "Before anyone sees."

Curiosity burns at me, but this isn't a conversation I want to be having right now, and certainly not one I want to be having here. We're out in the open, exposed, and for all I know that kid at the cash register is leaning out the door and hanging on our every word.

The guy — Julian — fixes me with a cold stare, the leathery dried skin of his face holding taut against the bone. Expressionless. Dead. Like something left in the desert to mummify. "I've been walking a good long while. Could be I'm done with walking. Could be I want to stay right here."

I could go back inside, risk the ire of the kid behind the counter. But if the guy comes in after me, starts blowing both our cover, I don't have a backup plan.

He interrupts my thoughts with sudden, rasping laughter that fades into another coughing spell. He hacks up another gob of who-knows-what from his lungs and stubs out the last of his cigarette. "I'm just fucking with you, kid. I know. I need to get on moving. Trust me, the last thing I want is to get taken back to the Lazarus House."

"…Taken back?"

"Where'd you think I came from? Fell from the sky just to spice up your day?" His lips curve back into a humorless smile. "You didn't think I've been dragging this carcass around town for years, did you?"

He has a point: Looking like he does, there's no way he'd have lasted long on the street. It's not always easy to tell when someone's Undead, but when they're pretty much a walking skeleton whose exposed bones feed into mummified flesh, that's a good indication.

"But you can't be from the facility," I say, feeling my sluggish brain struggling to make sense of this information. "You look like you haven't had a dose of Lazarus in…"

"Two months," he volunteers. He holds up two thin, knotted fingers of his good hand. "It catches up fast, when you've been dead awhile. I'm one of those who can still walk."

I stare at him, uncomprehending. There's a terrible image flashing in my mind, my dad's face pulled too-tight over a skull, his bones jutting out at odd angles under the surface of his skin. And then, suddenly, it's not my dad, it's Randy, his small frame grown frail and skeletal, pink hair sprouting from a bare skull, the dark brown pools of his eyes sunken deep in their sockets…

Julian tilts an eye in my direction, brow lifted, his tight dry skin tugging against the bones of his face with the expression. "They're not housing folk for free in there for no reason, kid."

Before I can say anything, someone pulls up into a nearby parking space, slamming their car door and heading inside. I cringe, shrinking against the wall, hoping to stay as hidden and innocuous as a shadow. No one pays us any mind — yet.

"You're a jumpy one, ain'tcha," Julian says, and lets out another wheezing laugh. "I'm not gonna bite ya, kid. Get outta here. I'll catch a ride."

"A ride to where?"

He shrugs. "There's places. You wouldn't want to know about that, though. Go on home to your nice cozy bed and whoever it is who keeps it warm and I'll keep slumming it out here. You wouldn't last five minutes if we swapped places. Just hand me another smoke before you go and we'll call it even."

He doesn't have to tell me twice. I leave the rest of the pack with him and scuttle off to the truck, and when I glance back he's faded into the shadows between the buildings, disappearing like some kind of ragged ghost.

Chapter 7

I'm sitting in the waiting room of the Lazarus House, that old converted trailer that serves as a front office. I've never quite figured out why they set it up this way rather than just using some of the old mission-turned-sanitarium for the same purpose. Surely there's plenty of space in the building, with its broad wings surrounding the courtyard. Surely there are old offices and lobbies and communal spaces inside that would work just as well or better than a dumpy singlewide in the parking lot. But I guess they have their reasons. Maybe they don't want any would-be clients seeing the Undead residents and getting cold feet about locking up their beloved relatives.

When I brought Dad here, I was still alive and the tour was jarring. That's when I met Chuy, who took me on a grand tour and told me so gently what a great place this would be for the corpse I'd left sleeping in the car. Things might have worked out differently for all three of us if I'd gotten a different first impression, if I'd decided that maybe this place wasn't so great after all. Maybe I wouldn't have died, and Chuy wouldn't have gotten attacked, and Dad would still be holed up like an angry, suspicious feral creature in the master bedroom, and maybe that would have been better.

Then again, I don't know that we would have ended up like this if I'd ever really felt like there was another choice. Going back, not knowing any of what I know now, I think I probably would still have made those same decisions. That's the thing about choice: it always feels inevitable once you see how it all works out.

They've tried to make the office space cozy, magazines and pamphlets strewn over a coffee table, a fake potted plant with a film of dust on the waxy leaves. I glance at my phone to check the time, and to see if Zoe's sent any texts about burning the house down or something, and then go back to my usual routine of fidgeting.

I have to see Dad this time. No excuses. After everything — the phone calls and the voice mails and that weird, cryptic warning from Julian — I just need to look him in the eye and ask directly what's going on.

An orderly comes for me after what feels like hours but, my phone assures me, has been less than fifteen minutes. He's a scrawny older guy with a few days of salt-and-pepper stubble. He greets me with a wide, genuine smile, like he loves working here and can't imagine anything better than talking to me now. I wonder if the Lazarus House makes a point of hiring outgoing people, if they've got some kind of personality assessment to go through. What are the criteria for working here, anyway? Do you actually need any kind of medical training to deal with people who are already dead? It had never occurred to me before to ask. When I came here the first time, I was just eager to get rid of my dad.

I imagine a paper sign taped up in the window: *Now hiring friendly, dependable staff to keep your dead relatives happy while they rot!*

If it's good enough for the tire shop, I guess it's good enough for this.

"These rules are stupid," the orderly says, by way of an icebreaker as he claps a hand over my shoulder to steer me out of the lobby and onto the grounds. "I'm sorry if they hassled you at the front desk. It's been getting harder and harder to schedule visits lately, I feel like."

I make a small, noncommittal noise of agreement.

"I get why we have to run things this way, though," he adds. "With all the security measures and rules, I mean. We're under-funded as it is, and we're constantly fighting against bad PR. I mean, we can't win. Either the human rights groups are saying such-and-such is mistreatment and abuse, or else the media is saying we're putting the state at risk by letting dangerous people run roughshod all over the place. It's a mess."

He heaves a sigh and leads me outside and across the courtyard to the old adobe building, toward the rooms they've got partitioned off for...residents?

Inmates? Patients? No term seems to really make sense. Curious eyes peer out at me from doorways. Out in the courtyard, there are a few Undead sitting at a picnic table, talking among themselves, but mostly the sudden cold snap has driven people back inside.

An old woman stares out at me from behind the small square window of her room. Her skin sags from her cheekbones, dragging down her lower eyelids, giving grotesque illustration to the term "hangdog face." Her skin is the color of an onion, and semi-translucent like one as well. I can make out the spray of blue-gray veins spiderwebbing across her cheeks and forehead. Her lips are curled back, revealing yellowed teeth riddled with cavities.

I hurry past and stop before the door to my dad's room. The guard moves out of the way so I can approach the door. I move to knock, but the orderly just shakes his head.

"No point. Just go in. He won't answer if he thinks it's me." He hesitates. "I'll just wait out here."

I give him an uncertain look, like I'm expecting this to be some kind of trap or test, but turn the knob and step inside anyway.

Dad's room was hastily converted from old living quarters for Spanish missionaries. A barely renovated antique space, looking ancient and dilapidated. There's nothing inside but a bed. He used to have some other things in here, a chair and a plant and a few books and such, but everything has been taken from him over time since he can't seem to stop "acting out" – a nice way of saying "turning objects into weapons for attacking the staff."

Just now, the room is dark, illuminated only by light spilling in from the hall. I squint into the gloom, looking at dad's sleeping form lumped up on the mattress.

"Dad?"

He was awake and perky when I called him to say I was coming, but that was a couple hours ago, and his moods can change like capricious winds. Sometimes he's clear and lucid; sometimes he's utterly incoherent, as if his corpse has remembered he's supposed to be blind stinking drunk.

"Dad," I repeat. A pause; he doesn't answer. "Dad! Get up."

The anger in my voice almost surprises me. But it shouldn't. The situation stinks of déjà vu. When he died, I was the one who found his body — slumped in the couch, head twisted back at an odd angle, mouth hanging open and vomit crusting his lips. It wasn't the first time I found him passed out, but it was the worst.

Now, in his room in this modern House of Lazarus, his eyes blink open. They retain that inebriated glassiness; his skin is still ashy and bloodless. But his eyes roll in their sockets, brown and bloodshot, and they meet mine in an uncomprehending stare.

"Davin?"

"Hey. I'm here."

He stares. He blinks, slow and labored, like he's trying to clear a hallucination from his field of vision.

"Dad. I talked to you on the phone, remember?"

He blinks again. His expression is suddenly slack, dumbfounded.

"You've been leaving me a ton of messages. You begged me to come and see you. You said I had to come down right away." My voice is low and cold and insistent, even though I don't mean it to be. I feel the orderly's eyes on the back of my neck and wish desperately that he would leave, or at least close the door. This is hard enough – humiliating enough – without a witness.

"It's late," Dad says, slurring. "Does your mother know where you are?"

"No, Dad. Mom's dead."

"Right…." He trails off, and I think he's done, before he asks in bafflement, "Aren't I dead?"

"…It's complicated." I heave a sigh. I can tell already, this is going nowhere. Of course. "Can you remember what you wanted to talk to me about?"

Sometimes it's like he's not even there, like his brain has checked out and left a glassy-eyed corpse in its wake. It's just my luck that he'd be like that now, that I would have hung my hopes on this visit only to be met with a drooling, barely-coherent joke. Anger burns in my chest, a match held to lighter fluid. How dare he. How dare he make me worry — how dare he make me care — only to fail so completely at even the simplest of things. It's not even that he's never been able to meet me halfway; it's that every time I try to go where he is, every time I cross over that center line and come to his side with my accommodations, with my understanding, it's like he backpedals even further.

He lets loose a stream-of-consciousness babble, punctuated by moments of silence as he starts to drift back to sleep. I shake him awake. His head lolls on his neck, boneless like a doll, but his eye is wide and staring. It rolls up in its socket to fix me with a bloodshot stare.

"They take them down the hall and they come back all wrong."

"Who, Dad? What are you talking about?"

"The rats."

I draw a hand over my face, taking a long, steady breath in an attempt to keep myself from screaming. What I want to do is give him a good, hard slap. What I want to do is raise my voice and tell him exactly what I think of him, and how I feel about this waste of time.

But I don't, because there are eyes on the back of my head.

And I don't, because a part of me is the same scared little kid who never stood up to him, who learned to stay out from underfoot and pick up messes and soothe hurt feelings. The little kid who learned how to de-escalate and find distracting games for his little sister to play so she wouldn't notice, because only one kid in a family should have to bear a burden that oversized.

Dad refuses to say anything else. He curls in on himself like a snail, a defensive ball huddled in the center of his bed. I can't bear to keep pushing. I came here with all these ambitions, thinking I would blow some mystery wide open — thinking I would interrogate my dad, figure out what Julian meant, lay to rest a half-dozen fresh anxieties that have swirled and eddied to the surface of my life in the past few weeks. But I can't even get my dad to string together more than two coherent sentences.

Back in the hall, the orderly makes a small noise, a quiet little cough. I glance back and he meets my eyes with a sad little half-smile.

"Sorry," I say, burning with humiliation. Shame rises like bile from my gut, hot and burning.

But he doesn't mention it. He kindly glances away, standing aside to let me take the lead back to the front lobby. I hear the jangle at his belt as he withdraws a key and twists it in the lock on Dad's door, sealing him in for the night. He does the same to each other inmate's door as we pass their rooms.

Just in case.

"When it all started," the guard says, without preamble. "Everyone thought it was only suicides. Remember?"

I'm taken off-guard by the question, but as the words settle in, I nod. I do remember. It was the running theory at the time: Only suicides came back from the dead. For a few weeks – maybe a month or two – that's how it seemed. Everyone believed it, planned for it even.

Somehow, that made it less frightening. If it was something you had control over – a thing you could prevent from happening to yourself – it seemed like less of a threat. You're never going to accidentally commit suicide. If you can stop your loved ones from doing it, if you can focus on that one single thing, you can prevent the Reanimation Virus from ever affecting you.

Well, they were wrong.

"I think a lot of us have lost someone this way," the orderly is saying, and I hear him hesitate over the word 'lost,' aware that it's not quite the right word. I know what he means. "For me, it was my brother. Not a suicide. Everyone in the family was shocked."

I hesitate, slowing my steps. I'm not sure why he's telling me this.

"He's here, in another ward. I'd already been working here, thought I knew everything I needed to know about the Undead, and then comes my brother and it's like I don't know anything at all. Life's funny that way, huh?"

Hilarious. Like a goddamn toothache.

"Anyway. It's probably a good thing you came when you did, to be honest." We're coming up toward the lobby now, and he slows, as if hanging back to talk. I match his pace. "They haven't made this public yet, but we'll be closing the ward soon – putting everything down on quarantine."

"What? Why?"

He looks over his shoulder, as if searching to see if someone is watching, and then shrugs. "Things are about to get…interesting. You didn't hear this from me, but that whole Lazarus thing is hitting us hard. It's looking like there's not going to be a replacement drug on the market for a good long while. And now that they keep sending folks to us…" His lips twist up, that wry smile freezing into place, but I notice that the humor has long since drained from his eyes. "The higher ups don't want a PR hassle, you know how it goes. So for a while, anyway, the doors will be closed. No new patients, no visitors – just the staff and folks already here, until we figure out what's going to happen longterm."

He pauses, and I reel, trying to take a moment to let that sink in. I'm trying to make sense of it. How would they even enforce the Undead-out-of-containment problem if no new patients are going to be admitted to the Lazarus House?

"So be happy you've gotten to see your dad, even if it wasn't much of a visit," he says, and there is definitely something in his eyes now, something hiding behind that unhappy smile. "You never know when you might get the chance again."

They used to say that about dying. They used to warn you: Tell your loved ones what they mean to you while you can, because you never know when you might lose them forever.

When someone was dying, it used to be a big deal to spend time with them, to try and squeeze those quality moments out of them at the end. Tie up loose ends, make some final memories – like photographs of those last days or weeks or years that you could store in your mind or heart.

These days, it's never a sure thing that someone might stay dead, and those final moments are cast in a different light when you know it won't be the end. It's that awkwardness of bumping into someone at the grocery store again and again, ratcheted up to a horrible eleven.

I thank the orderly for his help, and I make my way back to the car, feeling bone-weary and exhausted.

But just outside the outbuilding, I see something that sets my blood to freezing.

It's a huge frame, taller than me and easily twice as broad. A guy dressed in scrubs, built like a football player and with a no-frills buzzcut. There's no missing that silhouette.

I recognize him immediately, but it's impossible. It's like seeing a ghost.

"…Chuy?"

***

He turns to look at me, his expression temporarily caught in a configuration of surprise, then a grin spreads across his features. "Órale! Davin. I didn't know you were here!"

I gape at him. I can't find the words to make sense of this. Not the part where he's standing here, and certainly not the part where he looks happy to see me. What the hell?

"Last time I saw you," I start, but he shakes his head quickly, shooting me a meaningful look.

The last time I saw him he was being eaten alive from the belly up by a zombie. It's not the kind of thing you easily forget, and it's not something your brain can just make up. I know what I saw, and it does not reconcile with the image of him standing here now, whole and smiling.

He tugs up the hem of his scrub top. He's wearing a form-fitting shirt below, under armor or some kind of girdle — hard to say. It takes me a second, but recognition snaps my brain to attention. The form-fitting fabric isn't just covering the place where his guts were torn open. It's *holding it all together.*

"Holy shit," I breathe, little more than a whisper.

"Nothing's ever as final as you'd think these days," he says, and grins.

"Are you…are you still *working* here?"

"It's a good job. It pays well, and my sister just moved back in with her kids, and…" He shrugs.

I look around, searching for prying eyes and ears, but we seem for the moment to be alone.

"Didn't know if I'd see you again," he's saying, and I'm starting to realize the kind of danger I could be in now. Is that a threat? Is he going to tell someone about me, about Randy, our drug deal, the way it all went wrong? Has he already told someone? Is he in a position to blackmail me?

But then, if he did that, he'd be blowing his own cover, too.

"I'm sorry…"

"It's not your fault. Shit happens."

Shit happens. Right. Like having your body torn apart by teeth. Just a normal everyday occurrence, really.

"You didn't text me or anything," I say, still not really able to get over the shock. It's kind of weird to be shocked by people not staying dead these days, but the thought had never occurred to me that Chuy would have walked away from that. I don't know what I imagined. That he was eaten up like a kid in a fairytale. Ripped into pieces like something in a video game. What we saw happen was so horrific that I never once stopped to think about what might have happened afterward.

"You never texted either, man."

"Can I…do you want to meet up somewhere? Grab a cup of coffee or something?"

He lowers his voice. "I don't know if that's such a good idea. I think…it's probably best…if you stay away from here. For everyone's safety."

But I think I see something else in his eyes, some kind of silent communication or message. But it's gone before I have a chance to try to guess what he was communicating with a glance.

"My number's the same if you want to meet up," I say.

He hesitates, glancing over his shoulder at the building rising up behind us. Instead of answering, he says, "I'm sorry about your dad."

I don't think he's talking about the general status of being Undead. His words are pregnant with meaning that I can't parse, and before I can get any closer to understanding, the orderly who took me around back is passing by, eyeing us curiously.

"Okay," I say, the words empty, just something to say. "Well. Take care of yourself, all right?"

"I do the best I can."

He gives me a sad smile and shuffles away, leaving me alone and reeling in the parking lot.

Chapter 8

The drive home feels longer than usual, more lonely. A half dozen different trains of thought run brokenly through my head, swirling and eddying together so I can't see where one thought ends and the next one picks up — just one long chain of confusing ideas. Chuy's Undead now. The Lazarus House is going to stop taking visitors. And Dad's the same dead end as before, maybe even worse. All of the questions I came here with are every bit as unsolved.

The rain starts up as the Lazarus House drops from view in my rearview. It sluices against the windshield in a mist that's too heavy to ignore but too light for the wipers. Every few seconds, the wipers squeal against the windshield, and I turn them off so they won't streak and scratch the glass, only to turn them back on when the windshield gets too speckled with rain to keep going.

It's autumn rain, not like the violent deluge of the late summer — not like the storm that pulled the heavens down on top of me the night I died. It makes me nervous all the same. There's something about this stretch of highway that feels cursed at this point, after everything I've seen and done while crossing this highway.

When I was a kid, there were legends about this highway, too, but they were a bit more fanciful.

There were stories about the Spanish mission, long before anyone thought to buy it and convert it into a treatment facility. Stories about the ghosts that must have inhabited its flaking adobe walls, about teens trespassing to hold seances in the abandoned grounds. But those aren't what I'm thinking of right now. When I cross the desert alone, the thing that spooks me are the skinwalker stories I grew up with.

In the Navajo tradition, skinwalkers are shapeshifting witches. Those stories are a cultural thing, the sort of dark legend you don't mess with or take too lightly — and those aren't stories to be shared outside the tribe. But that's never stopped the idea of them from escaping out into local legend, campfire stories that twist and change with the telling, retold and adapted whether or not they've been understood. And those were the versions I grew up with, the bastardized urban legends told to me by my grandmother, who had her own version of every local tale. In her story, the skinwalkers were neither witch nor animal, but something in-between, something primal and inhuman. They crouched among the rocks of the mesa, naked and draped in furs. In her stories, they crawled on all fours and ate meat raw, and in the summer you could sit outside and hear their terrible howls and screams rising up into the warm night. Sometimes they would run across the road or keep pace with cars, moving inhumanly fast but with their proportions all wrong, limbs moving and bending in ways they weren't supposed to.

The sign off the highway lets me know the Rio de Animas is approaching. The night I died, the night my car ran off the road in the rain — I saw something on the bridge. Something inhuman, crouched over the remains of a deer. In my memory, I can see its silhouette, long tangled hair and eyes that flash in the dark.

I had swerved to avoid that shape, swerved and lost control, hydroplaned into the guardrail and over the side, and there had been no time to understand what I had really seen or if it had even really been there at all. I figure I'd been driven off the road by some kind of optical illusion, a shadow. Probably just a trick of the light. Probably just my mind conjuring up images stitched together from campfire stories about skinwalkers and La Llorona and El Cucuy and whatever other boogeymen are rattling around up there courtesy of an overly imaginative abuela.

But as I cross over the bridge, I catch something moving in my peripheral vision, and I slow the truck and turn to look, to reconcile what I think I just saw. I'm expecting to see a deer or a coyote, or maybe just a weird shadow against a rock or a bit of scrub. But what I see is a human shape, and it's not in my memory this time. It's right here in living color.

I pull off onto the shoulder just on the other side of the highway and stare. The figure in the desert stares back at me.

I think it's a woman. She's got long, wild hair and her clothes hang off her like maybe they'd been nice women's dress clothes at one point, a dress like something a person would be buried in. She's standing on a gravel path down off the shoulder, some kind of access road maybe thirty feet from my truck, and before I can really think clearly about what I'm doing I'm pulling back onto the road and looking for the first exit off the interstate. As my truck starts to move, the woman runs, bolting away from the highway and back into the desert, and I know I'm going to lose sight of her in a second but I think maybe I can catch up with her again. I think maybe I have an idea of where she might be going.

I take the first right turn I can off the highway, just a little ways past the bridge. It's not even an exit so much as a branch off onto a narrow path - an access road to one of the old natural gas wells that's long since run dry. There was a time when natural gas was booming and Los Ojos was full of tanker trucks and oilfield workers. But that boom came and went, taking the workers with it, and now all that's left are skeletons of old rigs: Abandoned tanks, lazy strings of barbed wire, stony access roads where the gravel has been overtaken by sand. If I were going to spend any time out in the desert, one of those old abandoned well sites is probably where I'd go.

What was it Julian had said about hitching a ride? About there being "places" he could go?

The path takes me away from the highway and loops backward, closing some of the distance between where the road let off and where I saw the woman — just like I'd hoped. There's no sight of her here, and I can't see that narrow gravel foot path, but I think I might be closing in on something. The path leads down into a little depression, a rocky hollow that'd be mostly hidden from view for the people driving past. There are no trees, but the scrub brush grows tall, and large blocks of sandstone are scattered across the landscape, worn down by wind and rain into smooth shapes.

Up ahead is a clearing, an empty space of sandy earth; rising from the center is a large cylinder, an old storage tank from the oilfield. Beside it, rusted drilling equipment, and a number of ragged dwellings.

Some are tents, or what could pass for a tent: tatters of fabric held up by poles. Others are small shacks built from cardboard, scrap metal, bits of particle board, things scavenged from the trash or picked up on the side of the road.

There's a fire burning in a metal barrel, and around it, a small group of people. Through a haze of smoke and drizzling rain, I can make out their faces. They are all clearly Undead, the kind who can't hope to pass for Breathers.

One is missing an arm. His raw, red stump is still oozing some foul-smelling, murky liquid. It dribbles down the side of his shirt. He's also missing a chunk of flesh from the side of his neck and face; a silvery fragment of bone is visible at his jawline.

Another guy seems okay except for the way his shirt clings to his torso; it hangs limp and sucked inward, way past where it should, the fabric damp and stained. I can make out the bulge of ribs under the fabric, and I'm pretty sure he's missing a big part of his body under that shirt. I can't begin to guess at what he's done with the guts that have probably spilled out already.

There's a lady holding a toddler in the crook of one arm. There's not a mark on the kid, so there's no telling whether he's Undead. Either way, he doesn't have much to look forward to, not if this is what his life looks like - eking out a living on the fringes of town, hiding from the authorities who would round them up and send them to the Lazarus House.

I look around for the long-haired woman, the one in the dress, and sure enough here she is — running, bent double, barely reaching this place at the same time I have. She rushes up to the side of one-arm and claws at his shirt. He wraps his remaining arm around her, and I'm not sure whether the gesture is protective of her or of me. From the way his muscles seem to strain and bulge under his skin, he's holding her pretty tight.

I turn off the engine, slowly open the door and slide out onto the ground.

"I'm not here for trouble," I say, keeping my hands up and visible.

No-arm tightens his grip on the wild-haired woman. The other guy takes a step forward, as if to shield the mother and the kid from my view. The kid makes a quiet, wheezy noise, breath rattling out of his lungs in an unnerving way, and I think: So maybe he is dead after all. Maybe he died of whooping cough or pneumonia or something. But there's no time to linger on that thought.

"That's a nice truck you've got," the guy with one arm says.

"You one of them? You working with them?" The guy with the sunken ribcage takes another step forward, tilting his head as he examines me like some kind of curious bird of prey.

I keep my open truck door between us like a shield. Under normal circumstances, my heart would be hammering, my terror would be beating in my throat. But my heart stays on its usual sluggish, faltering beat. It's just my guts that tell me this was a bad idea.

"I'm not a snitch," I say, which is a pretty pointless thing to tell someone, because of course a snitch would say that, but it's the first thing that pops out of my mouth. "I just. I saw your friend."

I nod toward the wild-haired woman, who I notice seems to assume a sort of hunched posture, her eyes bright and her lip curled like a snarl. I try to think of the words to explain what's brought me here, why I pulled off the highway to follow her. *I followed her because I wanted to make sure she was real*, sounds weird and stupid. *I think that woman is the reason I died*, sounds dramatic and accusatory. Neither of them really feel true, anyway. The reality is that I don't really know why I'm here, or what I'm hoping to get out of this interaction. I followed my gut, but now my guts are screaming at me to get away.

"Hey, look who it is," a familiar voice rasps, coming at me from my side. I spin around to see Julian limping toward me, cradling his broken-off stump to his chest. He grins, an awful yellow-tooth smile. "If I'd known, I would've just asked you for a ride. Save me some time."

The other two guys fix him with a questioning look. I stay silent, waiting — hoping — for him to smooth this over with them.

"He's all right. Just a dumb kid from town."

"How do we know he's not going to run and sell us out to them?"

"He's not. Trust me. I saw enough on the inside to know he ain't one of them. He'll behave." He rolls his gaze back to me, and I think I can spot some amusement there, a little hint of a smirk in the taut, leathery skin pulled tight across his teeth. "You're a good boy, aren't you?"

"I'm not here for trouble," I say. I'm still clutching at my truck door like it's a shield. I don't know why Julian is sticking up for me, or why he thinks he can trust me, but I'm glad he does.

When you're dead, you don't heal. You don't heal from the wounds that killed you, but you don't heal from any other damage you sustain, either. Not really. You can stitch up a bullet hole or bandage your guts back into your body and maybe the skin will kind of seal up on itself, maybe some blood will clot and plug up a little hole. But the torn skin, the broken bones — you're going to have those as long as your body lasts.

If this turns into a fight, I'm going to be feeling it forever.

Assuming they would let me leave.

"Anyway, kid, that's Elliot," Julian says, pointing at the no-arm guy. "And that's Duncan. They're in charge here, or think they are."

Duncan, the dude with the sunken-in ribcage, offers a little wave, and the hint of an uncertain smile. I realize he's younger than I first thought, maybe not all that much older than me. Maybe Olivia Nez was onto something when she said that Reanimation was hitting young people the hardest.

"Davin," I offer.

The little kid starts fussing, and his mom — or whoever that lady is — shushes him and steps away, jiggling him on a hip as she moves closer to the smoky fire. The other woman, the one with the wild hair, is still watching us with suspicion. But nobody's making a move to attack or anything, so that seems promising. I wonder if there's even more of them out here in this little community, hidden from view. How many people can a desert sustain?

A lot, actually, I realize. A lot of people can probably stay in these camps when nobody has to eat.

"And who is that?" I nod to the wild-haired woman.

"That's Gail," Duncan says. He seems to be the friendlier of the two, or maybe the dumber one; sometimes that's the same thing. He twirls a finger next to his head. "Shes loco."

Elliot shoots him a warning look, silencing him with a glare. If Gail heard or took offense to his comment, she doesn't seem to care; she's still watching me warily, her hands drawn up to her chest. Elliot's grip on her has loosened, and I see her yearning forward. Her nostrils flare, like she's trying to smell something.

"So, uh. You're all out here. Off the grid," I say, taking a stab at conversation. "Did you all escape from the Lazarus House, too?"

Elliot, the guy with one arm, shakes his head. "Some of us did, some of us didn't. We come from all over. Just getting by as best we can, you know."

I do know, or think I do.

I have the privilege of a house and a boyfriend and a community of Undead. If I didn't have that, where would I have ended up? If Randy hadn't found me on the side of the road after my accident, would I have still somehow made it back home to Zoe? If things had been just slightly different, would I have ended up out here, hiding from Coalition raids and surviving out among the weeds and ruins of abandoned well sites?

And they were already here the day I died. I'm sure of it now. That's what I saw on the bridge.

Were they watching me? Did anyone come to investigate? Did they think about taking me in?

"How haven't I heard about you before? We were up and down this highway selling Lazarus for months. I thought I knew every off-the-books Undead for a hundred miles. Unless…you're all off Lazarus?"

There's a social movement, or maybe just a little club, of users on one of those deep web internet forums about the Undead. They call themselves The Dusty Bones, and they're Undead who have chosen not to take any drugs. When I first heard about them, I figured it was some kind of fringe conspiracy stunt or something — because at the time, everybody knew that going off Lazarus was impossible. That you would come out on the other side a monster.

My gaze shifts to Gail, and I can feel the crease in my brow, feel the worry lines deepen in a frown that I did not mean to make.

Elliot laughs. There's no humor in it. "We get ours direct from the source," he says. "So we don't need any door-to-door sales shit here. Unless you need something, I'd like you to get back in that truck and leave us alone."

"Oh, no, I'm not…" I frown. What does he mean, direct from the source? The Lazarus House? I have a million questions, but I can also see that they've got my truck surrounded, a loose semicircle of Undead slowly converging on me. "I just had no idea you were out here. I had no idea anyone was living like this."

"Nobody lives out here," Duncan says.

"And we're not a petting zoo." Elliot drops his hand from Gail's side, taking a step sideways, and Duncan and the wild-haired woman advance. Julian is doubled over, hacking up thick gobs of black goo, and doesn't seem to be paying any attention to me or the others. "So I'm going to ask you nicely one more time, get the fuck out of our home."

I slide back into the driver's seat, pulling the door closed. Fumbling at the keys in the ignition.

Just in time; Gail lunges, slamming both fists on the hood with enough strength to leave two shallow dents. She doesn't flinch. Her eyes are locked on me, and up close I can see that there's something weird about them; her pupils are huge, absorbing the iris, taking up the whole eye like a cat on catnip. Her lips are curled up in a snarl and I think: That's just how Javier looked, before he tore into Chuy's guts.

I ease onto the gas and back away, pulling out until I find a space wide enough to turn. I glance in the rearview mirror and there she is, following after me until the truck starts picking up speed, like a guard dog chasing an intruder off the family property. Eventually I lose sight of her in the dust and the drizzling rain, but I'm certain she's keeping pace until I get almost to the highway.

***

I should have asked for more information. Now that I'm pulling away, now

81

that the immediate threat of a fight is fading, I'm realizing how stupid it was to walk away without answers. I should have forced Julian to explain what he had meant about the Lazarus House. I should have made him explain why he looks like he does, why he was so set on escaping. I should have asked Elliot what he meant about getting their Lazarus from the source.

I glance in my rearview again, even though I'm out on the highway, even though I've put miles between myself and their camp now.

There's nobody there. Of course there isn't. How would they have followed me?

Home's still a long way out, and now I'm buzzing with nerves, so I pull out my phone and tuck it into the center console, calling Randy on speed dial before putting him on speaker. He answers on the second ring, and I quickly fill him in on what's happened: Julian the Lazarus House escapee; the Undead camp in the middle of the desert; the way they've slipped under even our radar by getting their Lazarus right from the source.

I don't tell him about my dad. I don't tell him about his insistence about rats in the walls. I don't tell him about Chuy being Undead, either. Those are a different kind of horror, the kind I want some time to mull over on my own. They're different somehow than the Undead in the desert, whose existence is more of a puzzle, an enigma, than an open wound.

Randy listens, interrupting only to get clarification here or there on small points. It feels good to unload like this, to just relay back the facts as they happened; I can feel some of the tension starting to ease out of my shoulders. But it's short-lived.

"So there's a leak at the Lazarus House," Randy says, when I'm all finished. "Somebody, somewhere, is still selling."

"That's your take-away from this?" I can't hide the incredulity in my voice. How badly did I have to explain — or how badly did he have to listen — that this would be the place his mind ended up. "You're just going to gloss over the part where Julian said he's escaped from the Lazarus House? Where they're doing…whatever it is they're doing? Where he's obviously *not* getting any Lazarus?"

"I heard all that. I just can't see what it has to do with me."

"What it —" I cut myself off before I say something I know I'll regret. I clamp my teeth together so hard I can feel the roots shifting in my gums. "If there's something shady going on in there, if they're doing something bad…"

"You mean worse than picking people off the street and locking them up? Jesus, Davin, you don't have to go hunting for a conspiracy here. It's a detainment camp. It's already bad."

"All right. Fine. So the Lazarus. What's your point?"

He exhales, a long bracing sigh, and then draws a rattling breath. Sometimes his voice rasps, caught in the closed-up places where his throat was crushed by the rope. It's gotten steadily worse since we went off the Lazarus. "Okay. Let's think about it for a second. We know that going off Lazarus doesn't make you go crazy or lose your mind, because we're all fine. But to hear you tell it, this Julian guy looked like a mummy in — how long?"

"Two months," I reply, not liking where this is headed. "I don't know how he died, though, it might've…"

"Davin, unless the dude died from being packed in salt and left in the desert, I think it's probably pretty safe to assume that any…dessication…is happening because he's off Lazarus."

I sigh. He has a point.

When he speaks, his Southern accent is peeking through his words, the way it does when he's tired or excited or upset, when he loses his careful grip on enunciation. "What I'm sayin' is, great, maybe we ain't killing folks and eating their guts. But we're not exactly a hundred percent, are we? I know I'm feelin' it, and I'll bet you're feelin' it too. Like your body is falling apart."

I know exactly what he means. Being on Lazarus doesn't exactly feel like being alive, but it's a hell of a lot closer than what we're at now. I've never felt deader than I do today, and yesterday was worse than the day before. Every day is another slow spiral toward inevitable decay, and I know it and recognize it even if I don't want to admit it. Seeing Julian looking the way he does, seeing an in-the-flesh example of just why that group was calling itself The Dusty Bones? It's horrifying.

But what's the alternative?

Going back to being a criminal? Living every day in fear of being rounded up by The Coalition? Taking the risk of injecting a dose and losing my mind like Javier?

"Look. Lazarus might not be necessary for maintaining our humanity," Randy is saying. "But it sure as shit seems necessary if you don't wanna end up as a dried-out husk. And call me vain, but I think that's pretty fucking important."

There's something accusatory in his voice, like he's daring me to argue, but I don't have it in me to fight. The fact is that I don't know the right answer here. I don't know what I'm supposed to do, no better than he does.

Chapter 9

Friday comes at last, capping off what's starting to feel like the longest week of my Undead life — which is saying something. But Friday isn't about me, it's about Zoe, and the Underground, and achieving some semblance of normalcy in our routine, and I'm pretty committed to making that a success.

"You ready?"

"Just a sec." Zoe's perched on the edge of the couch, glasses sliding down her nose as she leans forward to watch the TV intently. She's wearing her favorite t-shirt, a faded emblem of a decayed hand thrusting up from the earth in a triumphant fist. "Have you been keeping up with this at all?"

I follow her gaze to the TV screen, where a black woman is being interviewed. The news-scroll caption beneath her name reads: Shaniqua Jones, mother of the deceased. The camera cuts from her to a scene inside a living room. Maybe it's a trailer, or an apartment — it's hard to tell for sure. But it's small and cramped, shabby furniture crammed into the dim space.

Taking up most of the center of the room is a long table — the kind of folding table you find in a church, thick plastic standing on thin fold-out legs. There's a bed sheet on the table, and laying on top is a teenage boy, probably Zoe's age or a little younger. He's wearing nice clothes, Sunday best, and his hands are loosely folded over his chest, his eyes sunken behind closed lids, mouth a colorless line. His dark skin has gone ashy with death, and there's something weird about his limbs, something bloated and swollen — lividity, the blood pooling from gravity and a heart that's long stopped beating.

A scene like that, you'd expect him to be surrounded by flowers, but there are none. Just some candles burning, flickering in glass hurricane vases.

The camera cuts away again. I reach for the remote, curious, and turn up the volume.

"…for eight days. No known reports of Undead returning after more than three days have been documented. Neighbors have issued a formal complaint, citing unsanitary living conditions as the body has begun to noticeably decay."

The camera changes now to a neighbor, another black woman with a toddler slung on her hip. The little girl has a pacifier in her mouth and is staring boredly off screen, but her mother is focused with laser-like intensity on the camera.

"It's not that I don't sympathize, because I do. I love my babies. They mean the whole world to me. I'd be devastated if I lost them. But it's like, girl, you got to know when you're done, and that boy ain't coming back."

The camera cuts away again, back to the reporter, a white woman with windswept hair and a tweed jacket, bundled up against autumn cold in some climate far from New Mexico. "While Shaniqua's case is perhaps the most dramatic, it does speak to an emerging trend. The CDC reports that fewer new Undead have risen this year than had by this point in the two years prior. The exact cause for this decrease in number is unknown, but scientists are speculating that new regulations governing Undead containment may play a role. Scientists acknowledge that it's too soon to be sure, but this unusual pandemic may have begun to run its course. This could be promising news for Governor Lynch's presidential bid, which has so far made a strong case for revising the policies surrounding treatment and citizenship of Undead…
"

I switch off the television.

Zoe turns to look at me, brows lifted. "Remember what Adrian said?"

"Let's get going," I say, realizing that I have so much to tell her now — about Julian, about the Lazarus House, about Chuy — and not knowing how to begin sharing something that big. It can wait until after the party, anyway.

***

We car-pool to the coffee shop because having too many cars in the lot after hours would be too suspicious. Randy insists on driving, so we're in the Mercedes, Zoe squished into the back seat and my knees pressed up into the dash. There are blood stains, long since dried, in the passenger seat, black-brown memories of when he picked me up off the side of the highway. There's a bullet hole, too, in the side panel, from that night where everything went wrong with Javier.

Randy could afford to fix these things, I'm sure, but he doesn't bother, for the same reason that he lets the trash pile up in the floor board. Because Randy likes to have nice things and neglect them; because suicide didn't work for him, but self-destruction is a hard habit to kick. We don't talk about it, but I know what self-loathing looks like.

All the same: It is a nice car, and it might actually be a little roomier inside than the truck.

CJ's is mostly dark by the time we pull up. If I didn't know better, I'd think the place was abandoned. The sign on the front door says "Closed Early for Special Event" in looping, spidery handwriting, and the double glass doors are locked. But the back door is open, a rectangle of yellow light visible beyond the dumpsters, and I pull the pickup into a space in the gravel back lot.

Ash is outside smoking when we arrive. The cigarette cherry glows in the gathering dark, and he casts a long shadow beneath the dirty yellow bulb lighting up the back door of the coffee shop.

We pull into the dirt lot and I tell Zoe to go on inside without us so Randy and I can have a cigarette before we go inside. She does, but not before stopping to give Ash a hug, as if this were a normal family get-together, as if it didn't mean anything at all that all of the important people in her life were corpses.

Ash is an older guy, sort of our group's de facto father figure. Unlike the rest of us, he died of natural causes, some kind of cancer, or maybe it was mesothelioma. You'd assume it was the smoking that did him in, but it was actually breathing in industrial waste through a lifetime of construction work. He didn't start smoking, he told me once, until after he'd died —

because at that point, why not? The nicotine doesn't do much, but it gives a little hint of a buzz, a ghost of the effects of Lazarus. Or maybe it's not even the nicotine. Maybe it's the formaldehyde. They pump that into bodies in the morgue, right?

I haven't seen Ash since our Lazarus supply dried up, and though he doesn't look as bad as Julian, he isn't looking great. His skin has a weird, brittle quality to it, yellowed and translucent like the outermost layer of an onion. Patches of his scalp are visible through his thinning gray-blond hair, and I can see broad dark liver patches staining the skin. He can't be much older than fifty, but he looks ancient now, as wizened and brittle as if he'd been alive for a century.

But he smiles when he sees me, and my heart aches at the sight because he could be my father. He's just about the right age. And, in a way, he's taken on that paternal role for all of us here in The Underground. When Randy found me on the side of the road, freshly resurrected and caked in mud and gore, it was Ash's house he brought me to. When we found out that the Lazarus was drying up and we were all facing withdrawal on our own, it was Ash who tried to give us reassurance. And now here he is, giving birthday hugs, being present, planning a goddamn party. It's not fair, and I guess I should be grateful for this family I've fallen into in death, but all I can think about is Dad's incoherent rambling, the way his room looks like a prison cell because he always has to ruin anything he touches.

"Hey Davin, Randy," Ash says. He stamps out a cigarette with the toe of his shoe and reaches to light up another. "Been a while."

"Yeah, sorry about that," I say. "Time has been kind of getting away from us. How are you holding up?"

He shrugs. "Well, I ain't dead yet," he jokes.

"We might have some good news in that department," Randy says, lighting up a cigarette and handing it to me before lighting up his own — a habit he's had as long as we've known each other. I take the cigarette he offers and before I can say anything he continues: "Davin's made some new friends who have a Lazarus hookup."

Goddammit. I should have known that Randy wouldn't let it go, wouldn't wait for me, wouldn't even talk to me about this before bringing it up and dragging Ash into it.

"Is that so?"

"I don't know," I say, hurriedly. And, before Randy can continue trying to tell my story for me, I lay it out in broad, swooping strokes: Seeing Gail in the desert, following her to a camp, meeting a group who said they were getting Lazarus from the source — whatever that means. "But honestly, they weren't exactly the friendliest bunch. They would have said anything to get rid of me. Probably the guy was blowing smoke up my ass."

"Let me see if I've got this straight," Ash says, resting an elbow against the wall below the light, cigarette still dangling between his fingers. Something about the pose and the shadows shifting across his features makes him look like a character from a 1940s film noir. "So you found a group of Undead out in the desert, and at least some of them claim to have escaped from the Lazarus House, yet somehow they've still got access to drugs that none of the rest of us can get?"

I nod. "It sounds far-fetched, right? And they're a whole freak show. Missing pieces, advanced decay. One guy looked like something out of an old monster movie. Practically a mummy." I feel a twist of guilt for describing them like this. But I feel a protective urge, a desire to keep those Undead in the desert away from The Underground — although I'm not really sure which group I'm protecting. Maybe both of them. Maybe they're just two worlds that I don't want to overlap.

Ash's brows lift up, surprised at this detail. He glances at Randy for confirmation.

He shrugs. "I wasn't there. I couldn't tell you. But I think it's worth looking into. You can't tell me y'all ain't the slightest bit curious?"

"It's all pretty weird," I admit.

"They sound like a rough bunch," Ash says, voice soft and thoughtful.

Randy doesn't say anything right away. He's frowning at the gravel underfoot, the scatter of ashes from several spent cigarettes. "Davin, you go up to the Lazarus House all the time — have you ever seen anybody in there who looks like those guys?"

"No." I think of the old woman with her hang-dog face. I think of the toddler I saw there once, tiny body purple and swollen. Chuy, looking alive enough to keep coming to work, his guts held in place with a girdle. I think of my dad, curled up on his bed like a snail. "But it's not like I go poking around in every room."

"Maybe we should."

I blink at Randy. He looks back at me, gaze even, and gives a little shrug. "Best way to find out, right?"

"There's no way," I protest. "For one, they've got security all over. You're not going to be roaming around there without supervision. For another, they're tightening it even more. The last time I was there, they said they might stop allowing visitors entirely."

Chuy might let us in, I think, but I don't dare say it. I don't even want Randy knowing that Chuy's still walking and talking. Considering we're part of the reason he's now a member of the Undead, I don't know if he'd be willing to put his neck out for us a second time — and I don't know that I'd ever want to ask him.

"I mean. It's the only way to know for sure what's going on, right? Seeing is believing." Randy smirks, a sly glint in his eye. "And it's the only place in town that still has Lazarus, right?"

I look uncertainly between him and Ash. Ash looks away, the way you politely turn your head and change your focus when you overhear people arguing and don't want to get dragged into it.

Randy says nothing, challenging me with his silence.

"No. No way. We're not...we're not criminals, Randy."

His brows lift.

Dealing Lazarus was different, I want to say. Reallocating prescriptions was not at all the same as breaking into locked doors or bribing officials or stealing from the source. But I don't know whether that's really true. And no matter what, we are all criminals — every last one of us from The Underground has an illegal freedom.

Before anyone can say anything, Zoe pops her head back through the coffee shop door. "Are you guys coming in or what? We're partying without you!"

Relieved at the interruption, I stub out my cigarette and head inside.

***

CJ's is a combination of coffee shop and gift store. The front half of the shop has novelties for browsing, a bar for ordering, and a few scattered tables. The back half, though, is all partitioned-off booths, private areas for discussion or study. Students come back here sometimes after school. There's probably an aspiring novelist or two in Los Ojos who comes to prod at their laptop. But mostly this meeting space is for us, the members of The Underground.

I don't know exactly how or why Delilah came to own the coffee shop that acts as the town's unofficial Undead meeting place. She's a Breather, so it's not like she's got personal stake in Undead rights or anything. But she's an old hippie type, New Agey but in a cool way — maybe that's it. Maybe it's just a rebellious spirit looking for something to latch onto.

When I go inside, Delilah is setting a birthday cake on the table. It's small, because there's only four people it needs to feed: Zoe, Delilah, her granddaughter Jo, and Ash's wife Lilith. Seeing them there, clustered around one end of the tables that have been pushed together banquet style, it strikes me how fortunate we are to have any allies at all. The Underground is small, but half of us are Breathers, and maybe that means something.

"About time!" Zoe says, looking up. She's grinning, her face flush with excitement. "We were waiting forever. Where are the other two?"

"We're here!" Randy calls, coming in behind me. He teases: "What, you're not done yet? Damn. Guess I better go outside again."

I hear footsteps, the door closing behind Ash. All present and accounted for.

No hint of the tension from outside follows us into the room, and I feel a rush of gratitude. My hand moves on its own, reaching for Randy's, and our knuckles brush, but he pulls away to investigate the celebration. Zoe's at the head of the table. Delilah and Lilith flank her, stand-in maternal figures. Jo is bringing in plates from the kitchen. Her girlfriend, Andrea, trails behind with mugs of coffee balanced precariously on a tray. Andrea's one of us — one of the Undead — and you can see the hints of decay in the lividity of her pale skin, the whispers of discoloration that mottle the inside of each arm. But her hair is clean and shiny, tied back in a high blond ponytail, and she's smiling as she sets a fancy whipped-cream-adorned coffee in front of Zoe.

I don't remember the last time we had a birthday party this big. It's possible that maybe we never did. Ours was never a big family; we didn't have a lot of cousins or close aunts and uncles like a lot kids around here. And growing up, neither of us had many friends. It was hard, with Mom's off-and-on bouts of illness, with Dad's erratic alcoholism. For a long time, the family was just me and Zoe, a couple of kids against the world, basically orphans no matter how dead or alive our parents might be.

"Well, that can't possibly be right," Randy says, pointing at the candles. "There are clearly fewer than 17 candles on this cake. Are these cheapskates trying to short-change you?"

Zoe giggles. For a minute, just a minute, she's not the citizen journalist, the passionate YouTuber, the Undead advocate. She's just a kid, a teenager with a birthday party, a cake and presents and a family. Lilith lights the candles and Ash dims the lights and we perform a self-deprecating approximation of the birthday song and Zoe's laughing so hard at our bad singing that she can barely find the breath to blow out the candles.

I take a seat at the table and Randy's hand finds my knee, fingertips gently tapping as he rests his palm against my thigh.

It's a good night, a powerful one. The last we'll have like this, as a family.

Chapter 10

T he party lasts for hours.

Zoe's gifts: A card-based party game with a political satire theme (Jo and Andrea); a shawl with a skull pattern crocheted into it (Lilith). Zoe wastes no time in sliding into the shawl, admiring it from every angle, running to the bathroom to take selfies in the mirror. It's a nice change of pace to see her documenting something from her own life instead of current events, but of course it doesn't last long. Within an hour of our arrival she's busted out her video camera and is asking interview questions of everyone at the coffee shop. Ash and Lilith leave a little after nine, but the rest of us linger, chatting, playing cards.

There's a TV bolted to the wall in the main part of the lobby, and Delilah turns it on as she starts in on the after-hours chores. I join her, grabbing the mop from the utility closet and starting in on the floor. Randy lingers in the corner, half supervising, half listening to Zoe try to coax a Lazarus withdrawal story out of Ash.

"I'm thinking of closing this place down," Delilah tells me, conversationally, as she wipes down the glass display for muffins and pastries. "Retiring."

"Yeah?"

"Business has slowed a lot," she says, not looking up. "Since it's all just coffee now."

CJ's had been our home base of operations for Underground meetings. It had also been an easy enough way to launder money and manage Lazarus orders among Undead throughout Los Ojos and surrounding areas. With that off the table for months — and more and more people seem to be getting rounded up by the Coalition — I can imagine she might be hurting financially.

I'm about to say something, looking for some comforting words to offer, when I catch an odd expression on Randy's face. He's staring over my head, gaze snapped to the television. I turn around to follow his eyes, craning my neck to see.

There's a man on the screen, well-dressed and affably charming in the sort of effortless way that older white men can manage, that easygoing manner that can hide all manner of nastiness below. He's waving at the camera and flashing a smile and I can't help but think there's something familiar about him, but I can't quite place what.

"Ezra Lynch, the popular District Attorney-turned-governor of Georgia, announced today his formal bid for a presidential run in next year's election," the broadcaster is saying, and Randy makes an odd strangled noise. I throw him a sharp look, curious and immediately on edge.

The television continues: "Beloved by his Republican constituents, Lynch is best known for his tough-on-crime policies, but his recent focus has been on the public safety threat of Undead."

The picture changes, footage of some kind of event or rally. It's out in the open, a park maybe, filmed over the heads of a small crowd clustered at the foot of the makeshift stage. I think it must be old footage, because the trees are still green, no signs of autumn touching them anywhere. But the man at the podium is the same as the last photo: well-dressed, affably charming, vaguely familiar.

"I'm committed to the safety of every living person. And if that means being cautious about the Undead, then that's what we have to do," Lynch is saying in a low Southern drawl, a rumbling voice smooth as sugar. "It's really no different than the precautions you'd take for any epidemic. It's not a political issue. It's an issue of humanity."

Randy gets up abruptly, without a word, and heads to the back door. The response is so uncharacteristic that I'm momentarily baffled. I shoot Delilah a brief questioning glance, and she just shrugs, looking as confused and alarmed as I feel.

Randy is not one to walk away from the news when it upsets him. Where is the witty comeback? The off-the-cuff analysis? Frowning, I get up and follow him to the back door, leaving the half-mopped floor behind. Zoe, who's sitting in a booth with Jo and Andrea, shoots us a questioning look as we pass, but I say nothing as I trail Randy outside.

Randy's leaning against the wall, an unlit cigarette in his hand, staring up at the sky.

"Randy…?"

"Nice night we're having," he says, breezily. His hands are shaking. I watch the white tube of the unlit cigarette flutter in his grasp.

Clouds have gathered in loose gray waves over the sky, like we're nestled down under a pile of feathers. It's cold. Or anyway, New Mexico cold, a dry chill that would raise goose pimples on my arms if my body had the energy left for such defenses.

"Uh-huh," I say. "Just had a sudden urge to come out and admire the stars, right?"

He cranes his neck, his head lolling in a loose-jointed slow pan as his gaze sweeps the sky. There's nothing visible up there but the clouds and, sliding between them, the blinking lights of an airplane.

"Somethin' like that."

"That guy on the TV," I start, sensing that I'm wading into dangerous territory. "He, um. You know him or something?"

Randy laughs then, a cold and bitter scoff, and he crosses his arms protectively across his chest, his unlit cigarette scissored between his fingers.

Something slides into place, some lazy synapse-firing in my memory. "That's not…that's not your *dad*, is it?"

"Ding ding ding, boys, tell him what he's won." The bitterness in his voice cuts like a knife.

I don't know a lot about Randy's dad. I know he's wealthy, and conservative, and ashamed of Randy for reasons both apparent and unknown. I knew that Randy killed himself, in part, out of spite, some misguided bid for sympathy or revenge. I know that his dad shipped him across the country to rot in New Mexico — out of sight and out of mind.

But I didn't ever imagine his dad would be a politician, much less one running for president. I don't know what to do with the enormity of that information. I know what it's like to have a shit dad. But the most damage my shit dad can do now is to himself, and maybe whatever Lazarus House employees he can traumatize.

"I thought I could get away from him," Randy says, and seems to remember there's a cigarette in his hand. He lights it, and takes a long, bitter drag, his body doing a shudder as if of revulsion, like he's been forced to touch something disgusting. "I really thought, if nothing else, the one bit of good in all this shit was that I could get away."

"You did, though," I say, because it seems like what I'm supposed to say, but it feels hollow even as I say it. I know what he means. The news, social media. It would be impossible to ignore his dad now, impossible to go through life without confronting him every day. I double down, even though I know I'm saying the wrong thing, because I don't know what else to do. "You got out. You've got a home here. Family. The Underground." Me, I want to add, but don't.

Randy's mouth twists into a smile. "There's one little perk to this," he points out. "If the media finds out about me, it will destroy him."

A thud of discomfort in my chest, my heart sputtering. "But they'd lock you up."

"Oh, don't worry," he says, flapping a hand dismissively in my direction. "I won't. The last of my self-destructive, spiteful impulses died hanging off a banister in the family foyer."

But I know that's not true, and a knife-twist of fear runs up through my gut and chest and throat, sharp like acid bile.

Because Randy is made of spite, and because — if this presidential bid gets serious — people will come looking for him.

And because if they find him, they'll find me. They'll find Zoe.

"Let's just go back inside," I say. My hand fidgets, fingers unfurling as if to reach out and then curling in on themselves like a wounded spider, a hesitant touch that never lands. I'm afraid to touch him, like he'll be white-hot, radiant with his pain and anger. I'm afraid that he'll push me away, and I'll be too fragile to handle the rejection.

"I'll be right there," he says, holding up his half-finished cigarette. "I'll just finish this."

I hesitate.

"C'mon. Go see if Zoe's just about ready to head home. I'll catch up with you in a second."

I head inside, but Randy never follows. When I go to check the parking lot ten minutes later, the Mercedes is gone.

***

Randy's phone goes straight to voicemail when I call, and he leaves my text on "seen."

Jo offers to give us a ride back to the house, and I gratefully accept. Her car, an older model Corolla, is downright spacious by comparison to the Mercedes, even with four of us — Andrea riding shotgun, me and Zoe in the back, her camera and card box and a take-out container full of cake piled in her lap, her new shawl tugged tight around her shoulders against the surprise chill.

"Thanks again for the ride," I say, looking again at my phone to check if Randy's responded.

"Of course. It's no big. Sorry you got ditched."

"I hope he's okay," Zoe says.

"I'm sure he's fine," Andrea says. "Randy just…gets like this sometimes. Something sets him off and then he's the only person in the world who matters. He'll get over himself in a couple days."

"It does suck he's dragging you into his shit, though," Jo says. "I know you guys have gotten close or whatever, but Randy's a hot mess."

She sounds protective, almost sisterly, and I appreciate the sentiment. But I can feel my nerves rising, that immediate knee-jerk desire to defend him. I quickly change the subject. I want to be pissed and hurt and worried on my own time.

Jo pulls up the curb, and I help Zoe with her armful of gifts. She's still riding high on the good birthday mood, and she sugar-crashes almost immediately.

I'm expecting her to get online like usual, but she's in bed and snoring within half an hour. I listen to her through the walls of my bedroom as I lie awake, staring at the ceiling and the ghosts of the stick-on stars that are long-since gone, and try to make sense of what's swirling around in my head.

***

At some point, I manage to sleep, and when I do, I sleep like the dead.

It's past noon by the time I wake up, but it's the weekend so I guess it doesn't matter — even by the standards of the living and the employed, you can get by with sleeping in on a Saturday. I'm out on the porch, sitting on the picnic table and smoking a cigarette, when Zoe pops her head out.

"Davin! Davin! Come check this out!" She sounds as excited as if she'd just discovered the secret of cold fusion.

I stub out the cherry on my mostly-spent smoke. "What is it?"

"I got it! It's not great, I mean, it kind of looks like ass, but I think it'll totally work!" She beams.

"Am I supposed to know what the hell you're talking about?"

"The footage?" She raises her hands in exasperation, as if I'm the biggest idiot she can imagine for not having already figured that out. "You know? You and Randy? Lazarus withdrawal? The video evidence that totally undoes literally everything the public is saying about the Undead?"

"Oh right," I say. "That footage."

She rolls her eyes. "Do you want to see it or not?"

I have to admit I'm curious. I know more or less what to expect, because I was there for it. But, in a real sense, I also was *not* there: Whole chunks of those long days are missing from my memory, like a black-out drunk who's lost a night of embarrassment. And, like the morning-after drunk, I'm a little anxious about what I'm going to see. But I follow her down the hall all the same, peering over her shoulder as she pulls up the footage in a video editing program with a dizzying number of buttons and readouts and options. But there, in a tiny thumbnail above a bunch of illegible rows of wavy lines, I can make out a grainy desaturated image of two people in a room.

"I left this running all night to compile while we were out. I've been reviewing it and putting the finishing touches on it all morning. Check this out."

Zoe clicks on the thumbnail image, expanding it to fill the screen, which doesn't do a whole lot to improve the image quality. It looks granulated, like the footage from the world's worst security camera. The angle is security camera-like, too, looking down on us with a fish-eye view, distorted around the edges. Between the brightness settings — which I can tell she's jacked way up to make the dark room more visible — and the grainy desaturation, Randy and I are almost unrecognizable. That makes me feel a little better.

"This looks like one of those zoo cams," I say. "Like we're pandas or something."

"Oh, hush. I didn't exactly have a studio to work with here."

The footage has been edited pretty extensively, fitting two days of torment into just a few minutes, speeding up and skipping long hours with dissolves and jump-cuts. But she's done well with laying out the timeline. A text overlay keeps track of the hours as they pass, marking milestones.

One Hour: I'm sprawled on the bed, arms flung over my face as if to block out a too-bright light. I roll from one side to another in hyper-speed, thrashing around like someone trying to get comfortable in a hot room, blankets on, blankets off. Randy's pacing the other side of the room, making small little back-and-forth trips across the floor from the master bath to the window and back again.

Six Hours: I'm at the door, barely visible in the feed. I'm pounding on it, clawing at it like a senseless animal. The whites of my eyes are visible, bright flashes in the distortion of my face. I crane my neck backward, staring up at the camera with wide unseeing eyes, mouth hanging open, swaying unsteadily on my feet. It looks like something from a horror movie, some low-budget art house zombie film, and watching it now I can feel my skin crawl.

Ten Hours: I'm sprawled on the floor, a vacant corpse. Randy is tearing at the curtains, shredding the fabric with his fingers like claws. The curtain rod falls, but he doesn't even flinch.

Twelve Hours: We're both dead asleep on the floor. We don't move, don't breathe, don't stir. We are two corpses.

Sixteen Hours: Randy is on the bed, disemboweling a pillow. He pulls out fistfuls of stuffing, tearing and shredding, his face a mask of rage. I'm back to clawing at the door. There's no sound, mercifully, but my mouth is wide open again, a silent primal scream.

Twenty Hours: Randy hangs over the side of the bed, vomiting something vile onto the carpet.

Twenty-Four Hours: We're both in bed. Randy's sitting upright, clutching the ruins of a pillow to his chest, rocking back and forth. I'm lying on my side. My hand reaches for him, and in the footage you can just barely see his lips moving.

"Did you edit out the audio?" I ask, suddenly sharply aware of what was being said in that moment, of what pain was being shared.

Zoe shakes her head. "I didn't record audio. I didn't think I really needed to since I was, like, on the other side of the door. And a webcam is a whole other thing than a microphone. Why?"

"Never mind."

In the footage, I've pulled close to Randy, and we've fallen into an awkward embrace. I can hear in my mind the words that are missing: His confession of pain, the suicide that offered no relief. *I wanted to see him grieve*, he'd told me. *I woke up alone, and I couldn't even cut myself down. And I thought, this is Hell. This is what it means to go to Hell.*

Thirty Hours: We're dead asleep in each other's arms, two refugees against the world, like lovers buried together to be unearthed by confused anthropologists.

Thirty-Six Hours: I'm stirring to life. The footage is brighter here, the daylight coming through the windows helping to make it clear. The room is a mess; I'm glad the footage is in black-and-white, because I remember waking up in that room painted in blood and bile and thinking it looked like a murder scene. It's a little better this way, a little softer. In the footage, I sit and stare for a long time, but that vacant zombie gaze, those milk-white fish eyes, has cleared. I look human again, in a way even the camera can pick up.

Thirty-Eight Hours: Randy and I have gotten out of the bed, disappearing into the bathroom. The camera stays trained on the empty, ruined bedroom.

Forty-Hours: We emerge, damp, wearing towels. In the present moment, I cringe. I remember pretty well what happened in the shower, too, and it's high on my list of things I will never, ever talk to my little sister about. But in the footage, at least, we look…clean. Presentable.

Zoe's edited it so that the final image is a freeze-frame, just a stray glance where I happen to look up at the camera. Pixelated though it is, it's a strong contrast with that feral-faced zombie who had been clawing at the door. It's footage that tells a story, and I'm impressed. No — I'm proud as hell. I also don't know what to do with it now that I've seen it.

"I'm sorry you had to see all that," I say.

She looks at me like I've suddenly grown another head. "Why?"

"It's…it's not a pretty sight, most of it." *What if that had been the last image she'd ever seen of you,* I'm thinking. *What if you had never come through the other side? What if forever, you were reduced to that wide-eyed screaming monster?*

"It is what it is," Zoe says, and shrugs. "Anyway, that's not the point. The point is that you're fine now. You start out normal, you go through this… I don't know, this feral phase or whatever. And then you come out on the other side and you're fine."

Is that what happened to Javier? Was that a temporary phase? Did he awaken at some point, blood running down his chin, and wonder what had happened? Could he taste flesh on his tongue? Was he ashamed?

But, by the same token: Those people on the news, the blank-eyed Undead cut down by police. Had *their* status been temporary? If they had been captured rather than killed, if they had been held with compassion rather than destroyed like rabid animals, would they have come through on the other side whole and complete and normal?

"It's just a withdrawal," Zoe's saying, with the excitement of someone who's solved a puzzle and is eager to explain it to anyone who will listen. "It's like coming off of heroin or something. Like, they look pretty scary, too, I bet. But it's just. A thing that happens. And we have it all here on tape. God. I can't believe I managed to get this footage to work. You have no idea how much…Davin?"

I realize I've been staring past her, barely hearing. My eyes are still fixated on that still image of me staring up at the camera, but my mind's elsewhere. I'm thinking of Gail in the desert, with her huge pupils and her lip curled in a snarl, lunging for my truck. I think of her crouched over a carcass in the middle of the road in the rain. I don't think that all of us come through the other side of this and remain entirely whole. Is it just left to chance? Could things have gone a different way for me — a path where I never return to myself, where I stay that slack-jawed, empty-eyed creature on the tape? Or is there some part of this that we're missing?

Zoe's staring at me.

"Sorry. It's. It's great. You did a great job. I'm proud of you."

"I'd really like to post it," she says. "I think it'd make for a really powerful episode on the show. My supporters are going to go nuts."

"I don't know if that's a great idea," I say, automatically. "I mean. My face…"

"It's pretty blurry," she says. "I don't think anybody's facial recognition software is going to pick that one out."

"I know, but…"

Her eyes narrow.

What I don't tell her: I don't know if it'll make any difference. If this is normal — if this is the real truth — then surely we're not the only people in the world who have figured it out. And that it's not front-page news already means that someone, somewhere out there, is trying to stop it. Someone is trying to cover this up, or else there's a ton of stuff like this already out there and nobody cares. Zoe thinks this is going to be the thing that blows some kind of movement wide open, as if the reason the police and the government are treating the Undead like they do is because they just don't know any better.

"Have you ever seen anybody else saying anything about this?"

"The Dusty Bones," she says. "Although, I haven't heard much of anything from them at all lately. I've never seen a video like this, though. Normally the videos are just…you know."

"Like the first couple minutes of this one," I say, and pantomine the silent bug-eyed scream, the grotesque twist of the head and wide jaws. When she doesn't laugh, I straighten my features. Zoe used to think I was both cool and hilarious, but I think we're long past that at this stage. She's gotten old enough to realize that she's always been the cooler sibling. "So what happens when somebody takes your video, cuts it down, reposts it to make it look like I'm a demonic monster, and then someone comes after us with a mob?"

"Oh my *god* Davin you are so paranoid."

"Am I, though? I think it's a good question."

She rolls her eyes, but I think I can sense some hesitation in her now. "They can steal it all they want. We've got the original."

"I'm just not super comfortable with it," I press, and, because I hate seeing the irritated disappointment on her face, quickly add, "not yet. I'll think on it. And you'll need Randy's permission, too."

"I bet Randy will think it's *awesome*."

She's probably completely right, but I don't want to tell her that.

✳✳✳

The video gives me as good a reason as any to try Randy again. I don't bother to call, just send a text: *Hey, Zoe got the footage of that night fixed. U want to see?*

No response for a while, and I set my phone down and get on with my day, cleaning moldy leftovers out of the fridge, sweeping up cigarette butts that have escaped from the ashtray outside. When I do go check my phone again, there's a new message notification, but it's not from Randy.

It's from Chuy:

Tell your boyfriend not to try snooping around out here again. It's not safe.

Chapter 11

"Christ, Davin, you're blowin' up my phone like a debt collector. What?"

Randy sounds tired when he answers, voice sleep-fogged and hoarse. Something in my chest unclenches immediately when I hear his voice, replaced almost instantly with annoyance.

"I've been trying to get hold of you all day."

"I noticed that."

"You didn't think maybe there was a reason?"

"*You* didn't think there was a reason I wasn't answering? I didn't want to talk. Shit. What is this, an inquisition?"

I can feel Zoe's eyes on me through the back door, and I shift my weight and lower my voice. I'm bent almost double on the picnic table, a steadily depleting pack of smokes next to me. "I just wanted to be sure you were okay."

"I'm okay," he replies, with an edge of snark like he's spoiling for a fight. Then he sighs, and, more softly, "I don't want to talk about my dad."

"That's not…" my cigarette dies, and I fumble to light another one. "You just left. Without saying anything."

"Yeah. I wasn't thinking. I came back, and I guess Jo gave you a ride by then already. Sorry."

"Did you…go somewhere today?"

He hesitates. "I went out for a drive, yeah." A moment's pause, and then, almost sheepish. "I went out past the Lazarus House. I was looking for those people you were tellin' me about. Which, for the record, we need a good nickname for. Didn't find them, though, if that's what you're freakin' out about."

"Did you stop at the Lazarus House?"

"Seriously, what's the deal with the twenty questions? <u>Yes</u> I stopped by. Nobody would let me in. They've got the place defended like Fort Knox."

"I'm asking because somebody <u>saw</u> you. Somebody who knows…" Deep exhale. "Chuy. He's Undead. He still works there. And I know because he's texting me some kind of threat about you coming around. So I'm going to really need you to explain what happened and why you haven't been answering my calls."

The line goes quiet for a minute, and I'm half afraid that he's hung up, but when I look at the screen the call is still live.

"So…were you planning on tellin' me that Chuy's still walkin' around, or was I just supposed to find that out on my own?"

"I didn't have a chance to tell you —"

"You told me this whole big story about these Undead living out in the desert and you didn't bother to mention the part about the guy on the inside who we know is good for a connection?"

"I don't think he is," I say. "I think…I don't know what his deal is. He's not answering his phone, either. Lots of that going around. But — he told me to tell you to stay away. It's not safe. That's exactly what he said. And considering…everything…I think we'd better listen."

Randy makes an irritated noise, but seems to relent. "Fine. Whatever. It's a dead end, anyway. Like I said, there's no getting close to that place now. Have you seen it lately?"

I was just there a few days ago. How intense could it be?

***

"Hey, Zoe. Have you heard from Dad lately?"

I come back inside after finishing off the last of the smokes. I let Randy go as soon as I was satisfied he'd told me everything, when I was reasonably sure he wasn't hiding some terrible event. But now I can't let go of that lingering feeling, some parts dread, some parts curiosity.

Zoe has definitely been eavesdropping. She crosses her arms over her chest, posting herself like a temple guardian in the hallway. "So, who's Chuy?"

"Never mind that."

"What were you and Randy arguing about?"

"It's nothing."

Her eyes narrow.

"So, no calls from Dad?"

"Nope. Not since you were up there last." She frowns. "Actually, he didn't even call me on my birthday. That's pretty shitty."

Shitty, and not entirely out of character. Still, it's not doing anything to ease my nerves.

"Do you want to go for a drive?"

✳✳✳

The Lazarus House sprawls dark against the horizon. The sunset bleeds over the adobe, painting the sandstone, casting dusky hues over the surrounding desert. Above the lines of crimson and gold at the edge of the horizon, the sky fades from deep blue to black, the earliest flickers of stars poking through the darkening sky.

But no lights shine within. It looks sealed up tight. If I didn't know any better, I'd think it was empty.

I hope it's not empty.

When I called, I couldn't get through on the phone. Just an answering service, the same recorded message on a loop: *"We're sorry, but no one is available to take your call at this time. For the safety of our staff, our patients and their families, we have suspended all visitation at this time. Thank you for your understanding. We're sorry, but..."*

I don't know what I was expecting when I drove out here, but it wasn't this. I think maybe a part of me thought, or hoped, that it was some kind of joke. That I could just show up and sort it out in person, maybe have a little argument with the lady at the front desk, maybe feed her some kind of bullshit and get inside anyway. But idling at the curb at the foot of the long gravel drive, that doesn't seem very likely at all.

The gate is closed, bridging the gap between two rows of lazy barbed wire fencing. Guards patrol the perimeter of the fence; not hospital staff, either, or the overweight gatekeeper I'm used to. This looks military. National Guard, probably, dressed in fatigues, armed. They look bored, not on alert, and don't spare us a second glance — but I imagine all of that's about to change if we linger here too long. All the same, I can't help but assume they're more concerned with keeping people in than out.

"What the fuck," Zoe whispers in the car beside me, pressing her nose to the passenger side window. She's got her phone out, trying surreptitiously to get some photos. I swat at her to put it down before one of the guards sees.

What a difference just days have made. It feels like a completely different facility from when I was there last. That guy had said they'd be changing things, but I wasn't expecting that change to be so abrupt, so surreal. The place looks like it's been transformed, a hostile takeover with the new warlord guarding the castle. It's hard to even wrap my head around what's going on here, how quickly a medical facility can shift into a prison.

"It looks deserted," I say, eyes trailing over the rough adobe face of the old building. The windows are dark, giving no hint of life or activity inside. I nod toward the guards. "Aside from, you know."

"Some lockdown," Zoe agrees, and she's holding up her phone again. I don't try to stop her. "You were here, what, three days ago? And it's already like this?" She gestures, a broad sweep of the hand to indicate 'this.'

"They had to have been planning this for months," I say, but I don't even know if that's true. How long does it take to get a military deployment like this? If the government wants to move, what's stopping them from doing it immediately? I honestly have no idea, but I know I'm so far out of my depth that I feel like I'm drowning. I don't need to breathe, but the pressure on my chest is suffocating anyway. "We need to get out of here."

The news stories about the violent Undead. The government assistance to put your loved ones into a facility. The advertisements. Everything pointing toward rounding up the Undead — and now here it is, the second phase, the part where they barricade the doors and keep everyone under lock and key.

Viewed this way, in hindsight, it's impossible to see it as anything but a malicious scheme. It's impossible to believe that the facility ever once might have had good intentions.

And I put my dad here. However much of an asshole he is, I was the one who put him here.

"And who knows what else there is inside," Zoe is saying. "Who knows what else they know that nobody is telling the rest of us."

Not long ago, I would have dismissed this kind of talk — this Dad-like conspiracy theorizing. But a broken clock is still right twice a day, and sometimes powerful people keep terrible secrets. Sometimes the conspiracies are true.

I don't know what's going on in there, and I don't want to know. But I know I don't want to linger outside any longer. I release the brake and peel out, turning around at the last minute, and realize that I could just walk away from all of this right now. Maybe I never need to cross the river, never need to drive past the place where I died. If I want, now, I could live my entire life on the other side of the Rio de Animas and pretend that the Lazarus House doesn't even exist.

A part of me wants to believe I could really do that.

***

I don't dare take Zoe to the Undead camp in the desert, but I return on my own two days later.

But first, Randy comes on Sunday, and we spend some time playing the card game Zoe got for her birthday — three people playing at being a family. I don't talk about my worries about what might be happening to my dad behind the double fences of his treatment facility, and Randy doesn't talk about the Lazarus. He asks Zoe about the footage and goes with her to watch it; I can't bear to see it again, so I go on to bed, waiting for him to come and slide in beside me. He does, finally, and his hands on me, under my boxers, his breath on the back of my neck, is enough to make me forget everything for a while.

When I wake up, Randy's gone, but he's sent some money to me through a phone app, with a string of incomprehensible emojis: man, money bag, smile with the cross-ways tape on its mouth, wrapped gift.

"Hey, Zoe. I'm heading out for a bit." I stop outside her closed door to tell her.

"Job app stuff?"

"Yeah, something like that."

It's not lying if she suggests it first.

On my way out of town, I stop off at the feed store that dabbles in sporting goods. It smells like warm leather and grain inside, and there's hay bales stacked up front displaying pumpkins, big orange ones and knobby mottled green ones and pale, squat white ones with protuberant ribs. I pass these and head to the back, where they keep their camping equipment; it's on clearance, lingering remnants of a long-past Labor Day sale. I pick up two large blue tarpaulins and a sleeping bag.

There's a small section of toys near the register, so I pick out a little plush toy from the shelf — gray and black, shaped clumsily like a roadrunner with the New Mexico zia symbol stitched into its breast and two long, floppy legs. I pay for the supplies, grimacing at the cost.

But it's an investment.

I hope.

I don't drive all the way out to the camp. Instead, I stop off just off the road, far enough from the highway that curious onlookers won't easily see what I'm doing. But far enough, too, that it's clear I'm not trying to invade on the Undead's territory. I lay out my supplies and weight them down with a heavy rock, toeing it sideways first to check for any snakes hidden underneath and then laughing to myself at the absurdity of being afraid of a rattlesnake right now. As if my blood were not already thick sludge in my veins. As if my heart wasn't already rhythm-optional.

I write a note and slip it into a plastic bag, sliding it down into the doughy rolls of the sleeping bag: *Maybe we can help each other. Tell me what you need.*

***

I'm not expecting Chuy to answer, but I text him anyway: *Hey. In the neighborhood. Want to meet up?*

But he does reply, and fast; my phone's vibrating before I have the chance to put it back in my pocket. It just says: *Casino?*

***

The casino is out past the Lazarus House, just inside the borders of the reservation. Midday on a weekday, it's pretty empty — mostly old folks gambling their Social Security checks. But as a meeting place, it has a few distinct advantages. One: It's loud. Every machine makes a different noise, clicking and tapping and chiming and blaring, and the speakers pipe in Golden Oldies to appease the retirees. The Platters are crooning "The Great Pretender" over scratchy speakers when I walk in.

Another advantage: You can smoke inside, and nobody really cares much about loitering. Especially on a weekday. Aside from old folks feeding money into machines, there's usually a few people lingering inside for free drinks and shelter from the weather. Nobody tends to pay them that much mind as long as they don't bother anyone and pretend to be interested in the slots when someone walks by.

Today, I guess we get to be those people.

There's a part of the casino filled with older, less popular games tucked away in a corner. Nobody's back there today, so that's where I arrange to meet Chuy, grabbing an ash tray and camping in front of a machine with a buffalo theme. The machine next to it is vaguely Halloweeny, with symbols like a bandaged mummy and a zombie with an exposed brain. I turn my back to it on principle and light a cigarette.

"You a gambler?" Chuy asks by way of greeting as he pulls out a chair two machines down, settling in like he's thinking of playing.

"No," I admit. "As a rule, never."

"That's smart," he says. "The game is rigged, you know? You might win a little sometimes, but if you stay long enough the house always wins."

All the same, he's pulling a 20-dollar bill out of his pocket and feeding it into the machine. He's wearing scrub pants and a sleeveless t-shirt pulled over the tight girdle holding in his guts. I guess he must have come straight from his shift. I wonder why he's finally agreed to meet with me, and I've got so many questions, I'm not sure which to ask first.

He sets the machine to the lowest possible bet, spending a penny per spin just to make it look like he's doing something.

"Nobody answers the phone at the facility anymore when I call," I say, finally.

"Yeah. It's this whole new thing. I guess there was this leadership change way up the chain? He came in to do some stuff different and try to renew that government contract or whatever. Some of the other places, in other states, were already kind of like that."

"So what's the deal? Is it just, like…"

"Just an optics thing, you know." He shrugs. The slot machine makes some kind of overtures like he's made a good hit, but it's just a dollar win. "Honestly, we hardly ever got visitors, anyway. I think you're in there more than just about anybody."

"Really?"

"Yeah, man. Nobody wants to see their family like that, you know. You take all the people who visit a prison, and subtract that from all the people who visit a nursing home, and that's about what you've got."

He goes silent for a while, pressing buttons and staring at the screen like he's deeply absorbed in his low-stakes game. I light up another cigarette. A woman comes by asking if we'd like any drinks, and I take a water bottle to be nice. It's small, half-size, with a cheap-looking custom label glued on. I roll it around in my palm and try to think of how I can ask the questions I want answered without giving away everything I know.

"Chuy…I'm sorry. For leaving you like we did. That was messed up."

"Yeah, man, that whole night was pretty messed up," he agrees, without looking up. "Probably in my top three worst nights ever."

I have a hard time imagining what could be worse than dying with somebody ripping out your insides. "What happened? After we left?"

"Well, Felix had a gun," he says.

I have to resist the urge to roll my eyes. Obviously Felix had a gun. I remember that part pretty clearly, considering he shot it at the car when we took off. The bullet grazed Randy and I had to clean up the hole and stuff it with paper towels from the casino bathroom.

"So he took care of Javier and booked it outta there, I guess. I dunno, man. I was out of it by then. Last thing I remember was Felix like, blam blam!" He pantomimes firing a gun, hands together, both forefingers extended. "Then I wake up and I'm in the morgue, you know? And I'm like, knocking on the door of that big fridge thing they've got me in."

"Wait. Wait. Hold up. So they know? You're registered and everything?"

"Yeah, man. There's a lot of us working there these days, here and I guess in other states too. Kinda like how all the laundry and cooking and shit at prison is all done by inmates. You knew that, right?"

My cigarette's gone cold in my hand because I've forgotten to smoke it. I'm staring now, uncomprehending, trying to wrap my head around that development.

"I mean not everybody, obviously. There's doctors an' stuff like that. Science guys. But the rest of us, all we gotta do is clean and keep the patients company and stuff, so…" he shrugs. "It's a pretty good deal, man. They let me come and go, too, as long as I'm back by curfew. I've got a bed, don't have to pay rent…best job I've had. If you want an in…"

"No!" I say, too sharply, and hurry to continue, "I mean, no, that's okay. I'm not…Chuy, have you told anybody?"

He laughs, shaking his head. "Davin, what kind of guy do you take me for? No way. I know you've got family to take care of, too, it's not my place to decide how you do that. I'm just saying, if you wanted…"

The idea doesn't sound terrible. That's the crazy thing about it, the really messed up part — I'm imagining that life, and it doesn't seem too bad. Money, a place to stay. Maybe a year from now, if I could last that long. Maybe Zoe could be okay on her own somehow. Could she stay with Jo and Delilah? The possibilities are blossoming in my mind so fast and so sharp that I've almost forgotten everything I came here for, all the answers I'd wanted to demand.

"That day in the park," I say, struggling to keep above water, fighting against the current of the thoughts now pressing through my head. "The thing that happened with Javier. Do you know why that happened?"

"I dunno, man. It's just a thing that happens sometimes. Every so often, you see people on the inside too — they just go loco."

"She's loco," Duncan said, finger twirling by his temple. Gail's wild eyes, flashing as she lunged for the truck.

"But why? What causes it?"

He shrugs, hitting a button on the machine. It spits out a ticket for $21.67. "Quit while you're ahead, see? Even if it's not by much. That's how you do it."

He gives me a friendly sort of punch on the shoulder as he passes by.

"I gotta get back. It was nice catching up, man. You take care out there. Tell me if you need a job recommendation, yeah?"

Chapter 12

I'm distracted all night, and the next day. Zoe asks if I've got any leads on a job and I have to fight back the urge to laugh, have to bite back the hysteria because, well, maybe? Maybe I do. But I don't say anything, because it's not something I want to talk about until I'm certain how I feel, one way or another. Because there's so much now piling up that she doesn't know, even though we never used to be the kind of family who kept secrets.

Randy comes over the next night, and we're in our usual places: Zoe tucked up into a chair, legs folded up under her, phone in hand and TV tuned to the news. Randy and I in the couch. He's fidgeting with a throw pillow, a distant kind of look on his face like he's partly somewhere else. I know the feeling pretty intimately, but it's weird to see him wearing it. He's always been so good at playing it cool.

But the TV makes it pretty clear where his brain is. It's the mid-week headline slump, and nothing makes better time-slot filler than election news. As the hour strikes for the national news to start, the headline story opens with a photo that's starting to become all-too-familiar: Ezra Lynch, his careful smile, his easy Southern charm.

Zoe's leaning forward in her seat, trying and failing to be covert as she searches our faces for a reaction. She hasn't figured it out — she's privy to fewer of Randy's secrets than I am — but she's starting to catch on. Randy's Pavlovian flinch at election news isn't exactly subtle. She'd have it worked out soon, I'm sure, but then the news goes ahead and blows it open, bursting the mystery like a pustule coming to a head.

A jump cut, and then there's a photo up on the screen, blown up so big you can make out the film grain. It's indisputably Randy, but it looks so different that all I can do is stare, trying to reconcile it with what I know, with the person sitting beside me. He's younger in the picture, maybe a teenager, with mousy brown hair that's been carefully cut and combed into an Ivy League haircut. His face is somber, no hint of his signature smirk, and his eyes have a cold, faraway look in them like he's drawn up inside himself and shuttered a protective hatch. He's dead now, but he looks a lot more alive than he does in this photo.

"Lynch's son, Randall, tragically lost his life just after his 21st birthday…"

I glance sidelong at Randy, seeing his eyes go wide, then narrow to slits. He makes a dive for the remote, cranking up the volume as he bends forward, almost double, like he'll see more of the TV if he leans in closer. There's an energy radiating off of him, a kind of miasma that seems almost tangible, a crackling electricity. I had thought he was angry when I caught up with him outside CJ's that night, but that was nothing compared to this.

The television, blind to the small-scale drama unfolding in the living room, continues with its bloodless report.

"…lost to a drug overdose, an event which shook Lynch to the core and solidified not just his firm stance against drugs but his faith in God."

"They say the Lord never gives you more than you can handle," Randy's dad is saying now on the TV, in a way that almost feels sincere. "But losing my only son rocked my whole world. I almost gave up on it all. But the Lord came to me and said, Ezra, you have work to do. And that's what I'm here for."

Randy's knuckles strain against the skin of his tightening fist, the pale skin a stark contrast to the couch upholstery where he's buried his fingers. A muscle in his jaw works and pulses. He's grinding his teeth so hard I'm afraid they might crumble.

Then all at once he's rocketing off the couch, an explosion of energy, and I wince and pull away, trying to duck the fall-out of a nuclear blast. Randy plunges his hand into his pocket, pulls out his phone. I can see from where I sit that he's visibly shaking, his hand trembling even as he punches in the number, but his face is a mask of tightly controlled fury.

The phone takes a while to connect. He waits in patient silence, rage slowly mounting.

"Hi. Yes. I'm calling for Ezra." Faux civility dripping barely concealed rage. His lips have gone thin and white, bared back from his teeth. I want to tell Zoe to go to bed, to urge her out of the living room, but we're both frozen in place, like Randy's a bomb that might go off if either of us move.

"Yes, I'm aware. Tell him it's from his son." The words twist, knife-point stabs of irony. "Yes. The dead one. You tell that son of a bitch that —"

Silent then, cut off, eyes gone wide.

He stares disbelievingly at the phone screen, as if astonished by the audacity of whoever had just hung up on him. Zoe and I watch him, shocked into silence, not knowing how to ask the obvious questions that are looming and not knowing what to do with this sudden agitation that rolls off him. He's shaking his head.

"I've gotta go," he mutters, turning for the door.

"Randy —" I reach for him, then, shocked out of my stillness. I'm out of the couch and halfway across the living room in two steps. My fingertips brush his elbow. "Stay. We should talk."

"I can't. I *can't* —"

He sidesteps my grasp, wheeling around and snatching his arm away like he thinks I'll hit him — or like he's thinking of hitting me. We're frozen like that, a half-second, him with his arm up, hand balled into a fist, me with my fingers still outstretched like some bad mock-up of the Sistine Chapel. Then he breaks eye contact and heads for the front door, and I don't follow.

He doesn't quite slam the door, but it closes hard all the same, the air pressure shifting with his absence, and I'm left standing there, feeling like I've fallen out of step with time, like I'm lagging just behind my body. Zoe's blinking at me, wide-eyed, like she's expecting me to chase after him. The television, at least, has mercifully moved on to other things, some sort of inconsequential sports news.

"You'd better go," Zoe says.

I don't know that I want to. There's a part of me that doesn't want the trouble — not the government scrutiny but most of all not the anger, that rage that closes doors and draws back fists. Not now when I've come so far, when my dad's locked away, when I've had a taste of peace. I don't need this. I don't need the drama.

That thought bumps uneasily in my brain, my gut giving a miserable lurch of realization. In this new world, without that aching need for Lazarus, without the fear of what I might do if I don't get a fix — is that the only reason I ever let him close? He found me on the side of the road like some kind of abandoned pet; he was the ferryman who drove me across the river of souls and into a new sort of afterlife. My salvation and my guide.

Is it really that easy to think about walking away?

It would be so easy. Let him go. Let all of it go. Go to the Lazarus House and let them take care of everything instead.

The low rumble of an over-souped sports car engine roaring to life out in the driveway. I lurch for the door and throw it open.

Through the windshield, I can see him, phone lifted to his ear, gesturing wildly with his free hand. I can't hear him through the glass, not over the sound of that purring Mercedes engine, but I can imagine the argument he's probably having. I imagine he's giving a piece of his mind to whoever mans his father's phone, whatever personal assistant or campaign manager or lapdog accountant has been given that odious task. Because I don't know Randy's dad, but I'm willing to bet he'll never take a phone call from his son again. I almost feel sorry for whoever's on the receiving end of Randy's rage.

I worry for a minute that he's going to back out, tear out into the darkening street, but the car stays in place. He hits the lock to let me climb in the passenger set, just as he flings his phone in the back. It lands carelessly on a stack of mail and papers, detritus that's been there who-knows-how-long, and slides down to the floorboard with a thud. I resist the urge to twist and reach back to rescue it.

"We should talk," I say, instead, and feel lame because I've already said this, because I can't think of anything else to say.

"Let's get out of here," he replies, which isn't an agreement, but it's not really a 'no' either. He pops the Mercedes into gear and backs out without looking. The back fender scrapes the asphalt at the foot of the driveway, where the incline is just a little too sharp, and the soft crunch sets my teeth on edge, but Randy either doesn't notice or doesn't mind.

I don't ask where we're going.

"There's a speed trap past that light," is all I say when he takes the turn out of the subdivision.

The car lurches a little, like a spirited horse given too much rein, but he eases off the gas and we pass the half-hidden police van without triggering the tell-tale camera flash. What I don't say is: Be careful, it's past curfew. I don't say: The Coalition patrols after dark now to pick up the Undead. I'm pretty sure any warnings like that I give are going to be received as a challenge.

"So." His knuckles bulge under the skin as he grips the steering wheel. He takes a side road, one that feeds onto an old county highway that doesn't get much traffic, and the anxious knot in my chest loosens just a little. "You wanted to talk?"

"Do you?" I don't know what I'd want if our roles were reversed. But it isn't helpful to try to imagine, anyway, because we're so different.

"I really, really fuckin' don't," he says, and the car trembles as the road gets rougher.

It takes me a second to realize he's pulling over onto the gravel shoulder. It's full-dark out now, the sky still a blanket of clouds, and the few brave lights of the pitiful Los Ojos skyline twinkle at a distance. Out here, once he cuts the headlights, it's pure dark, like we're out on the fringes of civilization instead of a couple miles from a subdivision. But the desert is a vast ocean, one that could easily swallow the town; drive a few minutes in any direction and you'll find it.

Randy shifts in the dark, and I hear a seatbelt unbuckle, hear the whisper of leather seat seats against his clothes, and then his hand is on me, pawing at the front of my jeans.

"Here?" I ask, and I can't quite tell if the anxious thumping of my ruined heart is from nerves or anticipation.

"I need…something," he says, leaning in, his breath on my neck. His voice sounds thick, half-strangled. "I need to feel alive. I need to feel *anything*."

His fingers work the button and zipper easily enough, and he nuzzles against the hollow of my neck. I'm still wearing my seatbelt. I'm still staring out into the darkness, waiting for my eyes to adjust so I can make out the shapes of cactus and bushes in the gloom. My heart flutters and stops, and I'm deathly still for a moment, a hard marble statue, unyielding and cold, but then I suck down a breath and concentrate on willing my body to react.

Randy kisses down my collar and tugs down the hem of my boxers and I shift my weight so I can free the arm that's gotten twisted under his body.

"Please," he whispers against my skin, and the weight of all the things he isn't saying, all those unvoiced demands, lies heavy in the word. "Make me."

My body reacts.

I tangle my fingers in the gelled spikes of his bubblegum-shaded hair and push his head down.

***

I can't keep it up.

I can feel his mounting frustration, the growing desperation, but I'm going softer with every passing second no matter the pressure or the rhythm or the angle he uses. He's running through every technique in his usual playbook with a fervor mounting on mania. It tickles, then hurts, a distant kind of pain that feels like maybe it belongs to someone else's body, and then sharper, more acute, and I push him away with an intake of breath hissing past my teeth. My dick falls limp and shriveled against my thigh, and I hurry to tuck it back under the waist band of my underwear.

Randy curls in on himself on the driver's seat, his skin stark white and pale against the dark interior. The moon is out, broken through the clouds in a fat white disk that bathes the car in eerie pale light. I'm amazed at how little space he takes up. He looks small, fragile, like some armored creature temporarily without its shell. I want to reach out for him, to comfort him, but when my hand moves he jerks away like I'm going to hurt him, and I freeze in place with uncertainty.

"It's not you," I say, and know instantly it's the wrong thing but it's too late to take it back. "I'm just. I'm distracted."

And I am. There's too much going on in my head, too much chatter that I can't silence.

But he's taking it as a challenge, an insult. A badge of failure.

Never mind it's my body that's malfunctioning. He's the one hurt by it.

"Let me," I say, leaning across the seat now, grimacing as my back creaks and my knee jams into the dash. "Let me make you feel good, at least."

He slaps my hand away with sudden violence, like an angry cat. "Don't fucking touch me!"

I realize that he's trembling. Beads of sweat, blood-pink, well up at his pale brow. The purple-black strangulation mark stands out starkly against his throat. The scar, that eternal reminder of his death, the hours he spent hanging from the rafters, resurrected but helpless, before the maid finally cut him down.

I'm shaking, too, but I don't know if it's for the same reason. If you could just pry someone's head open, I wonder, could you see their thoughts racing through it, blue tendrils of electricity coursing over the wrinkled gray surface? I don't know what's going on in his head, but his expression is closed-off, his dark eyes distant and glazed. He's not here, not in this moment, and I don't know how to bring him back to it.

I expect him to be breathing heavily, but of course he's not breathing at all. He's too distracted to remember.

"I'm sorry." I don't say: *You asked me to do this. You begged me. You begged because you wanted to feel dirty, you wanted me to make you feel like shit, so don't blame me for giving you what you asked for. How dare you turn this back on me. How dare you push me away.*

"S'okay," he mutters, thickly, but his dark eyes still have that faraway look, and I know it's serious because he's not making any wisecracks, he hasn't recovered with some witty retort. But he's not apologizing back, either.

But slowly, the trembling stops, and he starts to loosen the tight ball of his body. He turns the key in the ignition, and we drive home in silence.

✳✳✳

The house is dark by the time I get home. Randy is back in control of himself, his face rearranged to its usual sardonic mask. His hair is mussed, fluffy in all the places where my fingers had ruined the gel. My hand feels greasy, unclean, no matter how many times I wipe it on my pants.

"You can stay," I offer, when he pulls up to the curb.

"It's better if I don't." Maybe he senses some reluctance in my voice, or maybe he wouldn't have no matter what I said.

"Are you going to be okay?"

He shrugs. His lip curls in to a wry smile. "What do you think I'm going to do? Kill myself?"

He laughs, as though this were funny, but catches the look on my face and quiets.

"I mean, I tried that already. Didn't like it much. Not giving that old bastard the satisfaction of doing the job right a second time."

"I'll see you tomorrow?"

"Sure. Or whatever. It's no big deal." He offers me a smile. "See you."

He doesn't lean in for a kiss. I don't, either, and I don't reach for his hand. There's something between us now, some awkward, uncomfortable thing, like a plastic barrier, sticky and clinging and impenetrable. Something unspoken, and unspeakable.

I climb awkwardly from my seat, and he's pulled out and away before I reach the front door.

***

At first I think that Zoe's gone to bed, and I creep through the house in the dark so I don't disturb her. But as I pass her door in the hall, I hear the whispered sounds of mouse-clicks and staccato keyboard strokes, and pause to linger outside. The light over her door, the one she turns on while she's recording, is cold and dark. But there's no sliver of light spilling out from below the door, either. Do I want to know what she's doing there in the dark?

"Hey," she calls from the other side of the door. "Is it just you?"

"Yeah. Randy went home."

"He okay?"

I shrug, realize she can't see it, and then say, "I think so."

Fortunately, she doesn't seem to be in a hurry to press for details. I open the door and she spins in her computer chair to look, her face illuminated by the brightness of the dual monitors set up, casting their strange glow over the otherwise dark room. She's tied her hair back and changed into pajamas, but judging from the number of tabs I can see open on her screens, I don't think she's planning on sleeping any time soon.

"So I looked into Randy's dad, and he's a real piece of work," Zoe says, the computer screen shining white off her glasses in the semi-dark. "Like. Whoa. These crime policies he advocated, the cases he prosecuted. It's like he's been waging a war on Undead down there. Did you know anything about this?"

Not knowing what 'this' might be referring to, specifically, I'm left reeling a little. I don't know if I can handle any more revelations this week, not at the rate they're going. I shift my weight to lean against the door frame and try to decide what I want to tell her. It's petty, but I don't want her thinking that she knows more of Randy's secrets than I do, even though that's probably true. "I knew his dad was…some rich asshole, important somehow. I knew Randy killed himself and they covered it up by sending him out here. He's been getting hush money or whatever. The lawyer who set it all up is friends with Ash, introduced them."

"That's wild," she butts in. "I wouldn't have thought Randy was the suicide type."

I blink. Surely she had seen the scar on his neck, that livid purple bruise he half-heartedly tries to hide with high collars. "What did you think happened to him?"

She shrugs, and she sounds almost exasperated, but it's hard to read her expression in the dim light. "I don't know. I figured he was, like…lynched or something. He's southern, he's gay, it's still a thing that happens."

"Oh." I don't know what to say to that. It hadn't occurred to me, and I don't know what to do with the idea now that she's put it in my head. Then, reflex, I say the thing that he told to me the day we met: "Nobody asks you how you died. But everyone always finds out eventually."

She nods, frowning. Doubles down. "Yeah. I just…I didn't think he was the type."

"What type is that?"

She grimaces, shifting uneasily in her chair the way that someone squirms when they realize their beliefs are being challenged and that there's nothing behind them — that they're all just smoke and feelings and a lifetime of training. When she finally does speak, I know exactly what she's going to say because it's something Dad would say. "Cowards, I guess. People who won't fight or take responsibility for their lives. I didn't think…Randy's just really strong, you know?"

"I don't think suicide is weakness," I say, softly, but something is tugging at the back of my mind, some memory that takes a moment to slide into place.

Remember in the beginning, when we all thought it was just suicides?

That's what that orderly had said at the Lazarus House. Suicides. Patient zero — that teenager with a shotgun blast to his chest. Randy. Dad, too, maybe, in his way, suicide by self-neglect.

"Hey, Zoe?"

"Hmm?"

"The Undead Registration Act. That means there's, like…there's an Undead registry, right? Like somewhere there's a document with all of the known Undead on it?"

She nods, rolling her eyes at me like I'm an idiot for not knowing, and I guess that's fair. "Yeah, obviously. It's like the sex offender registry. It's public record. You can just pull it up. Here…" a new tab, a few clicks, and then there it is, a boring-looking government website that looks like it was designed sometime in 1995, which is ridiculous since the Undead have only even been an issue for a few years. "Why?"

"Just…" I hesitate, not sure if there's anything to this hunch, not sure if it's worth pulling her into it if there is. "Does it happen to list cause of death on the list?"

She shakes her head. "No. You'd have to cross-reference it yourself if you wanted something like that. It'd be kind of a pain."

"Oh."

She turns all the way around, spinning the chair on its axle to do so, and seeks out my gaze. "Why? What are you looking for?"

"Just…something I heard at the Lazarus House," I say, and instantly regret it because she looks so eager, so suddenly hungry for information. "About how at first everybody thought it was just suicides who came back from the dead."

She cups her chin in her hand, tapping the pad of her thumb against her lower lip. She frowns, thinking hard. "You know, there might be something to that." She spins back around and makes a few keystrokes, pulling open a window with some kind of bare-bones web forum in it. There's a logo in the corner, a retro-style black-and-white clipart skull. When did everybody start leaning so hard into 90s-era Internet nostalgia? What kind of ironic aesthetic have I missed in the last generational shift?

"What's that?" I ask.

"I'm enlisting some help. No way I can trawl through all of these results myself. So I'm gonna crowdsource that shit. Don't worry, people do stuff like this all the time on these forums…"

"Okay." I don't know what I'm expecting her to find, or hoping for her to find. It's probably a dead end. But I don't say that. I am suddenly unbearably tired, and I want nothing more than to crawl down into my bedroom and sleep my dead, dreamless sleep.

But Zoe looks excited, and she grins at me as I start back out of the door frame. "Thanks for the lead. I'll let you know what we dig up. You might be onto something, who knows."

"Yeah. That's great."

"Everything is okay with Randy, though? Like aside from the obvious?"

"Yeah, I think it'll be fine," I lie, backing into the hall.

"Cool. Well, goodnight."

"Yeah. Don't stay up too late." I close the door behind me and pad down to my room, barely managing to kick off my shoes before I face-plant into the bed, fully-clothed, puddling my body up on top of the blankets. I wake up twice in the night, disoriented in the darkness. When the light comes in gray and cool around the edges of my black-out curtains, I realize that my pillow case is stained russet from blood-tinged tears.

Chapter 13

I used to be someone who could hit "snooze" a half-dozen times before rolling out of bed. I used to have multiple different alarms set at different times, a multi-hour lead-up to the moment when waking up became a matter of dire need. Two-hours out, for the ambition of waking up early and getting something done before work. An hour out, for a workout and a shower. Half-hour out for breakfast. Fifteen-minutes to get dressed. Five minutes for pleading. The last one, the final straw: sleep past this and you won't be able to get to work on time.

Another, five minutes after, in case you didn't listen. Call that one the depression alarm.

Now, I don't bother with the alarms. For one, because since I died, sleep has been a binary state: on or off, sleeping or waking, dead-not-dreaming. A sound or a light or a touch in the night and if it's enough to rouse me then I'm up, brain switched on whether I'm ready or not. Also, now that I'm Undead and unemployed, I have no need of alarms because I have nowhere to go and nowhere I need to be.

So this morning, I'm more than a little disoriented when the sound jolts me awake, and it takes a few minutes of fumbling with my phone to realize it's a call, not an alarm. I squint at the name on the screen, second-guessing my alertness. It's early, barely 8 a.m. So why is Ash calling me?

"Hello?"

"Davin. Hey. Sorry if it's still early, I didn't know when you usually get up."

"It's fine." I blink a few times, trying to clear the crust from my eyes. Reddish-black flakes of blood-tinged tears, dried and goopy, drop onto the sheets. "What's up?"

"Were you with Randy last night?"

My gut twists. Apprehensively, not knowing where he's going with this or why he's asking, "For a little bit. Why? What's going on?"

"I think you'd better just come over."

"Ash —"

"It's not urgent, you can take a shower and get some breakfast for your sister and whatever else you need to do," he says, and now I can hear the weariness in his voice, some twinge of exhausted not-angry-just-disappointed paternalism. "But it's better you come on over sooner rather than later."

He disconnects.

I stare at my phone, disturbed to feel stillness where my heart should be hammering. My fingertips feel hollow and cold. I fumble with the touch screen and pull up Randy's number.

It goes to voice mail, twice.

I send him a quick text and then force myself upright, past the creaking resistance of my joints, past the rotten wood ache of my bones, and let momentum carry me to the door. I hesitate in the hall, hear the soft snores from Zoe's room, and debate whether to wake her. I decide against it. I don't know what I'm walking into, and 8 a.m. is early for her, too, especially if she was up late looking into the Undead Registry, which I can almost certainly guarantee.

I decide against the shower, after all, and just scrawl her a quick, vague note instead. I figure she'll call when she gets up if I'm not home by then. I wonder what could be happening that would keep me out late, and wonder what could be happening that Ash wouldn't just tell me over the phone. It has to be Undead business, I figure. Something he wouldn't want to say even on a burner phone. Something about Randy's dad?

Or, a more unpleasant thought: Something so bad it requires a face-to-face talk. Something you can't say over the phone because you need to look a person in the eye.

I drive to Ash's as fast as the speed traps will allow.

***

Ash's house has come to be like a second home, as much as Ash has come to be some new kind of father figure. It's a trailer, sun-faded and stained with the hard-water drip of the swamp cooler's exhaust, but the fenced-in yard of the trailer park space is always tidy, and Lilith keeps the worn-out interior immaculately clean. When I pull up, I catch some kind of warm, yeasty smell coming from an open window. Fresh bread or cinnamon rolls or something. It opens an ache way deep down in my core, some mix of nostalgia and longing and the kind of hunger that I can't sate anymore.

Randy's car is in the drive, so I have to park on the curb. Ash is outside, leaning on the low fence and smoking a cigarette. I wait for him to say something, to set some kind of tone for what I should be expecting.

"Sorry to call you over so early," he says. He steps aside so I can open the gate, and waits for me to fidget with the latch before he continues.

"Randy's car is here," I say, stupidly pointing out the obvious. I get the feeling like Ash thinks I know more about what's happening than I do.

"He's inside." He frowns, brows knitting. "He came over late last night, and Lilith is still real upset. I don't mind helping where we can, but you need to make him understand that we can't keep doing this."

I blink.

Ash continues, either not noticing my confusion or just not caring. "We were plenty happy to take you in when you needed help. We were grateful for the work you and Randy would do. But things aren't the way they were, and we can't carry on like this."

I'm frozen halfway between him at the fence and the rickety steps up to the trailer's front door, torn with indecision whether I should ask him what the hell he's talking about or just go inside and see for myself. I give Ash a long, questioning look, realizing as I do just how old he's looking now, how withered. His cheeks are sunken, sucking in so far with each inhale of his cigarette that the bones jut out like points. There are deep hollows under each eye.

I turn and let myself into the trailer.

It creaks and settles under me as I step inside, and I'm immediately hit by that fresh-baked smell, its intensity enough to freeze me in place. It smells like a bakery in here. Lilith is in the middle of the kitchen, fussing over something on the stove, and every inch of the trailer's minimal counter space is covered with flour and sugar and mixing bowls, pies cooling on racks, a tray of cinnamon rolls.

"Lilith?"

"Oh!" She stands up too quickly, wheeling around as if startled. There are big oven mitts on either hand, making her hands seem cartoonishly oversized. A wisp of gray hair falls over into her face. I try to remember if her hair has always been this gray. "Davin. Sorry, I didn't hear you come in. He's in the back room."

It it wasn't so long ago — barely a season — that Randy brought me here, freshly dead and delirious. I dead-slept on their couch for a day and night, a pitiful orphan. "What's all the baking for?"

"Just keeping busy," she says. "Once you get started it's easiest to just keep going."

I don't ask her what exactly she — the only living person in this house — is going to do with two pies and a pan of cinnamon rolls. It seems cruel. Maybe she has friends to share them with. Church ladies or a book club or something. Maybe The Underground needs its own support group, I think, a space carved out for the survivors who have to straddle our world and the land of the living.

"I told Randy this last night, but you tell him again to be sure it sticks," Lilith says, and catches my eye. There is no maternal warmth in her gaze, just a kind of low smoldering anger, feelings kept in check by years of practice in self-control. "Let him know this is his freebie. He pulls a stunt like that again and I'm not opening the door. This isn't our life anymore. It can't be."

I wish they'd just tell me what I'm walking into, but I figure I might as well rip off the bandage myself if no one's going to say it out loud. I make some noncommittal grunt in Lilith's direction and head down the hall to the back room, the singlewide trailer built like a funnel that leads back there. On the way, a stench catches my nose from the bathroom, and I linger there, nudging open the door to peer inside.

It's been cleaned, but there are still obvious traces of a tremendous mess. There's a brown stain like old, rancid blood smeared deep into the peeling linoleum of the floor, caught in the crevices of the baseboards. There's part of a handprint in the shower, smudged fingerprints, and a trash bag in the middle of the floor is bulging with stained towels. It smells like death and vomit and liquor, sick-sweet and sharp.

It smells like my dad's body, before whatever's left of his consciousness crawled back into it.

I close the door, reeling back and swallowing down a gorge that threatens to rise. It's utter cruelty that a body that has lost its need for food should still be able to respond to disgust; unfair that my reactions should still be so visceral. Like my body would be happy to turn itself inside out, to purge itself of whatever bits are left inside. Judging from the smell and the remnants of stains in the bathroom, that's exactly what happened in there.

"Randy?" I call down the last length of hallway as I approach the closed door. This must be Ash and Lilith's bedroom, and the fact that they gave it over to Randy is surprising and a little concerning. Did they tuck him back here for his comfort, or because they couldn't get him to move? I think of the scene in the bathroom and swallow and nudge open the door.

Randy is sitting upright in the bed, mostly naked. His clothes are nowhere to be seen, but a good look at him makes me guess they're in a trash bag somewhere like the stained towels in the bathroom. The blankets have been stripped from the bed, and he's sitting on some thread-bare sheets, knees pulled up to his chin. He doesn't look up when I come in, but he lets out a little grunt of acknowledgment.

He looks terrible.

His hair is disheveled, greasy pink strands pointing up at erratic angles. There is a big, dark bruise under one eye, a split down the center of his lip oozing red-black blood. There's something off-kilter about his posture, something asymmetrical, and I realize that he's leaning over to one side, hunched over a place where his ribs seem caved in. There's an old wound there, the gunshot from Felix on that ill-fated night in the park, that's torn its stitches and gaped open. Something pokes out, yellow-white like old grease in a pan, and I realize that it's fat oozing out of the wound.

"What the fuck, Randy."

"It doesn't hurt," he says, and he still doesn't look up at me. "Isn't that a bitch? I'm all fucked up, but I can't feel it. I can't feel anything."

"What happened to you?"

He shrugs, extending a hand to look at it. The knuckles of his right hand are scraped raw, skin peeled down to visible bone that flashes off-white through crimson gashes. "When I was alive, my dad was always putting me in rehab. I don't remember if I ever told you that."

I shake my head, uncertain where he's going with this.

"It was all bullshit. I wasn't addicted, not like the people in there. There's folks who need rehab, but they're sick with it, y'know? My thing was just that I liked to party. I liked to get fucked up. I'd go to a rave an' drop some molly and pick fights just 'cause I could, just 'cause it felt like somethin' different."

I move to sit on the edge of the bed. I want to reach out to him, but I also don't really want to touch him.

"I was always just too much. Too much fighting, too much drugs, too much sex with boys."

"Randy," I say, softly. "Did you get into a fight last night?"

He avoids my gaze, letting his split lower lip puff out petulantly.

I think of the mess in the bathroom, the liquor-scented ichor clinging to the grout. I narrow my eyes. "Did you try to get drunk and get into a fight and get the shit kicked out of you?"

"I used to be able to drink," he says, almost a whine. "I used to be able to drink an' even eat, sometimes, when I had some goddamn Lazarus."

That's all the confirmation I need. It's easy enough to fill in the details: Randy finding some bar, stirring up trouble, starting a fight, taking punches, drinking beers. Driving here. Getting sick all over the bathroom. I bury my head in my hands, massaging the sudden throbbing in my temples. "Please tell me you didn't."

"Ask me no questions," he says, with forced lightheartedness, and I hold up a hand to stop him because I don't want to hear it.

"Do they know what you are? Do they know *who* you are?"

He waves me off, lip curling up as if disgusted with the concern. "It's fine. Just some rednecks drunker'n I was. Nobody's gonna come lookin' for me or anything, if that's what you're worried about." He looks at me, then, and his eyes are dark and cold, as empty as night. "That is all you worry about, isn't it? Stay under the radar and play it safe. Like staying out of trouble means a damn thing when your life is…when this is all your life is ever gonna be."

I want to pull him close, to wrap him protectively in my arms. I also want to punch him in the face. I split the difference by doing neither, just stare at the bare mattress with its crumpled old sheets. "You're lucky Ash even let you in the door."

"Yeah, well. Lucky." He slowly unfurls, and it's there between us again, that invisible partition, something breaking or broken. "Lilith made it real clear I'm not welcome here anymore. I don't even know why they bothered to call you. What are you gonna do? Come in here an' make me feel bad? You think anything you say is gonna make me more ashamed than knowing I'm gonna be walking around like a battered housewife forever?"

He's pointing at the discoloration beneath his eye. It's not a proper shiner; bodies this dead don't have the energy for that kind of inflammation. But the blood vessels there are broken, the skin blemished like the smear of dead pixels on a broken plasma TV.

"If you had Lazarus," I say, tentatively. I don't know the science, how it works. But I know that the parts of me that he sewed up once, the ragged tears and broken parts left over from my death, kind of almost healed up. The scar on my face is more scar than wound, and it's got to be the Lazarus responsible for that.

He gives me a sharp look. "What are you thinking?"

"I'm thinking we know someone who might be able to help," I say, disgusted with myself for even suggesting it. "And if it'll get you to stop…being like this. If it'll get you back onto an even keel. Then I'll help you this one time. It'll make us even."

He smiles then, light coming into his dead eyes, his split lip gaping wider with his grin. "Davin honey, you're too good to me."

"I know."

Chapter 14

This was a bad idea, and it feels more and more like a mistake the further we get out of town.

I shouldn't have suggested it. It was a stupid knee-jerk offer, more pity than sense, and now that I'm thinking through the possible implications, I'm regretting it. But then, what have I been trying to build rapport with the camp in the desert for if not something like this?

I'm driving, and Randy's sitting in the passenger seat, bundled up into some of Ash's clothes. None of them fit, and he's sunken down into the shirt like it's a shawl, burrowing into the flannel. He fiddles with the radio dial for a while, but he catches me looking at his messed-up hand and retreats, pulling back inside himself.

We need to talk about what happened between us. We need to clear the air about what happened last night, that weird dark shadow that passed between us in his car and the choices he made afterward, those bad decisions that cascaded like dominoes into this moment. And maybe we need to talk, too, abut my meeting with Chuy, and the things that have been circling through my mind since. We especially need to talk so I can relieve some of the guilt of driving him further into such a desperate corner, and so I can make room for the anger that's rising up because how dare he make me feel like this.

We need to talk, but neither of us do.

Inaction is its own kind of choice.

"They might not be there anymore," I tell him. "So don't get your hopes up."

"Where else you figure they've run an' gone? The Ritz?"

That's not quite what I meant — more like someone might have picked them up by now, more like some wild animal might have made a meal of them — but I don't want to consider such dark possibilities aloud. They're bad enough lurking at the back of my mind, but speaking them aloud seems like taunting fate.

Even if they are there, I think, I'm not sure whether they'll even talk to us. Will they have received my offering in the desert? Will they have appreciated it, or been insulted? There's no way of knowing what kind of reception we'll get when we arrive. For all I know, the whole crew of them will turn on us like a pack of ravenous wolves. Maybe they'll tear apart the pickup to get at us. It's almost impossible to guess.

✳✳✳

I follow the old oilfield roads, the rabbit trail of gravel peeling off the country highway that breaks off the interstate, navigating my way by touch and muscle memory as much as anything. There's not exactly much else going on out here, and a plume of smoke rising up from their camp is the final beacon I need to find the place. I pass the place where I left the sleeping bag and tarps and see that they're missing. I hope that's a good sign, but maybe the wind just gusted up and carried them somewhere. Maybe a bear roamed through here and dragged them away.

We roll up onto their camp, and I'm honestly expecting to be met with open hostility, as if the Undead are going to come out and circle us with spears or guns or fingers curved into bony talons and gnashing teeth hungry for flesh. Instead, one of the guys — I think he'd said his name was Duncan — meets us with a little half-wave, coming around to the driver's side as I pull the truck into a sandy patch just off the main path.

"You lost?" he asks, with a bit of a leer.

"I don't know if you remember me," I say, stupidly, a feeble attempt at diplomacy.

Duncan's brow lifts. "Do you think we're idiots, kid?"

Randy hops down from the passenger side, cradling his wounded side.

But he flashes a friendly smile, one I realize uneasily that he inherited. A politician's smile for a politician's son. "Don't mind him, he's just tryin' to be polite and failing at every turn."

Right, of course, as soon as Randy has an audience to perform for, it's open season on me. I hesitate, thinking I might just stay in the truck, thinking that more and more I don't want any part of this. But I heave myself out anyway and follow Duncan back up to the main camp. Here I was, thinking I'd be out here brokering peace, negotiating a deal, but Randy's already smoothly slipped into the role all on his own. Elliot has already come out to investigate, and soon he and Randy have started talking, hitting it off like old friends within minutes of their introduction. Randy starts telling a story about what's happened to his face. It's funny, the way he tells it, and I can't stand the sound of Elliot's laughter so I pull away from the two of them to hide my irritation.

Of course it's like that. It was like that with my dad for a long time, too: The people who knew him least were the ones who liked him best. The only reward for getting close to him was feeling the radiant heat of his own self-loathing, that bitter black star at the heart of his universe.

"Where's Julian?" I ask, realizing I can't see him anywhere.

"He's over there." Duncan points at a makeshift tent, little more than a tarp drawn over a few rocks for shade. "He's not in great shape."

The women are nowhere to be found, either, but I do see the kid sitting over by some rocks, the stuffed roadrunner cliched in his hands. That makes me smile.

"We got your stuff. That was nice of you. Sorry we weren't so friendly last time."

"It's okay. I wasn't really expecting you to be."

I realize that Duncan is beating a path toward the tent where Julian is resting, and I follow him. He gestures to a wide, flat rock and takes a seat on another similar one. It looks like somebody dragged these out here on purpose, some attempt at assembling a sort of furniture. I think of the city carved into the stone face of the mesa, that ancient pueblo with its rock paintings and its many-roomed living space and wonder how long it would take to build something like that from scratch, whether a civilization living out in the desert would somehow stumble into making something similar on accident if they were left alone long enough.

"It's mostly just that Elliot gets real protective of Gail. She's…you know. Special."

I raise a questioning brow.

"I guess she wasn't always. I don't know, I haven't known these guys all that long, but I guess those two go way back. And she used to be, you know, normal. Well. I mean. Normal, in an Undead way."

"Then she went loco," I say. "After taking Lazarus."

"Yeah."

"But she can…get along okay?"

"She's not…really safe around Breathers, if you know what I mean? And kind of rough around strangers in general. But, I mean…family, right? What can you do."

What can you do, indeed.

It's just a thing that happens sometimes, Chuy had said, and now that I've seen it twice, in the flesh rather than on the news, I don't know what to think at all.

"It's that place," Julian says, and the sudden sound of his rasping voice makes me jump. I had thought he was asleep; he's so still and quiet under his tarp.

"What?"

"It's that place. They…do things….to you there."

He's interrupted by a coughing fit, and I get up from my spot on the rocks and crouch down next to him. Eyes roll, loose in their sockets, to fix me with a cool gaze. He'd been in rough shape when I saw him before, but that's nothing compared to the withered mummy he is now. He's eyeballing me now with deep suspicion, like he's expecting me to grab him, but he doesn't flinch.

"I won't go back," Julian says when he recovers, shaking his head. "I won't. I don't care."

"Go back to what?" I ask, carefully. "The Lazarus House?"

A small nod, almost imperceptible.

I bark out a laugh, squatting down next to him. "Oh, Jesus, no, I'm not… we're not here about that. I'm not going to rat you out. Why would I?"

A shrug, small but deliberate, as if the movement causes him great pain. It probably does. "Good. I won't let you."

I stare in disbelief. Those are bold words coming from a guy who looks like this — a guy who's falling apart, like some kind of scarecrow left to rot and molder in the damp. Like his guts are stuffed with leaves that go black and slimy with decay, spilling out and leaking down a tattered pants leg. He looks like a thing forgotten, and it's incomprehensible to me that there'd be something out there he'd find even worse than this.

"Tell me," I say, and the disbelief has shifted its weight to let the uneasiness start to bubble through. "What exactly happens in there?"

Does it matter? A nasty voice at the back of my mind asks. *Do you really care what they're doing to him there?*

Davin please they're hurting me they're doing terrible things please.

If it mattered so much, I think, *wouldn't you have done something? Wouldn't you have at least bothered to answer your phone? If you really believe that they're doing something evil, why did you give even a second of thought to working there? Why are you still thinking about it?*

"What do you think they're doing there, kid?" Julian rasps, and there's open derision in his voice. "What do you tell yourself it's there to do? Can't treat 'em. There's no cure for being dead. No light of recovery at the end of that tunnel." He looks away, averting his eyes toward the horizon, and for a second I think that's it, that's all he's going to say, no way to get him to open up and spill out any more. But then he continues, talking as if to himself, not clear if he even knows I'm listening or if he cares that I am. "No, you don't talk people there to get better. You take 'em there to forget about them, to let them rot away from everyone else, where they can't bother anyone with the stench. So what do you care what happens to someone you've already thrown away?"

"I didn't throw him away," I reply, sulky. I don't know why I'm rising to the bait. "It's hard. People have the right to walk away from things when they're that hard. They have a right to save themselves."

Do I really believe that?

Julian ignores me. "You don't care. That's the thing they count on. You don't care, and nobody else does either. That's how they get away with it."

"With what?" I ask, and grimace at the pleading in my voice. "Get away with what?"

He shrugs, vaguely, and then starts coughing, a long coughing fit that dredges up some slimy dark ichor from his chest; lumpy gobs of it dribble over his chin. "They call it the Lazarus House," he says, finally, wiping his mouth on the back of a hand. "Do I look like I've been taking Lazarus, to you?"

"They're withholding Lazarus?"

"For some of us, sure. We're better off than…the others. That group doesn't stop screaming."

My dad's words echo in my ears again, and a deep, terrible feeling of cold settles down in my gut.

"They keep them locked up. I've never seen them. I could just hear them. The screaming. The growling. It sounds like a dog pound, the way they howl. I don't know what they're doing to them, but I know it's worse than what they did to me." He holds out a shaking hand, the skin blackening and twisted across bony fingers. "And that's saying something."

"That other group. People…people like Gail?"

He nods. "Yeah. Inside. There's…different groups. Some get treated real nice. They let them wander around, go wherever they want. Some just get locked up in rooms to rot. But there's some of us who got picked for their… special project. Said they'd send money to our families if we participated. Don't bother telling you what it is they're really doing."

"They're experimenting." It's all, very suddenly, horrifyingly, starting to come together. "That's what you're saying. They're doing experiments to see…what happens if you go off Lazarus, or if you take too much, or try some other formula — something like that?"

"Something like that," he echoes, bitterly. "And now? Now if I try to go back on it, if I try to take the drugs, they don't even work. It's been too long.

All the Lazarus in the world isn't gonna save me now. Now how's that for an experiment?"

Is there some kind of Lazarus formula that causes the rage to set in? Some experimental blend? Did Chuy know when he brought it to the park that night? Or did he just bring it by accident, not realizing what his employers were actually doing?

Did they leak it out into the public on purpose? Or was it an accident?

Randy comes up on me then, touching my shoulder. I jump to my feet, wheeling around and making a quiet, strangled noise of surprise.

"Hey, sorry, Jumpy." He tries to meet my eyes, brows lifting in a question — an unspoken *Are you okay?* That I don't bother to answer. He continues. "We gotta roll. I need to show you somethin'."

"Yeah. Sure."

"You can come back if you want," Duncan's saying. "And if you want to bring more tents and stuff, that'd be cool. Or if maybe you've got an extra car? Or a trailer home? That'd be great."

I'm not super sure if he's being sarcastic or not. So I just say, "I'll see what I can do," and let Randy tug me away from the camp.

An absurd role reversal, Randy smooth and calm and back on the top of the world all of a sudden, but I'm too rattled to process my irritation.

* * *

"So what was that all about?" Randy asks when we get back into the safety of the truck.

I frown. "Julian thought we were coming to take him back to the Lazarus House."

I don't mention the other parts. Not yet. I want to hear his thing first.

"Yeah, the whole group of them apparently thought you were a narc at first."

"Wait, really? You looked like you were getting along so well."

"Yeah, well, I guess you won him over. Or maybe it was my charming personality." He shifts in his seat as I put the truck into gear, and I notice that he's got something in his hand, the size and shape of a ballpoint pen. He twirls it in his fingers, looking down at it thoughtfully.

"What's that?"

"A sample," he says. "Did you know there's only one company that produces Lazarus?"

"Sure, yeah. Pyadox. There's no generic formula. Zoe did a whole video about it."

"Right. An' one company means one supply chain. One factory, one fleet of delivery trucks, one set of warehouses. One point of failure. It's pretty stupid, honestly. Like they're begging to be sabotaged."

"So what's the deal with the pen?"

"Up-front payment for services to be rendered."

I glance at him sidelong, one brow lifted.

"They gave me this one if I agree to help them get more." He spins it around again thoughtfully, frowning. "Kind of shitty that these pre-filled Lazarus pens didn't take off. That would've been a whole hell of a lot more convenient. Then again, never got the feeling they were real interested in our comfort or convenience."

"I've never seen one," I agree. Never when I was giving Dad his daily shots. Never when we were brokering deals with pharmacists and outpatients skimming their doses.

"I think it's a promotional sample," he says, squinting at the label on the side. "Like, you know the kind pharmaceutical companies send to doctors? Just before the point where they try to sweeten up the deal with a steak dinner and a back-alleyway handjob?"

"I'm not sure that last part is a thing."

He shrugs. "Either way. That's my guess. Elliot said they got it off a truck. That's their whole system, actually. It's kind of brilliant. They don't bother stealing from the Lazarus House itself — he was saying some shit about how the stuff there is tainted, anyway? Like they tamper with it? — so they take it off trucks. Either stopping them out on the highway, or sneaking over when it's being delivered."

"Sure. What's a bit of highway robbery among friends. A bit of casual breaking-and-entering. Some lighthearted sneaking past armed guards, probably."

"That's the spirit."

I blow air out my nose, sighing an unconscious affectation now more than a biological reflex. I think about Julian, his wildly rolling eyes, and the weight of the reality if the things he said were true. "Julian says they're experimenting on people in there."

"That would explain the bad Lazarus," Randy says, not sounding the least bit surprised.

It would explain a lot of the crazy shit my dad's been saying, too, I think, and a wave of nausea rolls through me so hard I think I might have to pull over, but I swallow it back.

Randy pops off the safety cap on the Lazarus pen, examining the fine needle, no bigger than the point of a tack.

"You're not using that in here," I say, and my grip tightens on the steering wheel.

"What's the big deal?"

"The big deal is if you turn into a fucking monster, I don't want you in my truck. Let me pull over at least."

He grins. "Yeah? What are you going to do if I turn? Kill me?" A teasing brow waggle, and I hate that he thinks this is a joke.

"Stop messing around. Here. I'm pulling off."

There's a roadside rest stop up ahead, a faded sign bearing the symbols for a bathroom and a picnic table. The text below says WEIGH STATION - TRUCKS MUST STOP. I ease over into the right lane so I can take the exit, and Randy twirls the Lazarus pen between his fingers like a baton.

"What, exactly, did you agree to do for them?"

"There's a guy to talk to for details. We'll figure out the rest when we get to it."

I decelerate onto the ramp. "What do you mean, we?"

I can hear surprise in his voice, genuine, the sly artifice dropping. "I mean, that's what we do, isn't it? We've got a chance to get back in business. In case you forgot." He waggles the Lazarus pen. "It paid for this truck. It's paid for your utilities. And, y'know, that little thing called, 'keeping you from rotting on your feet.'"

"Here." I stop the car. I peer around the parking lot, looking for other cars, but I don't see any. "We can do it here. If you even think we should be doing it. Which I don't think that we should."

"This was your idea," he counters, and eases the door open, sliding down out of his seat. He half-turns to shoot me a look, daring me to argue.

He's right, but I don't want to hear it.

I get out, putting the truck between us so I don't have to look at him.

***

"Shooting up in a truck stop bathroom," Randy says, pulling up the hem of his shirt. "Now that really takes me back."

"Randy, if you'd ever done drugs in a truck stop," I say, propping the bathroom door open with my body so I can keep watch, "you'd know there's a difference between a truck stop and a weigh station."

He wrinkles his nose. "Fine, if you want to get technical about it."

There are long-haul truckers milling about out in the picnic area, smoking cigarettes and chatting up the weigh station staff. But there's nobody at the bathroom, and even if there were, I doubt they're paying much attention. Weirder things than this happen at truck stops and weigh stations all the time.

Unless, of course, he turns into a flesh-eating zombie and starts tearing through onlookers. They'll notice then.

Randy picks out a patch of pale, fishbelly-white skin over his hip and pinches it. He looks up at me, brows lifted.

"Hurry up if you're doing this," I snap, irritated. "Or else just toss the syringe and let's go."

The needle disappears into his skin and he presses down with his thumb, auto-injecting the contents with a single smooth movement. There's a sharps container on the wall across from the urinals, like there are in a lot of public bathrooms out here. Maybe because a quarter of the reservation is diabetic.

Maybe for the Undead, or the heroin junkies — take your pick. But Randy lets the Lazarus pen drop on the floor instead, bald concrete sticky with ancient dribbles of urine and black scuffs tracked in from outside.

His eyes slide closed, and he tilts his head back, jaw going slack, and for a second I think it was really heroin in there, some sick joke from somebody who thought it'd be fun to swap out a label. But then I see it, a bloom of color rising in his cheeks, parched capillaries opening and flooding tissue, and I see his shirt flutter with the sudden ferocity of his heartbeat and the twitching pulse that comes alive in the hollow of his elbow.

He snaps his eyes open, and my muscles tense. Fight-or-flight is more habit than instinct now, too, without any adrenaline left to pump through my veins. Instead of a rush of endorphins, I just have a sick spreading dread that creeps through my body like dry rot, that twists up the empty places in my guts. He's going to meet my eye and it won't be Randy staring out at me, it'll be something inhuman, some predatory reptilian brain pushing the buttons and handling the controls of its human vessel.

He's going to lunge for me.

He's going to rip out my throat.

He smiles, a lopsided grin that splits up one side, and the expression in his lidded eyes is one of utter satisfaction, contentment bordering on smugness. The shiner below his eye seems almost to fade, maybe just blending with the new color that's rushed into his cheeks.

"Christ, that feels so much better."

I hesitate. My gaze scans over his body, questioning, probing. I don't know what I'm looking for. It's not like his wounds are going to seal up, his skin knitting together. It's not like something is going to burst from his body in a shower of viscera and gore. This isn't some science fiction movie.

But there's color in his complexion where there hadn't been before, and the bruise on his throat is less visible, the edges softened, and the hollows under his eyes seem somehow shallower.

"You okay?" I ask.

"Okay? Shit, never felt better. Light me a cigarette, would you?"

"You know what they say about things that seem too good to be true?" I pull out two cigarettes, light both, hand him one.

"You know what they say about gift horses?" He takes it and draws in a long, drag, puffing his cheeks to blow smoke rings.

Chapter 15

I'm sitting in my bed, old laptop perched on my knees, browsing job ads in an increasingly frantic nightly ritual. I've been scrolling through listings for a long time, all of the words starting to blur together, prison bars of text across a white screen. The inside of my head is a low, dull roar, a white noise static of the same pointless circling thoughts: *You can't count on Randy for money. You're not going to find a job sitting in the dark in your house. You have to get back out there. You're going to get caught and put away. They'll find out that you're Undead. They're talking about taking temperatures at the door now. They're talking about doing body scans. It's already happening in the big cities, and it'll come to Los Ojos eventually. They'll know. You're running out of places to hide. You're running out of options. You can't count on Randy forever.*

And, always, that persistent nagging at the back of my mind: *You could call Chuy. You could take him up on his offer right now.*

Randy thinks things can go back the way they were. He thinks we can pick up where we left off.

But I can't see a way for that to be possible. Even if we follow Duncan and Elliot's lead, stealing Lazarus like a pair of highway robbers — what then? Who will be left to sell it to? If all of our buyers end up arrested or killed or squatting in the desert, then how are going to pay the bills?

The Lazarus House might be doing pharmaceutical experiments, but at least they pay people for them.

Zoe's silhouette darkens my door frame.

I look up, quickly shutting the laptop. "What's up?"

"You weren't looking at porn or anything, were you? Your door was open."

"First off, ew. Also, no. I absolutely was not."

"You closed your laptop really fast."

"Don't worry about it. Just…whatever. What'd you need?"

It's hard to see her face, the light glowing around her like a halo. But I think I can make out something strange in her expression, some mixture of reticence and excitement.

"So…remember when you asked about the Undead Registry? And the whole suicide thing?"

"Sure."

She hesitates in the doorway, takes a tentative step forward, and I scoot sideways on the bed and gesture to the foot of it for her to sit if she wants. She lingers, maybe measuring the awkwardness of being in her brother's bedroom, maybe not wholly believing me about my laptop activities, but relents. She perches on the edge of the mattress and folds up her knees under her.

"What made you ask that?" she asks.

I shrug. "Just something I overheard at the Lazarus House."

"Well, I looked into it. Or, I mean, the whole forum community kind of dug into it. We compiled a bunch of the data. And this shit gets weird."

"What do you mean?"

"For starters — yeah, suicides are crazy over-represented. Suicide makes up, what, 2 percent of all the total deaths in the world?"

I have no idea, so I shrug again.

"Yeah, well, it's about 30 percent of the Undead. That's what you'd call really statistically significant." She grins, then, and it's such a bizarre choice of expression for the information that she's revealing that I'm almost startled. "But it's even weirder than that."

"Okay…?"

"Come look." She hops off the bed and starts for the door, clearly expecting me to follow.

It's like when she was little and she'd build something in the backyard or draw something in a notebook and drag me out to admire it. She never showed her masterpieces to our parents — Mom was always too sick, Dad was never interested — so my opinion had to count for triple, but she always seemed happy with it. Thinking about that makes something in my chest hurt, some physical twang like heartbreak, but maybe it's just my body starting to fall apart on the inside.

I follow her.

The inside of her room has always been decked out like the combination of a film studio and a police precinct, one wall dedicated to pinned-up photos and news clippings and sticky notes. I notice now that the arrangement on the wall is different than it was before, things in different places than they had been, the red string making a different design than usual, but none of it makes a lot of sense at a glance.

"Okay. So like I said, we dug into all the registration information. And it's really basic, just ages and death dates and that sort of thing. Most of the personal information is redacted out. So we had to go through, and, like, manually check death records, and some of those were scrubbed so there was this whole thing and…well, never mind. The point is. Somebody had the idea to dig into the suicides to see if there was any sort of link, and it turns out that a lot of them had either been institutionalized at one point, or gone to a drug rehab, in the last fifteen or so years." She points to some papers on the wall — lists of names, highlighted in different colors. The colors, I notice, match to sticky notes that run up one side of the wall. "So we go digging through the records of those facilities and sure enough, there are a ton more people listed on the registry who have a similar background. And there's one company that keeps popping up through all of that."

She traces a complicated web of string connecting several papers on the wall to a single point. It's a company logo of a sunburst with the outline of a pill capsule at its center and the bold letters beneath it: PYADOX.

"The company that makes Lazarus? I didn't even know they were that old."

"Right? I don't think anybody ever really heard of them before Lazarus came out. But it turns out they're, like, this really old company. They were making all of these weird fringe treatments all through the 1950s and 60s. Like psychedelic research and stuff for mental illness, then in the 90s they got really deep into some crazy genome stuff, stem cell research in the 2000s.

Like, whatever the new cutting-edge controversial trend was, it's like that's what they were getting into."

"But nobody's heard of them."

"Yeah. Because, like…I don't think any of their stuff really worked. From what I could tell when I was looking, it seems like they were doing trial after trial and researching things that never made it to market, or didn't yield any results, or — anything. Just chasing a bunch of dead ends."

"But they stayed in business?"

She shrugs. "Yeah. That's suspicious as hell, right? And that's the other thing that's super weird, is I was trying to look into it and follow the money, and there's just…all of these angel investors and all of this secrecy, but also a ton of government grants? For things that don't do anything? But yet they keep managing to get partnerships with these facilities, and selling drugs to them."

"Okay, hang on." This is making my head hurt. I never had Zoe's appetite for conspiracy, maybe because I spent too long listening to Dad going off about crazy things. Or maybe just because I'm not as fast at putting things together as she is. "So what you're saying is there's this company that keeps selling experimental drugs to mental hospitals or whatever, and now people from those same mental hospitals are turning into zombies when they die?"

"That's kind of what it seems like, yeah." She finds a bare patch of wall to lean against, crossing her arms over her chest. Her glasses have slipped down the bridge of her nose, and she scrunches it up to try to push them back up. "I mean, this company that's been on the cutting edge of every medical tech but never seems to make anything good — all of a sudden makes this miracle drug that happens to be perfect for treating Undead? That's super suspicious, right?"

"I wouldn't call it perfect," I mutter, thinking of Javier, of Gail, of the madness in their eyes. Thinking about Julian, trapped in a decaying body. Thinking about the way my own body feels, and how it felt even when I was taking Lazarus every day. How it never made me feel alive, just slightly less dead.

Zoe ignores me. "So anyway, I think it's pretty obvious that Pyadox has something to do with the Undead. Like, they created the Reanimation Virus somehow. And then gave it to all of these people."

"Okay, cool theory. Except — how did I get it, then?"

"Well." She hesitates, like she hasn't really thought that part through. "The Reanimation Virus is a retrovirus, right? That's its whole thing, is it changes DNA. So maybe they did something to Dad, and you, like. Inherited it."

"He never even went to rehab, though." Randy did, I remember suddenly. He'd said that.

"He had to do that mandatory AA thing after he got all those DUIs."

"Okay, sure, but I was already born by then, so. That's a dead end."

"Okay. Well then — it's contagious. It got loose. That's not the part that matters." Her shoulders are rising, chin creeping up. She tightens the grip around her chest, body going on the defensive. "I'm onto something here, Davin. We don't have all the pieces yet, but this is huge. This could be the thing that blows it all wide open."

I stare at her conspiracy wall, the pieces laid out and labeled and connected in ways I can't really entirely wrap my head around. She's always been the smart one.

"What do you think would happen," I ask, tracing a fingertip along the New Mexico map she has pinned in the center of the wall, "if a pharmaceutical company specializing in really experimental drugs had access to a whole population of people who didn't have any rights or protections. What do you think they'd do?"

"…Whatever they wanted." She sighs, moving to flop down in her office chair. She pulls her knees up and spins, looking thoughtful. "I wish we'd kept some Lazarus. What if we could get it to some kind of scientist, leak the formula they're so secretive about? That'd hit Pyadox where it hurt, right?"

I don't tell her that I know exactly where we could get hold of some. I just don't see the point. What are we going to do? Find some scientist, analyze it in a high school laboratory, start making bootleg versions? Seize the means of production and take down big pharma? Get real. I can't imagine it's that simple, because surely if it were then someone would have done it already.

****

The story breaks in Friday's news:

Two Undead, detained and neutralized on the Rio de Animas Bridge

The two men were detained by Coalition officers after attacking a truck driver en route to the Lazarus House treatment facility outside of Los Ojos, New Mexico. Specific details of the altercation have not been released to the public, but it appears that these were rogue Undead that may have escaped the facility. The Coalition is working with local law enforcement and tribal police to continue the investigation.

It's all over social. I see it first in the paper Dad used to work for. He could have been the one to break the story, in another life.

I don't have to look at the photograph to know who it is, but it's there anyway. Two bodies sprawled, ruined heads blurred and pixellated, but I don't need to see their faces to recognize the missing arm, the unusual silhouette of the caved-in chest.

****

We pull into camp, with its sad lean-to shelter, its trampled brush and autumn-crispy weeds. No one comes to greet us.

Gail is gone. The other woman is gone. The kid is gone. I never even bothered to learn their names, and now I probably won't get the chance. They didn't say anything about them on the news, but that doesn't mean much. The news wouldn't say anything about a camp, Undead women and children living in the shadow of an old oilfield. It wouldn't fit the narrative.

Maybe they got scooped up and sent to the Lazarus House. Maybe they've moved on, scattering like dust in the wind, finding some other place to stay now that their leaders are gone. But whatever happened to them happened in a hurry. They didn't bring anything with them.

There are remnants of the camp left behind where they had been: the blacked-out husk of an old oil drum where the fire had been left burning. A mess of tarps and blankets, a half-ass attempt at a tent strung between spindling trees. The place seems abandoned. Randy's pawing through a heap of garbage, probably looking for more Lazarus, and I'm about to get annoyed at him for acting like a junkie when I hear the noise.

A dry, whispering rasp. A voice like air being pushed by a bellows — *chuff, chuff.*

Randy and I exchange glances, and I move toward the sound, curiosity overwhelming caution.

There, huddled against a stony outcropping, is the shape of what had once been a man.

Julian's mummified skin has begun to peel. Putrid black oozes from between the cracks. His lips are missing. His nose is partially gone. Both hands are gone now, leaving the yellowed bones of both arms poking through fleshless wrists. Two big black birds take wing as we approach, fluttering awkwardly and loudly into the sky, and I think I see a part of him go with them, a long pale strip of leather peeled from an exposed thigh.

He can't talk anymore, just lets out a rattling wheeze.

But his eyes roll in their sockets, round and staring, fixing on us as we approach.

"Jesus," Randy breaths, taking a step back. His eyes have gone wide, the whites showing in a pale rim around his dark irises. His throat bobs, adam's apple sliding under the bruised skin, swallowing back fear or disgust — I can't tell which.

I crouch down next to Julian. Hesitantly, I reach out a hand and lay it against his shoulder. "What happened?" I ask, not expecting him to be able to answer but wanting to ask anyway. Feeling like I need to say something. Acknowledge something. Wishing he could tell me, one way or another, what had happened. If the others got away. If they left him here — or were taken.

It's hard to tell whether he's smiling or if the skin has just dried taut into a rictus grin. His teeth are yellowed and bare.

I give his shoulder a gentle squeeze. My heart seizes up, like a fist is clutched around it. "Is there anything we can do?"

His eyes track sideways, looking past me. He looks at Randy, then back at me, expression unreadable. He lets out a hot, wheezing air sound, a rattle of dead air, but there are no words carried on it.

"Randy. Go check the truck. I think there's a water bottle."

He makes a vague, strangled noise behind me and then shuffles backward, at a loss now even for a witty retort. He comes back a moment later with the half-sized casino water bottle, warm to the touch. The plastic's probably leeched a dozen carcinogens into the water, but at this point I don't think that really matters.

I cradle Julian's head with a hand and trickle some water into his open mouth. His tongue, a shriveled purple strip of leather, snakes out over his bared teeth. It curls and seems almost to swell, a snail-like protuberance, and I wonder for a moment if he can even fit it back into his mouth.

His eyes roll up again, and I think I can read a request in them, so I give him more water.

Julian coughs, a rattling death-wheeze, and his eyes flutter closed. He falls still, and I stay crouched, uncertain, that heart-clenching tightness growing tighter like squeezing a ball. I don't know if he'll move again.

"Finish…it." He manages, finally, his voice more breath than sound. His eyes open, rolling once more in their sockets, looking past me.

Not at Randy, I realize, turning to follow his gaze.

But at a rock, an uneven chunk of sandstone about the size of a basketball, half-buried in the dust.

"No," I breathe, and my hand closes on his shoulder almost convulsively, squeezing so hard I'm worried the brittle bones will snap under my touch. "No way."

"Finish me," he says, breath hissing, and the force of the request pushing past those dead, cracked lips and bare skull teeth is frightening.

"This is so fucked," Randy says. There's an edge of something like hysteria in his voice.

The fist that's tightened around my heart loosens. My guts drop instead, the bottom-out feeling of dread and horror too big for words. I barely know this guy. He's certainly not somebody I would consider a friend. But the intimacy of the request is as undeniable as its monstrosity. When someone asks you something like this, you can't say no. You can't turn them down.

"Randy," I say, in a voice that doesn't sound like it belongs to me. It sounds far-off, like a ventriloquist throwing his voice, an empty sound that echoes and rattles through my body but doesn't belong there. "Bring me the rock."

"This is so fucked," he repeats.

But I hear the shift of dirt, the sounds of effort as he pries the stone loose from the sandy bed where it had sunken. He comes beside me, cradling the awkward package in both hands, holding it like a football he hasn't decided whether to throw. His shoulders are hunched with the weight of it, a weight far past the ten or fifteen pounds of the sandstone itself.

"I'll do it," he says.

"What?"

"I said I'll do it."

"Randy, you don't —"

Julian lets out an impatient whine, a frustrated back-of-the-throat noise. His bare-bone wrist scuffs in the dust, an involuntary spasm.

"Wait at the car," he says, and I meet his eyes. They're narrowed now, the whites retreated, a hardness crossing his pale features and drawing taut across his cheekbones, his lips pressed down to a thin line. "An' don't look."

I give Julian's shoulder a final, comforting squeeze before stepping away, reeling backward from the impossible horror. We shouldn't be here. We should never have come. It's my fault that we're even here, that we even met Julian, that we even learned about this place and its awful secrets. But Randy's stepping forward, lifting the rock over his head, and I have to move fast if I want to miss it, I have to nearly run, feet sliding and shuffling in the loose sand, and I just make it to the door when I hear the sound like a half-rotted melon smashing against a curb, and I'm bent over double beside the truck and my heart has gone still but my stomach heaves, heaves, useless and empty.

I cough up something dark and slimy and spit it out on the ground. I stare at it, focusing on it hard, trying to shut off all my senses, but it's not enough to keep me from hearing the stone fall a second time.

Chapter 16

Randy stops coming around to our house after that. Days pass without hearing from him, and I'm catching myself making excuses when Zoe asks about him. I don't want to tell her about everything that's happened between us — the awkwardness of the incident in the car, the awfulness of what happened in the desert. They say you can lighten a burden by sharing it, but sometimes the horror just spreads and grows and replicates instead. Sometimes trauma is a virus, infinite copies in infinite hosts.

He doesn't come around, and he doesn't answer his phone, so I drive out to check on him after the third day.

Randy lives in an apartment complex near CJ's, one of those pockets of "rich" neighborhood that sit in islands of decay. The route to his place takes me past a used tire store, a carniceria, and a neighborhood where the cars are parked on the street and a basketball hoop with no net sits at the end of the cul de sac. But Randy's apartment itself is nice, gated off, a three-story building that stands conspicuously tall against its surroundings. There are padlocks on the dumpsters, and someone pays the water bill to keep grass growing, although now it's mostly gone yellow-brown. The ornamental fruit trees planted by the perimeter are starting to turn, their leaves going red-gold.

Randy's car is the nicest in the complex, but at least it probably won't be broken into here.

I make my way up to his second-floor unit and stand outside of it for a while, trying to get up the courage to knock. The thick black-out curtains on his windows are missing, replaced by eggshell-colored blinds. I wonder if his landlord said something. This seems like the kind of place where they care how your windows look.

It takes a while for him to answer, and when he does, he just unlatches the door and steps back from it, inviting me in with a gesture. He looks tired. He's shirtless, and the dark bruise around his throat stands out lividly against the creamy paleness of his skin. The wounds on his side — the bullet wound I had sewn together so long ago now, the broken ribs that were fresh, the abrasions — look a little better. Not oozing fat, at least. Barely weeping fluid.

His apartment looks like something has been nesting in it. There's a sagging futon in the middle of the living room, flanked on either end by milk crates filled hodge-podge with books and random papers that leak out the sides. There's a gaming console and a television and a scattering of blankets and discarded clothes. There's a fist-sized hole on the wall by the kitchen.

"I'm probably not getting my security deposit back," he says, following my gaze.

"Has that got a story behind it?"

He shrugs. Instead of answering, he examines his hand, the place where the skin has sloughed off over his ruined knuckles. "You know what the first rule of dealing is, Davin?"

I don't answer.

"You're not supposed to get addicted to your product. That's the thing that always takes the junkies down — they get hooked, and they get sloppy, and then they get caught. Fucked up that we don't have any other choice, huh?"

He goes into the kitchen and returns with two slightly-dented beer cans. He offers me one and I accept even though I know I won't be able to keep it down. It's nice to have something to hold. He picks up an overturned chair and sets it down across from me, straddling it backwards and resting his chin on the back like a child.

"So are we going to talk about what happened?"

"You always say we should talk about things," he says, opening his beer and taking a defiant swig. We both know he's going to puke it up later. "But I don't think you mean it. I don't think you're a guy who talks about things, Davin."

I roll the beer can between my palms, frowning down at it. "Were you still going to try to go through with it? The Lazarus?"

"Is that your way of saying that you don't want to?"

A flash of memory, the last thing in the headlights before my car ran off the bridge: A figure crouched over roadkill, tearing at its skin with its hands. Except I know her name, now. I know that her name is Gail, and that she used to be just like us, and now she's not and maybe she never will be. I know that there were people who watched out for her, and now they're dead, because they were trying to get the same drug that turned her into a monster.

The wet sound of a stone cracking through a rotten skull. The way the skin pulled tight and dry across Julian's bones, and the way his wide eyes rolled in his head when he begged us to finish him. Abandoned in the desert — abandoned, or just overlooked by whoever or whatever befell the rest of his people.

Two Undead, their faces distorted, brains oozing out of their skulls. Neutralized. Dead on the pavement like so many others before them.

My dad, huddled and suspicious and rambling on his bed.

There are no good paths here. Every choice is just some new kind of horror.

"I can't," I tell him. "I can't be part of this anymore. No more drug deals. No more crime. No more digging into mysteries. I'm out."

"You think you can just quit? You think you can duck and hide and everything will go away? There's a dead mummy in the desert who shows real clear what the price is for not taking any risks, in case you forgot." He finishes his beer and crumples the can, the tendons in his ruined hand straining through the shredded skin. "Have you thought that far ahead? Because I don't think you have."

He pushes back from his chair and begins to pace the living room, making a tight circular path between the chair and his kitchen. He's agitated, shivery. Angry, I think, but that's not all of it. The Lazarus is working its way back out of his system. That dose wasn't enough to trigger a full-on withdrawal, but it's enough now to leave a path of agitation through his body.

I stay silent, watching him. Waiting for him to let it out of his system.

"You don't understand." His voice is heavy with a promise of pent-up anger, steam building up behind a release valve. "I can't do that again! You don't know what it was like for me, being all alone. For hours I hung there, and nobody came for me, and nobody cared. I thought I was in hell, Davin. I woke up and I thought I was in hell because the church was right all along — because I killed myself, because I'm a faggot, because I'm a sinner, pick your fucking reason — and my eternity was just going to be swinging there all by myself with nobody to care."

He's right. I'm always saying that I think we should talk about things, but now that it's actually coming out in the open I realize that I don't. Not at all. Something starts rising up in me, some volcanic combination of anger and pity and sadness and hurt, and I'm just sitting stock still in the chair trying to keep it all swallowed down.

"But it wasn't hell. It was worse than that. The maid came along eventually and she cut me down and do you know, she yelled at me? She just said, 'Oh, Randall, how could you. Don't you know the shame this will bring on your family! Your father will never forgive you!' That's what she said to me. I was dead and the only thing that fucking mattered was my dad. He didn't even talk to me that night. He didn't even acknowledge what happened. He couldn't look me in the eye. And you know what, that wasn't hell either."

He stops his pacing, glaring at me.

"Because that's the thing, Davin. That's the whole thing. I was dead. I was dead. And nobody gave a single goddamn. Because everybody dies alone. And there's nothing on the other side of that. You saw it too — you had to've. You die and it's <u>nothing</u> and I can't do that. I can't fucking die again."

"Randy, we're already dead," I say, exasperated. "What do you think is going to change? What difference is it going to make? I'm sorry your dad fucking sucks. Mine does too! But there's nothing you or I are going to do to change that, and it's not like…it's not like we're going to take some Lazarus and just magically live forever! You say you don't want to die again, but what you're doing is going to get us killed."

"I'd rather die with a bullet in my brain than wither up and rot like some kind of forgotten meat. Is that what you want? Do you wanna just dry up until you can't move an' shoo away the birds pecking out your eyes? You going to wait til I get that bad an' then it's you with the rock this time?"

"That's not fair." I flinch, the image of Julian flashing through my mind, searing into my thoughts. But I'm thinking, too, of the others, their bodies sprawled on the highway. I'm thinking of the armed guards patrolling the Lazarus House.

Randy pushes. "Who bashes *your* brains out when your time comes?"

I don't know for certain what was really happening with Julian — if his fate, his withered body, is the inevitable consequence of going without Lazarus, or some experimental result, the effects of Pyadox's pharmaceutical tinkering. But I do know for certain what happens when the Coalition finds you. I know for certain what lies at the end of the road Randy is proposing that we walk down, a risk I was willing to take when I was certain there was no other choice, a risk I can no longer justify now that I know there's even a slight chance of some other option.

I set the beer down on the floor, rising from my seat. "Fine."

His eyes narrow. He stops pacing and waits. The air between us grows cold.

"You want to get yourself killed by the Coalition, fine. You do that. But I've got people in my life who rely on me. I can't be running around like your crime buddy anymore. I'm out."

"People." He snorts derisively. "You don't have people, Davin, you've got one sister and she's got way bigger balls'n you. She wouldn't run away like this because she got scared."

"You're right. She wouldn't. And that would be stupid of her, and maybe that's a good reason why you shouldn't be around her anymore." My heart should be pounding right now. My body should be flooding with adrenaline. But it's not. It just feels sick and wilted in the absence. It feels shaky and hollow and spent. I realize I'm by the door, now, and I don't even remember moving toward it.

"What's that supposed to mean?"

"I'm not going to stop you," I say, the words forming themselves in my mouth. "But I'm not going to be part of this. And if you're going to do it, I don't want you coming around anymore or pulling me into it. I'm out. I'm done. We're done."

I don't want that to be true. I want him to come to me, to apologize, to bargain. I want him to beg for me to stay.

But he just glares at me, cold and defiant. "Fine. Then get out."

"Fine!" I step back and grab the door knob, forgetting it's locked. I fumble with the lock, burning and trembling in turn. You don't get a cool-guy exit in real life; you don't get the dramatic final line. I manage to get the door open and linger in the doorway, hesitating a spare second, waiting for him to tell me not go, and then I'm out into the darkness.

***

Who's going to do it for you, when your time comes?

Instead of sleeping, falling into that nothing void of dark at the shores of a vast and empty black sea, I lie in bed and try to imagine how it must have felt to be Julian. To be trapped in a body that simply would no longer move. To lie in the desert, parched and baking in the sun, birds pecking at your eyes.

I pull up Chuy's number on my phone and start typing out a message, then stop. Read over what I've written.

Copy it, save it down in my drafts.

Not yet, I think. It hasn't gotten that bad yet. I don't have to decide right now. I'm out. I'm safe. I can wait it out and maybe I'll still find a job somewhere, maybe I'll come up with some other plan. Maybe nothing will ever come of the Lazarus withdrawal. Maybe I won't be like Julian after all. But if it gets bad. If I don't have anywhere else to go.

Then I can send it. Then I can surrender.

***

When you're a kid, you think you always know when your parents are hiding

160

something from you, and you resent them for it. You want them to trust you enough to let you in on the secret. You want them to believe in you enough to think you can handle the truth. What you don't realize is that you've only scratched the surface of what they're hiding. It's not that they're hiding just a few small truths; it's that you're only catching glimpses of the places where their defenses have already cracked. The world is so much bigger and more terrifying than you can realize at the time, and the greatest privilege of youth is being shielded from it whenever and however possible.

Or, anyway, that's what I tell myself.

I don't tell Zoe that I know those guys from the newspaper. She fills me in with details about their deaths like she does with every Undead news story and I pretend that I don't know anything about it, pretend that I'm hearing everything for the first time, because I'm not ready to talk to her about this yet. I'm hoping that, maybe, I'll never have to talk to her about some of what's happened, some of what I've seen. Because she deserves to be shielded from it — or because I'm too much of a coward. Either way, it all ends in the same place.

I take her to the bank on Monday.

She's suspicious, like she's expecting this to be some kind of setup, but she also knows better — as Randy would say — than to look a gift horse in the mouth. Because she's still a minor and I'm her legal guardian, I have to be on her account. But I promise that I won't touch her money, and we bicker about ground rules: about the money, the videos, the fans. I have no idea what rules are appropriate. It's not like anyone gives you a handbook for this sort of thing. So mostly I ask questions and raise objections and let her come up with the way to fix them, and it all sounds good enough to me.

It's fall now, true fall, and the colors have changed in the mountains. It's patchy down in Los Ojos proper, but there are still pockets of color. You can see the gold in the cottonwood trees growing on the river bank. The imported ornamentals, the fruit trees landscapers love to plant outside banks and apartment buildings, have gone crimson. It's not exactly cold — it's still in the fifties during the day — but there's a bite of chill to the air, that specific scent of fall.

Instead of going straight home, I take the long way back, slow-rolling through what passes for downtown. There are Halloween decorations up in shop windows. The chile roasters outside the grocery store have been replaced by huge cardboard boxes bulging with pumpkins. In a few weeks, they'll have blocked off Main Street for the vendors and the mariachi music and the dancing, people selling sugar skulls and painting faces for money. The Day of the Dead hits a little bit differently now that the dead don't always stay that way, but I guess like most holidays the celebrations are more about the aesthetic anyway.

"Davin?" Zoe's looking at me sidelong, like she wants to ask something but is scared to. There's some of that frightened rabbit in her again. She's wearing her birthday shawl, the perfect defense against the not-quite-cold, and she adjusts it around her shoulders. "Something happened, didn't it? Or something's going to happen?"

"Things are weird with Randy," I admit, because that feels safe to tell her, and it's true.

"Did you two break up?"

"I'm not entirely sure we were ever dating."

"You were definitely dating."

I shrug, admitting defeat. "Well. I don't think we are anymore. I don't know."

"That sucks."

Silence blankets back over the truck, and I pull into the grocery store parking lot on a whim.

"When was the last time we carved a pumpkin?"

"What?"

"A pumpkin. When was the last time we carved one? For Halloween?"

"Oh, shit, it's been a while." Her brow furrows, thinking about it. Then she puts on an impression of our mother that's heartbreakingly accurate, "They're a waste of money and just an excuse to make a mess. Why buy something just to cut it up and let it get moldy?"

"Well now we have to."

She grins. "Do you think R—" stops herself, course-corrects, "Jo and

Andrea would want to come over? We could turn it into a party."

"Hell yeah we could."

We buy four pumpkins. Zoe insists on paying for them, and I tease her, calling her 'big spender' and 'high roller' and she eats it up because even though she's seventeen, even though she's twice as smart as I'll ever be and the internet's leading expert on Undead conspiracies, she's still just a kid, and I want that to be true for her as long as I can.

Chapter 17

I call Randy the next morning. It goes to voicemail.

The next time I call, the phone rings and rings, but doesn't connect. Eventually I hang up. I send a text instead, just a noncommittal "Hey" to test the waters. I sit waiting and watching for the 'read' notification and give up eventually. If he's got me blocked, if he's going to be childish about not talking to me, then fine. I'm done. I'm feeling bad about how we let things end, but I'm not chasing after him. Not even to say goodbye.

I doze on and off throughout the day. Zoe doesn't say anything about it, but I figure she's just assuming I'm moping about the breakup. She's probably pissed at me. I don't know what any of this means for The Underground. Does The Underground even exist anymore? We used to be united for a single purpose — we used to exist to keep each other safe and flush with Lazarus — but what does that even mean now? Ash didn't want to be involved with Randy's shit anymore. He said as much. Delilah's shutting down the coffee shop and she and Jo are breathers; they can walk away any time they like. Andrea? Who knows. Maybe we'll split right down the middle, one of those breakups where you take your friends with you. Maybe Jo and Andrea would take my place in Randy's inner circle, and I'd go back to being alone.

It doesn't matter.

I'm out. I'm out of that world, and I don't have to go back.

Julian was just one guy, one fringe case, and there's no guarantee that things would have turned out like that for anyone, no indication that I'm doomed to the same fate. It was a fluke.

A fluke — that's what Randy said about Javier, too.

So which is it? Does taking Lazarus turn you into a monster, or does *not* taking Lazarus turn you into a mummy?

And if it's both — if it's becoming a monster or rotting away piece-by-piece into dust — which is really worse?

Even if Pyadox is using experimental Lazarus formulas, does it make much difference? It's not like there's another option. I could sit out here and wait to fall apart from Lazarus deficiency, or I could go get paid to do it on the inside. Chuy said it's a good job. He said they're taking care of him and sending money home to his family. Even Julian said he'd been given an option. He consented to be a lab rat in exchange for the money. And, hey. Maybe some good will come out of it. If they're really running experiments, if they're really using the Lazarus House as a way to study the Undead instead of just keeping them locked up and off the street, then maybe they'll figure out better ways to help people.

It's the right choice. It has to be the right choice.

I hear Zoe rustling around in the kitchen, the clatter of pots and pans, and I think: I should get up, I should go talk to her, I should tell her everything. I've never kept so many secrets from her in her life, and it's stupid to think that it's even possible to keep secrets from somebody whose whole life is about turning over stones.

I curl up in bed, cocooned in my blanket, and feel feverish.

It's not fair. I didn't even use the Lazarus when Randy did. I can't blame this feeling on withdrawal. It can only be some kind of grief.

I got sick once, withdrawal from Lazarus when I was so stupid I thought I could ration it, when I thought I could do everything by myself. Randy came, he swooped in like a savior and he gave me my drugs and brought me back to the living and I thought that made him my savior. But what if he hadn't? What if I'd wept my bloody tears and sweated out that dark ooze, like that liquid that pools at the bottom of a refrigerator where the meat's all spoiled — what if I'd stayed in bed and weathered the storm and come out on the other side realizing that everything was fine?

What if there had never been any Underground? What if there had never been any Lazarus distribution network, any deals in shadowed parks, any gunshots cleaned and sewn in bathrooms? What if I'd never had to see someone turn into an animal and rip into someone's body like meat? If I'd never had to hear the sound of a skull crushing under the weight of a stone?

Would that have been better? Or would it have been worse?

Violence or decay. A bullet in the brain or a body crumbling to dust. Everyone dies, and everyone dies alone, so what difference does it really make how you get there?

The microwave bell dings in the kitchen, and I hear its door open and close. Zoe takes her food and pads down the hallway. I hear her footsteps stop in the hall, an uncertain lingering, and then her door opens and closes and soon enough I hear the sound of keys, the sharp clickity-clack through the wall.

I fall asleep, or what passes for sleep, and dream of nothing.

***

The phone rouses me, and I grab for it clumsily, not looking. It's Randy, I'm certain, and I answer through a fog of sleep. "Yeah?"

"Mr. Montoya. This is Lara Santana from the Lazarus House."

I sit up in bed, something hollow dropping through my core. There is an absence in my heart, a place where it should be beating frantically with sudden terror, but all I can feel is the reluctant sludge of old, dead blood creeping like oil through dessicated veins.

It's early. The light at the edge of the window is pale and gray. I've slept through the night without realizing.

"I'm so sorry. There's been an incident. We're going to need you to come down."

An incident?

What does that even mean? Images flash into my head, muddled. My dad escaping, fighting, hurting someone. A clench in my ruined guts. Would they refuse to let me work there because he's such a troublemaker? What if they're going to make me take him home, I think, with a kind of sleep-clogged logic. What if they're going demand that I take him back? The whole scenario plays through in my mind, the impossibility of it — me and Dad and Zoe and Randy, all smashed absurdly under the same roof, my dad and Randy drinking cheap beer and puking up their rancid guts, some twisted funhouse sitcom vision. The whole idea is so awful, and so ridiculous, that it almost makes me laugh.

Except Randy wouldn't even be here. I'd forgotten. Dad's going to come back and fill his space and time will revert back and it'll just be me and Zoe and Dad and it's going to be just like it was before except somehow even more awful.

"Mr. Montoya? Can you hear me?"

"Yeah. Yes. Sorry. What's this about? What did my dad do this time?"

Hesitation on the line. I can just make out that electric hum of static, of breathing. "It's really best if you can just come talk about this in person with one of our staff —"

"Just tell me what he did so I know what I'm walking into for once. Please."

"Mr. Montoya, I'm very sorry. Your father is dead."

An absurdist laugh tears out of my throat. Is this a fucking prank call? Of course he's dead. Obviously he's dead. He's been dead for years, that's why he's there. But —

"I'm sorry, I don't think I'm following you. What do you mean, 'dead?'"

"If you can just come down —"

"What happened?"

"There was an incident with a staff member —"

That word again. Incident. My mind is racing with ideas of what that could mean, of how an "incident" could lead to my Dad being a deader corpse, what could possibly bridge that gap between walking-dead and forever-dead, but really all I can think about is the way he looked that day on the couch, the tilt of his head and the crusty froth of vomit around his mouth, the way finding him dead in the living room had seemed both so inevitable and so devastatingly unreal. The image plays on a repeat loop in my brain, a white-noise buzzing threatening to overtake my senses, and I realize I've missed some of what the lady on the phone is saying. I struggle to parse her words, but they're more sound than meaning.

"Yes, I understand," I say into the phone, speaking on autopilot. "I'll be right over."

She says some more things, a buzzing fly against the plane-engine drone in my head, and I drop the phone onto the bed without disconnecting. It bounces, the screen flashing a confused beacon, then going dark as she leaves the call. I stare across the room. This feels like the worst of Lazarus withdrawal all over again. Alone in a darkened bedroom, the world tilting away beneath me as my thoughts go blank.

But I don't get the terror or the reprieve of lost consciousness to save me, here. Just thoughts looping like a scratched record, infinite repeats without meaning.

My dad is dead.

My dad is really dead.

Forever dead.

Pulling the marionette strings of my corpse takes concentration and effort, and right now all of my thoughts are focused inward. I can't move and think at the same time. I sit and stare.

I can't put a word to the emotion fluttering through my ruined gut. Is it grief? Is it fear? Is it...relief? A guilty, twisted relief, an oppressive weight being lifted but only because the thing causing that weight has been snuffed out entirely. No more phone calls. No more fielding his insanity, no more delusions, no more worrying about him escaping or attacking or...

...an incident with a staff member.

I find control over my legs and I make it to my feet. I shamble stiff-jointed for the door, none of the pieces of my body moving together correctly. In the movies, they make that herky-jerky zombie movement with camera tricks, but it turns out that all you need is a body that won't listen to your authority.

"Zoe?" I stop outside her door. It's so early. There's no way she's awake, and I think, why am I waking her up? Is this an emergency? How much of an emergency can it really be for someone to die a second time?

I knock. Wait. Knock again, louder.

A muffled "hmmmph?" from the other side.

"Hey, Zoe. I need....It's about Dad," I say, finally finding my voice, trying to dredge myself back into the present, pulled clean of the mire in my thoughts. The words "incident with a staff member" chase round and round in my head like a dog spinning after its tail, an echoing overlay to the image of him dead and open-mouthed on the couch, opportunistic fly buzzing over. "The Lazarus House called. They…I need to go down there."

A questioning, sleepy noise.

Should I go inside? Should I explain through the door? Should I just leave now and get it over with while she's gone?

"He's, uh." Saying it out loud — having to explain it — seems impossible and exhausting. I realize my hands are shaking. Zoe. I'm going to have to tell Zoe, if not now, then later; there's no way past this moment. And when I do, she's going to cry, she's going to grieve, because Zoe's emotions all live right at the surface. Because Zoe is tough as hell but she's not hard, she's not cold. Not like me. I've spent my whole life trying to protect her from things, but the truth is she'd be better at dealing with most of them on her own. "I need to go. I'll fill you in when I get back."

"Nnnf."

"Kay. I'll lock the doors behind me. If you need anything…" *Call Randy,* I almost say, but I don't know whether that's true, whether that's even safe. "Text me."

I don't think she's heard any of this, not really. I keep standing outside the bedroom door and hear soft movements, quiet rustling, and then a low snore. I don't blame her. It can't be long after dawn.

I grab my keys and splash some water on my face and head out the door.

Chapter 18

I stop at Randy's apartment on my way out of town.

I don't mean to do it. My head feels stuffed with bees, a low warm buzzing that blocks out the noise of my thoughts, and I drive on muscle memory alone. I'm parked outside his unit before I realize where I am. I don't see the Mercedes parked in its usual spot. Maybe he's out. Maybe he's talking to the rest of The Underground, trying to get someone else on his side. A replacement in crime.

Maybe he's parked further up the lot. Maybe I want him to be gone so I can be mad at him.

I get out of the truck and make my way up to his door, driven by inertia. I knock. I try the knob, just to check, but it's locked.

Something like a low-burning rage sears through my chest. Something wounded and betrayed. He has no way of knowing I'm here, of course, no way of knowing what's happened or how I feel — but all the same, how dare he. How dare he not be here right now. How dare he ghost me like this and leave me to face this alone.

I knock again, more insistent, and I see the blinds rustle on the unit next door, a pair of suspicious eyes peeking out through the slats. It's so early, and here I am, pounding on the door like an angry lover. Maybe they think I'm police. Or maybe they'll want to call the cops on me, figuring I'm up to no good. I don't know if people worry about the cops showing up in this neighborhood like they do in mine.

I back away from the door, sparing the briefest of glances back to the neighbor's window. They step back hurriedly, letting the blinds fall back into place. Best not to linger here in case they decide I look too rough for this neighborhood — although, wouldn't there be some sweet irony in that? But my mind's racing ahead as I climb back into the pickup, a thought clear and worrying enough to pierce through the persistent hum of white noise that's blanketed over my thoughts.

It's hardly dawn.

If Randy isn't at his place at this hour, then where the fuck is he?

There's no way he's left this early to do anything. If he's not here, it's because he's been out all night — I'm certain of that.

So where?

***

The drive out to the Lazarus House is too long to be alone with your own thoughts.

My mind flips between static and rumination, thoughts chasing themselves round and round in circles. I let them go. It's too exhausting to try to corral them, to impose any sort of order on them. A miserable bone-aching weariness has set in, a kind of deep-set exhaustion that battles against a crawling electric hum that rolls like ball lightning up and down my skin. Like my body's throwing everything it has at its own broken down machinery, a robot's weak struggle to self-repair.

Dad is dead.

Where is Randy?

Flashes of things I don't want to think about: The snap of the old woman's bone in the grip of the Coalition agent. The sound of the stone crunching through the dried-out bone of Julian's skull. Javier with a mouth full of blood and gore, looking up wild-eyed from Chuy's guts. Gail looking like some thin, mangled thing crouched over the body of roadkill in the middle of the highway. Elliot and Duncan, dead on the pavement, gunned down by police.

It's too much. How much horror can you take in before you can't handle any more?

The defining category of humanity is resilience. You pick up where you are and you deal — that's how I've gotten this far, how I've kept on putting one foot in front of the other, how I've managed to navigate when every day is a new disaster. But when does it end? Does it ever end?

Where the fuck is Randy?

I turn on the radio. The station is staticky out here, an in-between place where no radio towers broadcast clearly. The snow overlaid on the music sounds like the crunching white noise in my head.

The last time I felt like this, driving along the road, I crashed my car and died.

I grip the wheel harder, sit up straighter.

I might never have to make this trip again. Dad is dead — *dead*, fully dead, totally dead — and I never have to make this drive to visit him, never have to roll up to deal with some new drama, never have to make excuses for his behavior. Dad is dead and I don't ever need to think about him again.

Something wet crawls down my cheek and I swipe at it with the back of a hand. It's a red-black smear, tears. I didn't realize I was crying.

Great. I'll have to get cleaned up somehow before I can show my face at the Lazarus house. I'll have to work hard to hold back any tears, because as soon as they see this, as soon as they notice the bloody black goo leaking out of my eyes, they'll have me locked up in a room and I won't be needing to make this drive ever again after all but for a wholly different reason.

Would they still give me a job, I wonder? Or is that offer only available if they don't arrest you first?

I pop the truck on cruise control and lean over to paw through the glove compartment, fish out some napkins. I swipe at my face with them, feeling a sudden surge of anger.

Angry at my body for crying. Angry at myself for caring so goddamn much.

I never cried when Dad died.

From the moment I found his body, to the moment I got the call that he'd awoken in the morgue, I felt nothing at all. Just a cold shocked numbness. If I'd had more time, I told myself, I would have been able to grieve. But there hadn't been time to grieve, not really, not when my life was suddenly so busy with so much else: doctor's appointments and paperwork and talking to social workers and talking to lawyers and giving Dad his drugs and taking his abuse and finding a job and trying, every day, always, to shield Zoe from all of it.

So I hadn't cried then.

But it feels traitorous to cry now.

What am I even grieving for at this point?

You wait too long to grieve and it starts to feel almost garish. It starts to feel like melodrama, some kind of production. If your heart wasn't broken before, why is it hurting so much now? There's a time limit to it, a statute of limitations. There has to be, because otherwise once you open that door, when does it ever end?

If you let yourself weep for every injustice, every trauma, every miserable goddamn thing that gets heaped up on you, then you'll never stop crying. You'll be like La Llorona in the story, a wailing woman, sobbing forever at the banks of the river between life and death.

I squeeze my my left eye tightly shut, screwing the napkin into it with such ferocity that I'm half-worried the eye will just pop and start oozing jelly. But it doesn't, and I open it, blinking away the last of the sticky dampness. I shift my grip on the wheel and apply the napkin to the other eye with the same intensity, plugging the tear duct the way you plug up a bloody nose.

I blink again, both eyes clear. I exhale through my mouth, breath hot and dry and rancid in the closeness of the cab. Morning breath is worse when you're a corpse. I paw through the center console and find a mint, sliding it under my tongue and holding back the roiling disgust as my body recoils at the sugar. But I hold it there and let it dissolve, dry tongue sandpapering along the walls of my mouth, and by the time I get to the Lazarus House, I can pass as presentable.

∗∗∗

The guards eye me warily as I pull up to the gate.

My heart should be hammering with fear, but it's all still and quiet in there, dead inside at last. There's something freeing about it, this disconnect from fear, the separation that's driven its wedge down between my body and my mind. I'm too tired even for that sick, rotten dread that lives in my ruined guts. I'm just empty.

Maybe they see that emptiness in my eyes. Maybe that's why they don't ask me too many questions. Or maybe they're just not trained for it; shock troops designed to intimidate, not to carry conversations. Lucky me. I give my name and explain my business in a few terse words, broken sentences because I don't have the energy for a monologue right now.

"Davin Montoya. They called. My dad. Tell them I'm here. I'll wait."

Zoe is at home, I think. Zoe is home and if this takes long enough, she'll be awake and curious, and she'll want to talk to me when I get back and I'll have to find the strength for words, so I'm going to save up as many as I can for her. Nothing short of that is worth the effort.

Two armed guards stand outside my car, long rifles slung across their chests. Is this what killed Dad, I wonder? Did he try to escape and get cut down by a storm of bullets? I try to imagine him like that, body cut apart by the impact of a hundred rounds from a semi-automatic, holes spurting red-black gunk, his head arcing back and brains blown clear from his skull like something from the news. I try to think of him bleeding out in the gravel or in pieces on the asphalt, but I can't imagine it.

I can only think of the way he looked on the couch that day, mouth crusted with vomit, a fly crawling over his unblinking eye.

A guard says something into his radio, and something garbles back, and then the gate's being opened and they're gesturing me inside. I drive slow, forced to creep along behind the men in front and beside the pickup. They herd me like a stray calf into a parking space and wait, again, for me to shut off the engine and climb out and head inside.

They lead me past the waiting room, heading down the hallway to the back of the trailer of the administration building. There's a closed door with a sign - BATHROOM - and a piece of paper pinned beneath reading ASK FOR KEY. They lead me past that to a door at the end of the hall, the master bedroom converted now into an office space, and I realize: This is Ash's house. It's the exact same model, the identical blueprint. Maybe they were manufactured in the same place. This thought strikes me as extremely funny, and I have to stuff my knuckles into my mouth to force the laughter back down my throat. I cough to cover for it, and swiftly wipe my hands on my pants before they can see the unnatural hue of the rancid sputum.

The door opens, and they let me inside, closing the door behind me. I listen for the sound of a lock, like this is an interrogation room, like there should be one-way mirrors on the walls and a big steel table. But there's not. Just regular cheap office furniture, a generic desk and padded chairs like the kind at a bank. There's a bland painting on the wall, pastel sand glued to canvas in some simulation of a Southwest sunset.

The man on the other side of the desk seems familiar somehow, but I can't place him. Maybe I've seen him on the news. He's an older guy, wisps of hair combed carefully over the bald spots, bits of shiny scalp visible beneath. He has long sideburns and a bare face that's the same width as his neck, like somebody added some accessories to a pencil eraser to make a puppet.

"Mr. Montoya," he says, but doesn't extend a hand.

"Davin," I say. "Mr. Montoya is my father."

He lets that hang there, like he's waiting for me to be embarrassed or to acknowledge the irony. But we just stare at each other, and he clears his throat.

"Sit. I know this must be difficult for you."

I don't sit. I stand, arms at my sides, and watch as he pulls out his own chair and folds into it. He folds chubby hands in front of him on the desk. There is a paper beside him, carefully stacked and arranged with a pen on top, staged for signing.

"What happened?"

"My name is Alan Decker," he says, ignoring me. "I'm the acting general manager of this facility, and I'd like to extend my greatest condolences to your family on the loss of —"

"Acting manager," I say. "So you're sitting in on someone else's job. Where are they?"

"Please sit," he says, and I think I can make out an imperceptible little twitch in the corner of his eye. "The Lazarus House is restructuring, actually. There's an acquisition in the works. But keep that one under your hat, would you? We're not quite ready to reveal all the details to the public." He winks, tapping his forehead, as if sharing this makes him my friend.

"My dad."

"Of course, yes. Again, I really just want to say how deeply sorry we all are. The safety and wellbeing of our patients —"

I grab the back of the chair and lean forward over the desk. I don't usually use my height for intimidation, but I hope I'm looming. "Cut the shit. Just tell me why you called me here."

The corners of his mouth twitch down. His frown lines crease deeply through the fat of his jowls, doing nothing to reduce his resemblance to a puppet. "There is paperwork that must be completed. Official death records for the Undead Registry, a release form for the ashes, a waiver of liability…"

"Aren't you, though? Liable? Isn't that your entire job?"

"The waiver is a formality," Decker says, and I'm almost impressed at how good he is at talking right past questions. "Or, I should say, more of a reminder of what you already signed. Surely you recall when your father was brought here?"

I think back. It's a little hazy, remembering the details, considering a few hours later I was lying dead in a river.

"At any rate, it's all very standard. We provide the greatest possible standard of care, but our patients do pose some unique challenges. It's a very uncertain world, handling the Undead. We learn new things every day."

"Challenges." I push back from the desk, crossing my arms, cradling my permanently broken ribs so he won't hear them creaking and grinding as I straighten. "What did my father do? Did he try to escape again? Attack another guard? Just cut the shit and tell me. You don't need to hold my hand."

Decker blinks, his head wobbling like he's been slapped. His brow furrows. "Oh goodness, no, no, Mr. Montoya. Whatever violent end you're imagining…oh no. There's been a terrible misunderstanding."

"There was an *incident*," I say, pronouncing the word carefully, scathingly. "That's what I was told on the phone."

The furrow deepens, but his eyes go hard, that mr-buddy-nice-guy persona sliding right off his face. "You were misinformed, and I will talk to the employee responsible. Perhaps she was confused. I am very sorry for the distress that must have caused."

Now it's my turn to blink, incredulity stirring some kind of life back into my guts. "Then what happened?"

He hesitates, holding up his hand as if in a gesture of careful consideration. "It's what we might call, a failure to thrive. We've been seeing it more frequently. Undead quite simply grow resistant to the Lazarus and, eventually…" he shrugs.

"I've never heard of that." I'm surprised to hear the anger in my voice. "Excuse me, but that's a bunch of shit. First people say that if you don't take Lazarus then you go crazy. Now you're saying if you *do* keep taking it, it just…stops working? And then what?"

"And then, well…think of it as like being on life support."

"Life support doesn't kill you unless somebody pulls the plug."

"…you are absolutely correct. My apologies, that was a bad metaphor."

"Or that's exactly what you meant."

"Mr. Montoya, I'm going to need you to sign these papers."

"Let me see him."

"That is not possible. The body was sent to the crematorium this morning."

The room seems to rotate around the edges, like the floor is slowly turning. I hug myself tighter, afraid that I might lose my balance if I let go, afraid that I might launch myself across the room and do something that I'll regret with my hands if I let them loose. "You can't do that."

"We can, actually, and we have. If you'll reference your agreement —"

"You can't!" I yell, and then it's over, I've lost my grip on myself in every possible sense. I'm across the desk without realizing that I've moved, my hand wrapping tight around the collar of Decker's button-up, pulling his face close enough to mine that surely he can see the poor stitching on my face, surely he can smell the rot on my breath that can't be hidden by a mint. He's close enough to know that I'm not alive, and in this moment I don't even care. "Did you kill him? Did you fucking kill my father and burn the body? Stop lying and tell me the truth!"

He fumbles for a button on his desk, and almost instantly the door bursts open, the guards burst through, and I've got hands on my arms, dragging me back, the fabric slipping through my fingers as I lose hold on Decker's collar. This is it. They're going to kill me. Forget working here. Forget walking away. They're going to drag me down the hall and lock me in a cell; they know what I am, and they're not going to let me walk out of here. I can see it in my mind, clear as day, can see them dragging me from the room and taking me out to the grounds, and maybe they don't even bother with the cell, maybe they just duck behind a stone wall and bash my brains in here and now.

Zoe's at home. She's waiting for me to get back.

She'll belong to the state.

I go limp in their grasp, all of the fight leaking out of me. I'm as quiet and meek as a puppy, and I let them pull me backward.

"I can understand that you're upset. Grief is a terrible thing. I'm sorry, Mr. Montoya." Decker smiles, and it's an unpleasant, leering sort of smile. "I'll have the papers delivered to you. We will need them returned before we can release the ashes. I recommend that you do not return. You will not be welcome on these grounds again."

I want to scream. I want to tear out of their grasp and wheel on these guards and unleash every bit of Undead fury I can. I want to gouge out their eyes and dig my teeth into them, and it's not Lazarus doing that, it's just pure, natural rage.

But I don't, because they're not man-handling me out into a holding cell. They're not yelling for backup. They're not even, really, treating me like an Undead.

Just a guy, crazy with grief. Just a customer service problem. An issue to resolve.

And because of that, they let me go when I get to the truck. They warn me to move along. But they don't stop me from pulling away.

I get a few miles down the highway and pull onto the shoulder to scream. There's nobody to hear me out here.

Chapter 19

When our mom was dying of cancer, Zoe made it a point to learn everything she could about the disease. There was a book she bought in the hospital gift shop, a picture book for explaining terminal illness to kids. It was obviously far too young for her, too simplistic, but she read it solemnly in the waiting room and then went back to the gift shop to scour the shelves for more. When she ran out of options there, I took her to the library so she could learn more. For a little while, it looked like she was studying to be an oncologist, a teenage prodigy. She crammed her brain with information, facts spilling out at odd moments.

In the car: "Did you know that the early Egyptians were diagnosing cancer as early as 1600 B.C.?"

In the waiting room: "Did you know that naked mole rats are immune to cancer?"

At the dinner table: "Did you know that there's a type of cancer that dogs can spread like an STD?"

Our own living encyclopedia of macabre facts.

Mom died, and we buried her, and she stayed in the ground. People still did that back then. It wasn't a very big funeral. Mom had some family, but they weren't interested in our lives; they'd never approved of her marriage with our dad, never saw why she'd stayed with him through the ebb and flow of his drinking, never saw why she'd choose to stay in Los Ojos instead of finding some kind of opportunity and moving up, moving on. Dad was late to the funeral. I was trying to make excuses for him, and the funeral director was nice about it, even as Dad came in reeking of whiskey and the funeral home staff had to strong-arm him into a separate room until the service was over so he didn't disrupt anyone with his howling. The funeral director said that kind of thing happened all the time, that grief is unpredictable, that no one should be judged for the way they handle their pain.

But the way Dad handled his pain left more for me to do, so I was too busy to pass judgment anyway.

Someone has to be there to write the checks, to answer the questions, to shake the hands and smile like you mean it when people tell you how very, very sorry they are. Someone has to be there in the moment to keep it all together, because there's a lot of work to the business of dying. And in the end, everybody went home, none of the people who promised they'd call or write more ever did, and we swept the condolence cards into a box and hauled the flower arrangements out to the dumpster and got on with life, the way you do because you have to.

Zoe stopped sharing cancer "fun facts" after that. Not because they were ghoulish, I don't think, but because they had stopped having any utility. They weren't a thing she needed anymore. She had learned enough about cancer to find some sort of peace, make some kind of sense about the cause-and-effect, and she cried and spent some time looking at old photos and making a little memory album and then she was done. Just that easy. And I was so jealous then, and could never understand how it is that my little baby sister could have learned to grieve when I could never get the hang of it myself.

***

I'm glad, for once, about the long drive home from the Lazarus House. Grateful that it gives me time to roll the guilt and the shock and the anger around and around like smooth stones, grappling them and swallowing them down. My skin feels like it's buzzing, an electric tingle that shivers up and down my arms in waves, deadened nerves sending ghostly signals back to a brain that's increasingly ill-equipped to listen.

But I don't know what I'm going to say, and I don't know what to expect, even as I open the door and kick off my shoes and see Zoe sitting at the table, eating cereal out of a piece of tupperware because nobody remembered to run the dishwasher. I stand frozen in the entryway, not ready, not prepared to confront this moment, knowing I'm never going to be.

"Hey. Where'd you go?" She waves me over, gestures with her spoon at an open chair.

"Zoe. Something's happened."

She stiffens. "Is it Randy? Is he okay? Did you guys have a fight or something?"

The question is so completely off-track that I falter, almost laugh. "Randy's fine," I say, but that could be a lie. I don't even know where he is, much less how he is. But that's something I can't find space to worry about right now. "It's about Dad."

"Oh." She sounds disappointed. She shovels more cereal into her mouth.

I pull up a chair and sit, because it feels weird to stand and say this while she's sitting there eating off-brand cereal and reading something on her phone. The cereal box is sitting on the table, a cartoon mascot of a cheerful blue sea lion staring at me with big blank eyes and a wide stupid grin, and I turn it around to face the other way. It doesn't help. The same character is on the back, balancing a ball on his nose at the top of a maze, a spiral dotted with cereal ingredients — wheat and sugar and nuts and milk and fruit.

"He's. Um. The Lazarus House called. I had to come down to…" there's no amount of editorializing that is going to make this easier. I want to make this make sense for her, but it doesn't even make sense to me. I reach a hand across the table and catch Zoe's arm, the one not wielding a cereal spoon. I lay my wrist over her phone, wait for her to look up to meet my eye. I can read suspicion in her expression. "He's dead. Full-dead. They…they cremated him this morning."

The words are harsh and bald and cold.

She drops her spoon. Milk splashes from the bowl, a small spray of drops. "What?"

"I know." I search for something else to say. And, lacking any embellishments that will make this any better, I end up just saying everything. "I don't. I don't know what happened. They said at first some kind of incident.

Then the other guy said some bit about 'failure to thrive.' It all sounded like bullshit. I got…I got mad, they dragged me out of there like I was…like…I don't know."

"You're not joking."

"I would never joke about this."

Her eyes go wide, shimmery, magnified behind her lenses. She grabs her phone off the table and before I can stop her, before I can ask her what she's doing, she's got it up to her ear and has pulled away from the table, made for the back door.

"Hi, yes, I'm Zoe Montoya," I hear her say, with the kind of fake cheerfulness that you adopt when you're talking to customer service. "Yes, I'll hold."

She ducks outside the door and her voice goes muffled. I sit, left alone with soggy cereal. The sea lion on the box looks unbearably smug, and I take a swipe at it. The box flies, somersaulting in midair, showering a rain of cereal in an arc all across the table and floor. It skids to a stop beside the refrigerator.

If I were Randy, I would throw the bowl off the table, too. I would throw it at the tile and hope that it shattered.

And if I were my dad, I would leave it all there, soggy and sticky, leave it for the flakes to be crumbled to dust and tracked deep into the carpet.

But the thing about making a mess is that somebody needs to clean it up. It doesn't matter how angry you are, how sad you are, how fucked up the whole world around you is, how bad you're hurting — the ants don't care. The carpet doesn't care. And you can only get away with making your emotions somebody else's problem if there's somebody else around.

I get up and retrieve the broom and dust pan and start sweeping, and I don't realize that I've started crying again until I see the dark spots splashing onto the tile, falling and making a mess even as I'm bent over trying to fix the last thing, and that's it. That's the breaking point. There's no wrestling back control this time. There's no dabbing at tears and plugging them up before they can ooze out. There's no stopping these from coming, so I don't even try. I let the grief take the wheel for once. Give myself over to it. I had wanted to surrender, right? Well. Here's my chance.

I hit the ground and I'm huddled up against the cabinet, my face in my knees, when Zoe comes back inside.

She's been crying, too. But of course, her tears are clear, glistening damp streaks down each cheek, not the disgusting mess that's seeping from my eyes. But if she notices the splatters on the floor, or the scattered cereal, or the broom and dustpan lying abandoned beside me, she doesn't say anything about them. Instead she sniffs and pulls off her glasses to clean them on the hem of her shirt.

I wipe my eyes with the back of my hands, streaks painting my wrists. Something clear leaks out of my nose. I don't know if it's snot or cerebral fluid. I wipe it on my shirt either way. I'm shaking, the way you shake when you've been throwing up for a long time and your body's all emptied out. The way you shake when you don't have anything left to give but your body is demanding more.

"I called them," she says, voice hollow. "It's like you said. They wouldn't really talk to me."

"I'm sorry."

"It's not your fault."

"Yes, it is," I say, and the words are ripping up through me like I'm vomiting shards of glass. Every one hurts, but I can't stop. "I'm the one who made him go there. I'm the one who didn't take care of him here. I'm the one who — who — let him die."

"Is that what you think?"

"I knew he was bad off," I say, and it's not the Undead version of him I have in mind. It's not the walking corpse that I'm envisioning. "I knew it. I shouldn't have left him alone. I should have been watching out for him. I just…I couldn't stand to be around him for one more minute so I just…I just left him alone and I should have known."

I pull my knees in tighter and hear the crack and shift of my bones. My stomach sucks inward, the muscles bending at unusual angles to fill empty places where organs used to be, purged out of my body now to make room for something else, something rotten and festering. I cover my eyes, pressing the heels of each hand in hard to try to stem the flow, try to stop it from leaking and oozing out, but with my eyes closed all I can see is that living room, the sun streaming in, the dust dancing in the light; all I can see is my dad lying on the couch, a fly crawling over his open dead eye.

She flops down next to me on the floor, leaning her head on my shoulder, and we sit there for a while, not saying anything. I wait for her to say something comforting, to trot out some kind of platitude, but she's too smart for that. So instead we just sit in silence, the last survivors of the family disaster, a couple of shipwrecked kids, and she doesn't say anything about my gross Undead tears and I don't say anything about how she's smudging her glasses every time she tries to clean them.

Eventually I get up, taking her hand to pull her up to her feet. When I sweep up the cereal, she holds the dust pan steady.

"I'm supposed to be the one comforting you," I say, waiting for her to shake out the cereal into the trash.

"Yeah, well, you suck at it," she says, and flashes me a grin. "It's okay, though. You're good at a lot of other stuff. Are you okay?"

"I think so. No. I don't know."

"Yeah, me neither. It's some shit." Zoe hesitates, then catches my arm. "Mom and Dad dying, you know you didn't make that happen, right? You're not, like…god or something."

I look up. She meets my eye.

"If anybody's at fault for anything here, it's those sketch-ass Lazarus House people. If they…if they did something, then we'll find out about it and we'll destroy them. That's how we make this okay."

She's already started to pull away, to head for her computer, prepared to find some keyboard warrior way to take on the world, and I'm partway convinced that, given the opportunity, she'll be able to do it. But she's missing some pieces.

"Zoe." I catch her before she goes. "There's…some stuff I gotta tell you."

***

Slowly, over the course of hours, it comes out.

184

Julian and the Undead in the desert. His dessicated body and the awful final request. Gail, who used to be like the rest of us and then, somehow, had become something else. The experiments at the Lazarus House. The money they promised to families in exchange. Chuy, walking and working and living at the Lazarus House. The job offer I had considered.

I don't tell her everything. I don't try to explain how things have gone so sideways with Randy. Because it's not all my story to tell, maybe, and because it's not her problem to fix. But I tell her more than I ever would have thought I could, even though it takes a while, even though it all comes out in a jumble.

I ask her if she wants to record this. If she wants to have it all on video for the documentary.

She tells me it's all right, that we'll fill it in later. Once we have the rest of the answers.

"The viewer will need all the dots connected," she explains, but I think maybe she's just too caught up with hearing it all.

We're out on the back porch. I've been steadily working my way through a pack of smokes. She's wrapped up against the wind chill, shawl tight around her shoulders as she sits on the corner of the table and stares at the sky, listening to me as I explain, only stopping for clarification or questions when I veer too far off track for her to follow.

"I'm sorry I didn't tell you everything," I say, when I've run out.

"Were you really thinking about going and working at the Lazarus House?"

"Yeah."

She's quiet a while, and I'm not sure what she's going to do. Start yelling at me, maybe. She'd be well within her rights to. Instead she just shakes her head like she's disappointed. She gives me a look with an expression that's hard to read. I think it might be pity.

"You dipshit," she says, and her voice is hoarse, like maybe she's going to cry again, but instead she just leans over the table and punches me in the shoulder. Then she slides down to the ground. "All right. Well. At least you came to your senses. So lets take those fuckers down."

***

It's still daytime, but I can't think of anything else to do so I go back to my room and flop fully-clothed in my unmade bed, staring at the ceiling. There are outlines of stars imprinted in the ceiling. There used to be glow-in-the-dark stars up there, little luminescent decals, but I took them down when I was a teenager. Zoe had always loved them, coveted them, and I gave them to her for her room, but we couldn't get them to stay stuck anymore. All the adhesive had worn off. We even tried super glue, but they still fell off, ripping off bits of plaster, like little glow-in-the-dark meteors bringing down the ceiling with them. We gave up and threw the stars away. But you can still make out their ghosts on my ceiling, the little outlines made by leftover adhesive and years of blocked light, and I stare up at them now with unfocused eyes and trace constellations between them.

I can hear Zoe in the other room, clicking and tapping at her keyboard.

The house is so quiet that the sound seems amplified, like a mouse gnawing in the dead of night.

Rats in the walls. Dad had been ranting about that. I wonder now if that was true. I think of a fat gray rat sliding its oily body up onto his bed at night, nibbling at an exposed toe. I imagine them pouring from a hole in the wall, a little furry tide of them rushing in to scavenge a corpse that, by rights, shouldn't be able to fight back.

Or, when he talked about rats, did he mean *lab* rats? The people being experimented on? Was he one of them? Julian had made it sound like it was voluntary — like he was bribed into it with promises of money, not coerced — but what if that's not true? What if they started experimenting on my dad just because they could? Because he was a pain in their ass. Because he was always causing trouble.

What if he was causing trouble because they were hurting him?

I roll over onto my side, curling into a protective ball, trying to block out the noise with a pillow. But it doesn't do much for the noise in my head, which is a competition between the snowy white-noise static and a relentless cycle of thoughts and images chasing around in circles.

I screw my eyes shut and try to silence the thoughts.

When I open them again, the light has shifted on the wall, the glow behind my black-out curtains changed in color and tenor. I must have fallen asleep, but I don't remember; I don't remember visiting that place I always seem to go in my dreams, that little island of light in the deep void of nothing.

I reach for my phone. Dial Randy's number, and get no answer.

I send a text instead, weighing the words carefully knowing that they could be intercepted: "Did you still want to do the thing?"

I hit send, hesitate a moment, then send: "I'm in."

I watch the corner of the screen, waiting for the 'read' notification, forgetting to breathe. But it pops up, and I exhale a sharp hiss of relief.

A moment later, his message pops up: "About damn time."

Chapter 20

We agree to meet up at a 24-hour diner because I need to get away from the house for a while but I can't stand the thought of Randy's sad bachelor apartment on top of all the other misery. Besides, in all the movies, the grand capers and heists always get planned at a place like this. Maybe they're onto something.

It's a greasy spoon place, the kind frequented predominately by truckers and homeless people, and there are some of both there tonight. A homeless guy sits at the bar, wearing too many layers for the ambient temperature, slowly drinking a cup of coffee. The trucker has pulled his cap down over his eyes and is lightly snoozing in a corner booth, waiting on his food to arrive. It's an off-hour of day, not quite lunch rush, no longer really breakfast, so I'm not expecting many other patrons. All the same, the waitress takes her sweet time with checking in on our table, which actually suits me fine.

"So what happened to change your mind?"Randy asks me after the waitress has walked away with our drink order — two waters and a pot of coffee to share.

"My dad died," I tell him, because he needs to know and because I need to practice saying the words aloud until they make sense to me. "Forever, I mean. This time."

"Oh." A silence, hesitation. "He was kind of an asshole, right?"

He was, he absolutely was, but hearing Randy say it sends a shiver of anger through me. Some kind of instinctive reflex to defend him. I can talk shit about my family, but nobody else gets to do it for me — that's the rule, unspoken but universal. Or at least it should be. Then again, Randy's dad is a politician, and that twists all the rules. Maybe at a different time I'd cut him some slack; maybe I'd even be sympathetic at how much it must suck to have your family be right there in the public to get dragged through the mud. But right now, my emotions are an exposed nerve in a raw, gaping wound, and I close them off and seal them up deep inside because I don't want to share.

"He was my dad."

"Okay, okay, fair 'nuff." He raises his hands, a sign of surrender. "But you're in?"

"Yeah. Kind of. But, um…" There's an impulse to explain everything, to share every fresh anxiety and regret, to tear open the ugly scab healing over my fresh grief, but I can't. I think he'd understand. Maybe better than anyone, Randy should be able to understand what's going on in my head, which is why I can't bring myself to say any of it. Not now. Later, maybe, when this is done, when we've finished everything. And there is a lot to do. "Where were you yesterday? I came by your place. On my way…when I drove out there."

"Oh. That." He grins. "Well, as it happens, I was meeting with somebody who might just be able to help with exactly the problem that we are having."

The waitress is back with a tray loaded with water, mugs and a coffee carafe. She asks if we want any food. I order a breakfast burrito, thinking I might bring it home for Zoe. Randy asks about the pie options, listens with relish as she lists them all, and then says he'll think on it and might order a piece later. I'm tempted to kick him hard under the table but I hold it in.

"As you were saying?"

"Right. Yeah. So remember how I had that chat with Elliot before… everything?" He makes a vague hand gesture meant to envelop the concept of 'everything.' I nod. "Right. So he gave me the information for his connection, who it turns out is a weigh station attendant. Every truck that comes through there has to stop and be weighed and have its papers checked, which means that any delivery coming through that corridor of highway gets diverted to the weigh station."

"Including the Pyadox trucks."

"Precisely. So this guy's got routes, license plate numbers, arrival times, the whole nine. Elliot would figure out the relevant information and set up a trap, using the bridge as a choke point. A whole Robin Hood act. Kind of over-the-top if you ask me, but hey, whatever works."

"It didn't work out too well for them after all," I remind him, thinking of the news story, the photo of their corpses.

He shrugs. "Well, it worked out fine every time until it didn't, right?"

That's not a comforting thought. "How do we deal with the driver? I don't want to hurt anybody."

"I had a feeling you'd say that."

"It's a valid concern."

"Sure. So we skip the trouble and just do it at the truck stop. Get him distracted and out of the truck."

"How do we pull that off?"

"Money talks." He shrugs. "I think I can work something out. It won't have the dramatic flair of a highway robbery, mind you..."

"All the better."

The waitress is back with my burrito. Randy tells her he does want the pie after all, ordering cherry — warm and a la mode, of course — with a good-hearted wink, and this time I do kick him.

"So why the sudden change of heart?" he asks, leaning forward on one elbow. "I mean. I get the thing with your dad sucks, but...?"

I glance around. The trucker is now shoveling a plate of bacon and eggs and pancakes into his face. I doubt he cares much about listening in. And the homeless guy is too far away, even if he cared, which I doubt. All the same, I keep my voice low. "Zoe really thinks there's a chance we can make something happen if we get hold of a sample. Like, if we could get it to a scientist, get the formula leaked, something like that. She thinks that's a way to hurt Pyadox."

"Do you think that will work?"

I shrug. "I don't know. I don't know what I think. But..." I prod at the burrito, like it'll make any difference to the waitress whether I pretend to eat it or not before I ask for the box. "I keep remembering what you said. About who's going to kill me when my time comes. And for a while I thought, maybe

I'll just turn myself in. Maybe that's the way to save anybody I care about from getting hurt — I can just go into the Lazarus House and disappear."

"But that didn't work for your dad," he says, softly.

He reaches a hand across the table, covering mine, and I let him even though my body tenses up at his touch. There's a lot we still need to talk about. There are things about us — our relationship, or whatever this is — that we're going to need to address and repair. There's still some of that barrier between us, that semipermeable membrane, and I'm not going to pretend that there isn't.

But this, at least, this specific thing, is something that he understands. And it means something that he does.

"I don't know what happens without the Lazarus. I don't know how long I'll have before I start to fall apart without it. But if having it means I'll have more time to figure everything out, then that's what I have to do."

The waitress comes back, and this time I'm grateful for the interruption. Grateful not to have to try to explain any further, to self-examine any deeper under the scrutiny of Randy's dark eyes. My thoughts are straying back toward my dad, and that's not a safe place for them to be right now. I have to keep busy. I have to stay focused on the plan, because that's what's going to get me through these next few days.

The waitress leaves, comes back a moment later with a check and the boxes, tut-tutting at the melted ice cream soaking down into the pie, at the mostly-full coffee carafe. Randy slides her a big bill and assures her we won't need any change. I put my wallet back in my pocket, too slow on the draw.

"So this change of heart," he says, and a hint of a sly smile creeps back into his face. "Is that just about the Lazarus or…"

"One thing at a time."

***

We knock out the finer details of the plan, absurdly, while carving pumpkins on the living room floor. There are only four pumpkins to the five of us — me, Zoe, Randy, Jo and Andrea. So somehow I've gotten stuck with the clean-up part, the scooping-out-guts part, while the others sketch out designs and alternate between discussing the plan and making small talk as though this were the most natural thing in the world.

"It'll give us something to do with our hands," Zoe had said in defense of her idea, and she's right. There's something almost soothing about keeping my hands busy as we talk through the plan and its contingencies. But I can't shake the feeling that the real reason we're doing it this way is so we have something to hold onto if it goes bad. One last memory.

"So we keep Zoe at our place," Jo's saying, twirling a marker between her fingers. The sugar-skull design she's drawn on her pumpkin is going to be painfully complex to carve, but I don't know if she's thinking that far ahead. "But it's a just-in-case thing, right? Like you definitely are planning on coming home after? No offense, just making sure I've got the plan."

"Yeah. If everything goes correctly, we get in, we get the Lazarus, we leave before anybody really notices,"I say, picking seeds apart from pulp and spreading them out on a tray. I can't eat them and Zoe doesn't really like them, but it seems like a waste not to roast them all the same. I'm feeling a sudden aching camaraderie for Lilith and her stress baking.

"That's one perk to doing this at the weigh station instead of messing with the Lazarus House. No fences, no armed guards, no bullshit." Randy frowns down at his own pumpkin, fidgeting with the paring knife in his hand. Sinew moves beneath the ruined skin of his knuckles. "And, considering the time of day, there really shouldn't be a lot of bystanders to have to try to avoid, either."

"For the record," Andrea says, "can we just acknowledge how sketch it is that they always get their Lazarus shipments into the facility in the dead of night?"

"It is a little weird," Randy agrees. "Although, I mean, Wal-Mart stocks at midnight or whatever, right?"

"Sure. But it's not like there's customers to avoid or anything? I don't know. It just seems really weird."

"Well, I guess we'll see. Everything goes according to plan and in a couple of days we'll all be back here talking about exactly how weird all of this was."

And if it doesn't go according to plan, of course, maybe we'll never be here like this again

***

"You ready?"

It's late, and the highway is dark. The only world that seems to exist is the one inside the glow of the headlights. We're in the Mercedes. Randy figured it would be faster, in case we need to make a getaway. The trade-off is that it's flashy as hell, so we compromise by deciding to park a little way past the exit, pulling the car off onto an access road, and walk the rest of the way up an embankment to the weigh station.

There was a time when walking up this hill would leave me puffing and out of breath, smoker's lungs protesting with the effort. But now my body just complies, hauling itself as tirelessly and relentlessly as its weathered joints will allow. So I guess that's one mark in the "Undead perks" column.

It's a pretty small column.

"All right. So. The truck gets here at..." he glances at his phone "...11:45, give or take. The attendant calls the driver out and into the office area to go over something about the paperwork, or whatever excuse he thinks up on the fly. That gives us a few minutes to get the truck open, grab some Lazarus, and get out."

"And if the truck is locked?"

Randy pulls something out of the pocket of his hoodie — a small pair of bolt cutters. "If he's bothered, which I bet he won't, it'll be a padlock. I was looking at the truck model online last night and that seems to be the consensus about keeping it secured. You got the box cutter?"

"Yep." I grip it hard in the pocket of my own hoodie. We're assuming the Lazarus will be shipped and stored on pallets, plastic-wrapped and stacked. There's no way we'll make off with a lot, but even if we just cut through and get one box, that'll put us in way better shape than we've been in.

The parking lot for the rest area is mostly empty. There's a few scattered lights, but there's plenty of shadows. Good news for us — we'll have places to hide. But bad, too, if there's anyone else out here lurking. *There's no one,* I tell myself, even as I look behind me again, paranoia tingling its way up my spine. *Why would there be?*

The weigh station building sits on one side of the parking lot, with the drive-through scale area beside. A separate outbuilding houses the bathrooms, with some picnic areas between. Behind it all, in the dark, the embankment slopes down into the desert, dirt and gravel and scrub separating out the space from the access road where we parked. We settle in a shadowed spot just over the embankment, a little ditch filled with bits of trash blown over from people picnicking in the rest area.

"This is the kind of ditch my grandma would tell me not to play in," I whisper, trying to get in a vantage point where I'll be able to see the truck coming. "La Llorona will get you. That's what she'd say."

"Well, if La Llorona is the worst of our worries, we're doing all right."

I fall silent, watching the road. Headlights flash occasionally on the highway, but nobody pulls off at the exit. Time slows to a crawl. It feels like we've been out here for a million years, but when I ask Randy he says it's been less than ten minutes. I hold my breath. My heart is still. In the perfect silence, crouched here in a ditch, I'm hyper-aware of the desert. The smell of the sagebrush beside me. The distant yipping howl of coyotes. The rushing noise of tires over concrete passing by on the highway.

"I don't think they're coming —"

"Look!" He elbows me in the side, pointing. A pair of headlights at the off-ramp, and then it's rolling in, a box truck, and my first thought is: Just how much Lazarus do they go through that they need a truck that big to ship it all? The truck is unmarked, the kind of nondescript vehicle that you pass a thousand times in a year traveling up and down the interstate. I used to see trucks like this all the time pull into the pumps at the Kwik-Gas I worked at and never gave a second thought to what they were carrying or where they were headed.

It's weird, now, to think of how much hope I have riding on the contents of this one.

Randy leans forward, tilting his head to listen better. The signal will be the driver door opening. If the driver doesn't get out — if our friend in the weigh station office can't lure him out or decides not to do it after all, bribe or not, then we'll bail. That was the agreement. We'll try again or come up with some other plan.

I'm keying myself up for that, bracing myself for the disappointment, running through the possible alternatives, when I hear the door open and slam shut. When I see the movement of shadows beside the truck, hear the indistinct sounds of the driver talking to someone.

Holy shit, I think, feeling that hollowness in my chest where my heart should be pounding. *He's actually doing it.*

And then Randy is up over the side of the embankment, hissing at me to follow, and I climb up beside him. We cross the space quickly, quietly, watching for any eyes on us. But the coast seems to be clear; just like we planned, we're all by ourselves out here. The driver's inside the weigh station building, a closed door and some distance between us. Just a couple minutes to cut the lock and pop open the truck and we're free.

I stand watch as Randy hops up onto the back bumper and snips at the cheap padlock holding the door closed. So far so good.

He has to jiggle the handle a few times to loosen it, but then it's free, and the roll-up door creaks and rattles open.

Chapter 21

"What the *fuck.*"

The back door of the truck slides open, a shearing creak, and even though we can't afford to stand and stare — even though we have only seconds before we'll be found — neither of us can move. Randy's gone wide-eyed in horror.

I don't know quite what I was expecting. Crates and boxes, probably. Shrink-wrapped pallets filled with little padded containers of medicine vials, their sides splashed with "keep upright" and "fragile." But I do know what I wasn't expecting, and seeing it here feels so awful, so impossible, that my brain's threatening to seize up in defiance against it. Like if I just shut down right now, power off like a robot, I won't have to see and process and understand what I'm looking at.

But I don't have that option.

I have to see this.

The back of the box truck is filled with people.

Or, to be more specific: Undead. There are dozens of them, maybe close to fifty, crammed in like cattle. Cattle trailers are least have those slats on the side, ventilation holes for them to breathe and peek out wide-eyed at the highway. These have been left in the tight, airless dark. A smell like sweet rot rolls out of the truck like a plume, an earthy stench like fresh compost and decaying slime.

"What the fuck," Randy repeats, and that seems to break the spell, at least for a minute. He drops down from the truck and waves at the dazed human cargo. "Get out. Come on."

The people inside shift uneasily, and it's hard in the gloom to make out any specific features in the crowd. They all blur together, a seething mass, a zombie horde. In the movies, the zombie horde is always hungry, always eager. But these Undead just look frightened and confused. There's blood and bile and bits of people that have fallen off or been vomited up, the truck painted in gore.

As my eyes adjust to what I'm seeing, even if my brain still refuses to make sense of it, I realize that many of them are missing parts of themselves. Arms. Legs. Scraps of torso, sides of faces.

"Where are we?"

"Is this New Mexico?"

"They said they were taking us to a different facility. They said they were taking us to New Mexico."

Terror is giving way to confusion for some of them. When they talk, I hear hints of accents from places far from here. But I'm not paying much attention to that. I'm paying more attention to the way these people have been hurt. How many of them are injured, and how those injuries don't all seem to have happened in transit. There are bandages and stitches on some of these broken parts, soaked through with red-black blood.

Parts that were cut off after their death. Parts that were cut off of bodies that will never heal.

"We're here to help," I say, stepping forward to drag out the loading ramp from the truck, grimacing at the sound of the metal scraping. It doesn't matter. I extend a hand for the person closest to take. "But you have to hurry."

This was supposed to be a shipment of Lazarus.

The first Undead takes my hand, meeting my eyes with a frightened gaze, blank-eyed and staring, not really comprehending.

"What have they been doing to you?" Randy is asking, with a mounting mixture of anger and horror and disbelief.

"They cut us up," someone replies, a rasping voice muffled by the shifting noises of people in the truck. "They cut us up until there aren't any pieces left. They need the tissue samples to study."

And that's it. That's the awful truth, the reality of it suddenly and terribly falling into place.

Julian and Elliot and Duncan, all missing parts of themselves. The screams and howls in the Lazarus House, those rats in the walls. The experiment isn't just to watch and see what happens when you take their drugs. Like good little scientists, they have to get their hard data. Of course they do. Tissue samples. Regeneration. Vivisection has been forbidden for over a century, but it doesn't count if your subjects aren't alive. It doesn't count if your subjects can't feel the pain of a knife. Never mind that we walk and talk and worry. Never mind we can still feel the pain of terror and loss. Never mind that whatever you do to us becomes a scar we'll carry forever, a wound that won't heal.

I hear the weigh station door open, hear the surprised shout of the driver, but that's not the thing that's worrying me the most.

Because in my peripheral vision, there's a flicker of color, rotating beams of red and blue.

"Goddammit," Randy pushes past me, peering around the corner of the truck and watching the squad cars roll in. "Coalition. No way they came on accident. That motherfucker sold us out."

You know what they say about things being too good to be true.

Duncan and Elliot, I think, caught by cops out on the highway — gunned down before they had a chance to run. Was that a setup, too? Is their connection playing both sides, happy to take our money and play along until we're good and trapped? Maybe he didn't think we'd be as speedy with the bolt cutters. Maybe he didn't think we'd have the truck open and the cargo spilling out so fast, even as his cop friends come rolling in.

Did he even know what was in this truck?

Does he care?

It doesn't matter anymore, because we're found out, and it's a long run back to the car.

***

The bobbing beam of a flashlight, the sound of approaching feet.

"They're coming!" Randy hisses, gesturing for the people to hurry.

They're climbing down, but moving slowly, bodies creaking and protesting and sometimes breaking in the process, leaving pieces behind: flesh that snags on exposed hinges, tearing free; skin that's melded with the hot metal of the truck and rips away like tissue paper; limbs that snap with the jostling effort of many Undead shoving past and climbing over one another as fear ripples through the crowd, cattle preparing to stampede.

It's grotesque. It's awful. And it's necessary, if they want any chance at all of getting out of here.

There are a lot of us, but the numbers don't count for anything against the Coalition. Not when those officers have guns and training and body armor on their side. What are a bunch of unarmed Undead going to do? What can a horde of broken bodies do against a rain of bullets? Numbers aren't an advantage right now; they're a liability.

"Come on, come on, come on," Randy mutters. He's moved to the side of the truck, standing vigil as I try awkwardly to help people down, try to move them. We could cut and run, leave them here to fend for themselves. Both of us know it, surely, but we wouldn't dare. I'm a coward in a lot of ways, but even I couldn't walk away from this, not without trying.

"They're moving as fast as they can," I say, trying to keep my voice low, calm, trying my best to stall against the mounting panic that's threatening to send this scene into utter chaos.

"Stop and put your hands where we can see them," an officer yells. More lights flashing — they've called for backup. There's got to be at least four armed officers on the scene now, and that's not even counting whatever trouble the truck driver and the weigh station attendant could cause us if they decide to jump into the fray. We are out of time.

"Run!" I yell, all pretense of sneakiness lost now. "Just go! Scatter! They can't catch all of you!"

I hope to god that's true.

I shoot Randy a look, and he looks back, hopelessness fading to determination, eyes going narrow and cold as he sets his jaw. In a split second, he's made a decision, and as soon as he does, everything in his countenance has changed. He grabs for my hand, pushing the keys to the Mercedes into my fist.

Undead are starting to run, a stampede that shambles past us on other side. A temporary body shield. An officer raises his weapon, taking aim, but the shot misses its target. Hits a woman in the shoulder instead, spinning her around, but she stays on her feet. Broken bodies can sustain a lot of damage. There's another tally in that small advantages column: Until the brain is damaged or the body is totally destroyed, we can just keep soldiering on, miserable and broken and dessicated but stubborn as hell.

"Get out of here," Randy says. "I'll stall them."

"You can't —"

"Go! Get them fucking out of here!"

"They'll kill you!"

"They won't," he says, and fixes me with a lopsided grin. Something dark and determined and dangerous flashes in his eyes. "They won't dare. But even if they did, I can think of worse ways to go."

The last people who are able to move are climbing down from the back of the truck. There are a few who aren't going to make it, too broken and fragile to clamber down on their own, and I can't think about that right now because I need to make sure that the others get out of here, I need to make sure that I can get out of here, I need to get back to Zoe, I need to survive even if it's just through this night so I can know that something, anything, good has come out of this awfulness.

I grab Randy's shirt, balling the fabric of the button-up in my fist, and tug him close. I kiss him, my mouth on his, a quick and hungry and sloppy communication of all of the things that I don't know how to say and don't have time to put into words.

I let him go and reel backwards, stumbling over someone who has fallen into the dirt.

Randy strides out away from the truck, directly out into the light, his hands held out to either side. He shakes his head, the hood falling away, his pink hair blazing in the dim light. He pushes his way out calmly to the front of the line, past the bodies that are surging and scrambling past.

The last person in the truck is a kid, just a fucking toddler, one fist jammed in his mouth, the other clutched tight around some small filthy toy, and I grab him and throw him over my shoulder and we're running. There's no time to look back. There's no way I can stay and watch, not if I want any chance at all of escaping this place. There's no second-guessing or changing my mind now.

"OY! Fuckers!" I hear Randy yell, loud, defiant in his confidence. "Do you know who my father is?"

And then I'm too far away to make out what happens next. I can't hear anything over the sobbing of the kid wheezing into my ear. My legs are screaming, my arms are screaming, and with every step I think I'm going to crack in two, but my bones hold.

I haven't heard any more gunfire, but I don't know if that means much. I can't hear much of anything through the haze of my panic and the kid sobbing on my shoulder, and besides, there are other ways to kill a man, ways that are quiet and terrible.

But I have to think that he's okay. I have to imagine that if anyone can talk his way out of this, it's the politician's son, the rich white kid whose story is so strange and so strong that nobody would hurt him until they knew it wouldn't be their head on a platter if they did.

The Undead have scattered. Some have crossed over the embankment and made a break out into the desert. Others are looping back around toward the highway. There's no way to control their movement, no order to impose on them, and even if I could take charge I wouldn't. The only thing that will save some lives now is knowing that a handful of Coalition officers won't be able to chase after dozens of people all running in different directions. Let them shoot. Let them try to shoot us all in the head in the dark. Let them try to follow after us in the desert, running over sand and stone and cactus. Let them get tired and weary chasing after a prey that will never get winded.

They'll get some of us. But they won't get us all.

My free hand tightens its grip on Randy's keys.

I hear a woman screaming, sobbing, calling out a name again and again, and the kid starts to yell for his mommy and I think, oh thank god, at least I'm not taking him home, at least I haven't adopted a kid in the middle of this. I let him down and double over, hands on my knees, watching him run unsteadily towards her, and the enormity of this all starts to creep up on me. The reality of what we've just done.

I see them there together, mother and child, and my heart gives a sudden aching lurch. They are strangers to me, imported from some other state, dragged cross-country from some other facility or holding cell or prison or whatever people in places that aren't Los Ojos do with people like me. But they're not so different from another mother and child I know, a mother who Duncan protected with his body, a mother who disappeared when her companions were murdered out on the highway.

The scrap of fabric in that kid's hand, the filthy toy he's been clinging to for dear life. It's not a roadrunner. But it could be.

The mother makes eye contact with me against the darkness and mouths, "Thank you."

"Go," I tell her. "Hurry."

The Undead have scattered, and there's no way to know how many will get away for good, how many will find one another or find some safe place to stay or find some way, any way, to rebuild, to survive, to find something like freedom. I'll need to look for them. I'll need to try to find them, to know for sure that this made a difference, but right now I need to get back to the car and get out of here.

I need to get home.

And I need to get packed, because home isn't going to be safe to go back to much longer.

***

It's the only story the news wants to run this week.

It's everywhere — the local broadcast station, the city paper, social media. We're even there on the national news, the first and probably only time that anybody has ever heard of Los Ojos, New Mexico.

MASS BREAK-OUT OF UNDEAD DURING TRANSIT FROM SECURE TREATMENT FACILITY

PRESIDENTIAL CANDIDATE'S SON: AN UNDEAD DIRTY SECRET?

UNDEAD THREAT LOOMS LARGE IN SMALL SOUTHWEST TOWN, VIOLENT POLITICAL GROUP SUSPECTED OF LEADING ATTACK

REPUBLICAN CANDIDATE EZRA LYNCH CAMPAIGN THROWN INTO QUESTION, SON APPEARS TO HAVE TIES TO UNDEAD TERRORIST GROUP

The stories pile up, getting more outlandish with each iteration. I'm surprised but not entirely displeased to find out that I'm the leader of a clandestine and violent terrorist organization.

The news footage rolls, and in some of the clips I can see Randy, his pink hair impossible to miss even in the background of a scene.

Randy, cuffed and being led into the Lazarus House, the news ticker rolling at the bottom of the screen explaining how he's being kept for questioning.

Randy, glancing over his shoulder, smirking, making eye contact with the camera.

Making eye contact with me.

***

They send us Dad's ashes, like they said they would.

Or, well. They send us something, anyway. I guess I have no way of knowing whether the gritty white-gray powder is really my dad. Fragments of bone in it seem almost to sparkle, crystalline, the way that veins of quartz shine in a mountain face — so they're someone's bones. They could be whatever grit is left over from a mass incineration. Maybe Dad's in here, or maybe it's a mixture of all the Undead they've sent to burn.

I guess, for this, it doesn't really matter.

If there's something to be learned from being a walking corpse, it's that your body doesn't mean all that much about who you are.

We drive up onto the mesa, our picnic spot that overlooks the town. It seems like the right place. The trees up here are mostly piñon and scraggy junipers, evergreens that doesn't know about the changing seasons. But looking down on the town, I can see the patchwork of color, the oranges and yellows and greens and all those wide swaths of dusty brown. I can see the roads and buildings, the trailer parks and highways. A whole little world down there, kind of like the little world painted in miniature on the rock face of the mesa. All of it is quiet and still. Dad never talked about what he'd like done after he died. I think when he came back we all kind of forgot that one day he'd die again.

It's just the two of us, Zoe and me, and in a way, that seems right. I wish that Randy were here. I kind of wish that Ash and Jo and the rest of The Underground were here, too. But they're our family now, in a sense that Dad never was, and it makes sense somehow that we would give Dad his last farewell here alone, closing the book on the last chapter of our old life.

"It's time," I say, stubbing out a cigarette that I've been smoking slowly. I've spent the last few minutes just staring out over the city, thinking about all the people down there, shrunken down by distance, living their tiny ant lives. Thinking of the Undead in the desert, and Randy in the Lazarus House, and The Underground scattered in hiding. Thinking about how to make this right.

"The wind isn't very strong," Zoe says, looking skeptically into the cardboard box and sealed plastic bag that holds what's supposedly left of our dad. "I don't think it'll really, um. Scatter."

"Not that. I mean. It's time to post that video. All of them. Everything you have and you're ready to share — if you still want to go public, it's now or never."

She looks up at me, confusion battling hope on her face. "What? Really? You're not worried about being found out and…everything?"

"I'm fucking terrified," I admit. "But you know what you're doing, right?"

She shrugs, suddenly modest.

"Damn right you do. So you tell me — what do we need to do to make that documentary?"

We spend the rest of the day planning, some ideas that aren't going to go anywhere, some that we'll need to do right away. We might need to leave the house behind. We might need to drive halfway across the country looking for answers. But we're not sitting on this anymore. I'm not letting fear keep us in a cage. Not when the stakes are this high. Not when we've come too far now to turn it around.

We're showing the world what's happening here, what's happening to us. We'll force them to pay attention.

And whether it takes a lawyer or an army or an angry zombie horde, we're getting Randy back, too.

About the Author

T.L. Bodine writes dark fantasy and horror of all kinds, from the zombie novel RIVER OF SOULS to the Wattpad-exclusive gothic, THE HOUND. She's interested in uncanny, fantastic things, and the way real people with real problems interact with them.

When not writing, she can usually be found watching horror movies, playing story-heavy video games, or experimenting in the kitchen.

She lives in New Mexico with her husband, David, and two small dogs.

You can connect with me on:
🌐 http://www.tlbodine.com
🐦 https://twitter.com/glassratmedia

Subscribe to my newsletter:
✉ https://tlbodine.substack.com

Also by T.L. Bodine

River of Souls

Undeath is a manageable condition.That's what the media says, anyway: with the help of the miracle life-extension drug, Lazarus, the Undead can retain their humanity and live normal, happy lives. Without it, they become violent, mindless walking corpses. Davin Montoya was eager to believe all of that. Forced to drop out of college to take care of his teenage sister, Zoe, after their father drank himself to death, he was more than happy to sign the no-good alcoholic over to the government's Lazarus House for treatment. That was one less thing for him to worry about.Until an accident left him joining the ranks of the freshly deceased himself.Now, keeping his death a secret is the only way to keep his sister out of foster care. But to do so, he must venture into the underground society of Unregistered Undead - a dangerous world of drug deals and government resistance. But when their access to Lazarus begins to run dry, the truth starts to unravel...and it's not what anyone expected.

The Darkness of Dreamland

When 7-year-old Nathaniel Weaver is kidnapped by his imaginary friend, the only person who can find him is his social worker.

Child welfare agent Adrian Montgomery lives a life of routine, reason, and careful compartmentalization. But his search for Nathaniel leads him through a door in reality itself, slipping into Dreamland: A faerie realm fueled by human dreams, where unseen monsters sweep through in the darkness to eat away at rational minds. Lingering too long in Dreamland means losing himself entirely, but escaping means finally confronting his worst nightmares — literally.